PRAISE FOR NIK COHN

'A thrilling, inspirational read'
– *Guardian*

'Set the template for a whole new style of rock journalism, informed, irreverent, passionate and polemical'
– *Choice Magazine*

'The book to read if you want to get some idea of the original primal energy of pop music. Loads of unfounded, biased assertions that almost always turn out to be right. Absolutely essential'
– Jarvis Cocker, *Guardian*

'Cohn was the first writer authentically to capture the raucous vitality of pop music'
– *Sunday Telegraph*

BY NIK COHN

I Am Still the Greatest says Johnny Angelo (1967)
Awopbopaloobop Alopbamboom (1970)
Market (1970)
Today There are No Gentlemen (1971)
Arfur: Teenage Pinball Queen (1973)
King Death (1975)
Rock Dreams (1974)
Ball the Wall: Nik Cohn in the Age of Rock (1989)
The Heart of the World (1992)
Need (1997)
God Given Months (1997)
Yes We Have No: Adventures in the Other England (1999)
20th Century Dreams (1999)
Soljas (2002)
Triksta: Life and Death and New Orleans Rap (2005)

King Death

NIK COHN

NOEXIT2

This edition published in 2017 by No Exit Press,
an imprint of Oldcastle Books Ltd, PO Box 394,
Harpenden, AL5 1XJ
noexit.co.uk

A CIP catalogue record for this book is available from the British Library.

This is a work of fiction. Names, characters, places, and incidents either are
the product of the author's imagination or are used fictitiously, and any
resemblance to actual persons, living or dead, businesses, companies, events
or locales is entirely coincidental.

ISBN
978–1–84344-897-6 (print – double edition with *Johnny Angelo*)
978–1–84344–979-9 (epub)
978-1-84344-980-5 (kindle)
978-1-84344-981-2 (pdf)

2 4 6 8 10 9 7 5 3 1

Typeset in 13.25pt Sabon
by Avocet Typeset, Somerton, Somerset TA11 6RT

Printed in Great Britain by Clays Ltd, St Ives plc

For more information about Crime Fiction go to @crimetimeuk

TO ELVIS AND JESSE,
THE PRESLEY TWINS; AND
FRANNY MAE LIPTON

King Death

1

One day, towards the end of a long dry summer, Seaton arrived in Tupelo and stopped at the Playtime Inn. It was a stifling afternoon, the town lay in a stupor and, for lack of anything better, he stood at his bedroom window, half-hidden behind a net curtain, looking out across the street.

From where he was stationed, he could see three shopfronts: a Chinese laundry, a pool hall, and a saloon called The Golden Slipper. Between them, they occupied perhaps a dozen yards of sidewalk. In addition, if Seaton craned his neck, he could just make out the first three letters of a gilded nameplate – WIL, as in WILKES & BARBOUR (Noted Upholsterers).

Within this frame, the action was severely limited. An antique Chevrolet was parked outside the pool hall, a mulatto woman was scrubbing the steps of the saloon and a mongrel lay panting beneath a lamp post. In the doorway of the Chinese laundry, there stood a man in a heavy black overcoat, black gloves and a black slouch hat, and between his legs there was a small black suitcase.

Seaton watched, and time dragged by very slowly. He

felt sticky and unclean and, from time to time, to ease his boredom, he would turn away and flop down on his bed, or splash his face with lukewarm water, or help himself to a cigarette. He was an Englishman born and bred, and at the bottom of his suitcase, there was Wisden, the *Cricketers' Almanack*, for 1921; three old school ties, all different; and a photograph of the Queen Mother.

So the afternoon passed. Propped up behind the glass like a tailor's dummy, Seaton began to nod, and a large blue fly settled on his nose. The Chevrolet drove away, the mulatto maid finished her scrubbing, the mongrel wandered off round the corner. Finally, only the man in black remained, and even he was lost in shadow, all except for his shiny black boots, which protruded an inch into the sunlight, toecaps glinting.

Possibly Seaton drifted off into a doze, perhaps he simply ceased to register. At any rate, when a siren sounded on the corner, it took him by surprise and his head jerked, his eyes opened wide.

It was past five o'clock. The sun had lost its force and his sweat had turned cold on his flesh, a sensation which made him shudder. Wincing, he shook himself and stretched and yawned, and he was just on the point of moving away when a stranger in a blue pin-striped suit emerged from the pool hall, and began to stroll down the block.

He moved with bent head and slouched shoulders, and it was not possible to make out his features. From a distance, however, he seemed roughly the same age and build as Seaton himself – squat and stubby, slack-fleshed – and he did not walk so much as amble, splayfooted.

As he came abreast of the laundry, he produced a cigar and paused for a moment to light it, holding it up to his nostrils, rolling it lovingly between his thumb and forefinger.

Immediately, the man in the black overcoat stepped out from the doorway, hand outstretched, as if to proffer a light, and the stranger half turned to meet him, inclining his head.

At this moment, something odd occurred. The two men, as they touched, appeared to mesh. There was no noise, no semblance of a struggle, but the man in black, flowing into the stranger's flesh, seemed to pass straight through him and come out on the other side, all in one smooth motion.

For an instant, as he stepped clear, his face caught the light and his eyes were seen to gleam and sparkle, like tiny mirrors refracting. Before Seaton had time to focus, however, they had dimmed again and he had turned his head. Stepping down from the sidewalk, momentarily eclipsing the WIL of WILKES & BARBOUR, he tucked his black suitcase underneath his arm and, sauntering, he disappeared off the edge of the frame.

The man in the pin-striped suit was left behind. For several seconds, he hung without moving, cigar still halfway to his lips, head still inclined towards the empty doorway, as though he were listening to something very faint and difficult, which required his utmost concentration. Seaton could hear dance music playing on a radio, saw a flutter of pink silk in the depths of The Golden Slipper. Then the stranger gave a sigh and, folding gently at the knees, he slid down on to the sidewalk, where he twitched three times and was still.

That same evening, when night fell, Seaton crossed the street to The Golden Slipper, where there were blondes in tight red dresses, slow sad country songs on the jukebox and men who drank to forget, and he sat down alone in a dark corner booth, consuming large brandies.

Once, he had been a choirboy; in all his childhood

snapshots, he appeared as a perfect dimpled cherub, pink and round. But now he had reached his middle thirties and that first pure glow was dulled. His pinkness had grown mottled, his dimples had turned into embryonic potholes and, though he was not exactly fat, he sagged, like puff pastry gone wrong.

Tonight he wore a blue naval blazer with shiny brass buttons, cavalry twills and a pair of chukka boots, made in Japan, which had been polished so hard and so often that they gleamed bright lemony yellow. But his shirt was soiled, there was a button missing from his cuff, and his tie, though Old Carthusian, was stained with tomato ketchup.

Inside The Golden Slipper, soft glowlights turned from midnight blue to purple, from gold to fluorescent pink, and the blondes, both strawberry and peroxide, were ranged in a spangled line along the bar, silently filing their fingernails.

Seaton got drunk to make time pass. When the jukebox played a song about honky-tonk angels, one of the blondes slid in close beside him, softly squeezing his thigh. 'Stranger', she called him, which pleased him very much. But she smelled too strongly of liquorice, her eyes were too red from weeping. So he gave her a dollar and told her to leave him be.

When he looked up again, he saw that the man in the black overcoat was sitting at the bar, sipping Dr Pepper through a straw. Even off duty, he still wore his black hat, black gloves and shiny black boots, and his little black suitcase lay snug between his feet.

For forty-seven seconds, the Englishman did not move. Then he crossed the floor and sat down on the next stool. 'I saw you,' he said. 'I was standing at my window, I saw you in the doorway and I watched everything that happened.'

The man in black did not reply, made no move, gave no sign of anything. Impassive, he took another sip of his Dr

Pepper and gazed at the reflections in the back-bar mirror, where he saw, on the stool next to his, a small rumpled party with a wet mouth, wet puppy-dog eyes and fingernails bitten down to the quick. 'I witnessed every detail,' Seaton said. 'And I felt I simply must tell you, I was overwhelmed.'

'Thank you,' said the man.

'I've never seen anything like it; not on TV, nor even at the movies. The way you flowed right through him, all in a single movement, and he did not struggle in the slightest – if I hadn't seen it with my own eyes, I would not have believed it.'

'You are most gracious,' said the man.

'I was thrilled. Perhaps I ought not to say that, perhaps it isn't quite dignified. But my blood began to roar, my temples began to pound and do you know, when you had departed and the stranger was still, I felt as limp as a dishcloth.'

At this, the man in black, who did not take his eyes off his own reflection, made a minuscule adjustment to the angle of his hat brim, drawing it just a fraction lower across his left eye.

There was a brief silence; then the Englishman stuck out his hand. 'Permit me to introduce myself,' he said. 'My name is Seaton Carew and I come from across the seas.'

'They call me Eddie,' said the man.

And the two of them shook hands.

Flushed with triumph, Seaton ordered another large brandy for himself, another Dr Pepper for his new friend, and he raised his glass in a toast. The blondes chewed gum, the jukebox played a song about lost love and loneliness: 'Eddie,' said Seaton.

'Mr Carew,' said Eddie.

And they drank.

Eddie's voice was a softest Mississippi drawl, hardly more than a whisper, but his language might have come from anywhere. When he turned towards his companion, his face was entirely bland and empty, bereft of age or meaning. From deep inside his overcoat pocket, he produced a pair of knucklebone dice, and he began to roll them on the bar, idly noting their progressions. Meanwhile, Seaton drank and watched.

Several times the Englishman opened his mouth to speak, only to check himself at the last moment. In the end, he shut his eyes and drank off his glass at a gulp: 'Would you think it an impertinence? Would it cause you great offence?' he said. 'But I'd like to ask you something personal.'

'Such as?'

'How does it feel?'

'Does what feel?'

'Umm,' said Seaton. 'To kill.'

Reflected in the back-bar mirror, Eddie tumbled his dice and threw eleven. Then he made another adjustment to his hat. 'But it isn't,' he said.

'It isn't?'

'Killing,' said Eddie. 'It's Death.'

This was not a reply that Seaton had expected, not remotely, and it flustered him. The tip of his nose went white, his ears burned crimson and, raising his glass again, even though it was empty, he drank deep and long. 'I don't understand; I'm afraid that I fail to follow you,' he confessed. 'What is the distinction?'

'The difference between night and day,' said Eddie. 'Killing is for amateurs, Death is a profession.'

'Amateurs?'

'Hooligans, thugs and crazy men: wild animals, who live

off pain and slaughter, and their only pleasure is destruction.'

'And Death?'

'But Death is a science, and also a vocation,' Eddie said. 'We are craftsmen, and we loathe and despise all viciousness. Inside the industry, we are known as technicians or mechanics, sometimes as eliminators. But we are not butchers, you could not rightly call us criminals. For my own satisfaction, I'd like to think that we are performers.'

All the while that Eddie was speaking, he did not cease to flick his dice and, since his face was masked by the angle of his hat brim, his voice seemed disembodied, an illusion which made Seaton sweat. The glowlights moved relentlessly through their cycle, from baby blue to aquamarine, from burnt sienna to twilight rose. 'Violence sickens me,' he said. 'As God is my witness, I bear no hate for any man alive, and every act I commit, I render it with love.'

'Just the same,' said Seaton. 'Death hurts.'

'She does not.'

'What then?'

'She thrills and transports. If only you trust her, she provides the greatest treat of all.'

Behind their backs, a drunk slumped forward across his table, overturning his glass, which shattered on the floor; and Eddie laid his black-leather hands palm upward on the bar, so that there could not possibly be any tricks or concealments. 'You've seen for yourself; in your heart, you know I don't lie,' he said. 'The way I work, there is no question of carnage or suffering. Every detail is quick and clean and merciful. From the moment I take charge, the subject knows that he is in safe hands and does not try to hide. Instead, he relaxes and lets go, drowns in pure sensation, and the whole transaction is over in a flash. Inside the profession, we call this a completion and, nine times out of ten, when you look into the subject's eyes, you will see that he's smiling.'

Seaton mopped his brow with a large red-spotted handkerchief. Beneath the breast of his blazer, his heart beat fast. Too many brandies had made him dizzy and he felt a little bit sick. 'A treat,' he said. 'I never thought of that.'

'Of course not,' said Eddie, not unkindly. 'You have been brainwashed just like everyone else. You've swallowed the propaganda and all the hysterical headlines which make Death sound like a plague, and you never took the time to look beneath the surface.'

'I suppose I didn't.'

'Who could blame you? People believe what they're told and every time you hear of Death – in the papers, on the screen or even in real life – you're taught that she is evil. All these amateurs have ruined her reputation; she has become a dirty word. Professionals like me are known as monsters, perverts and scum – that's the only picture that you've ever been shown and so you accept it automatically, without even thinking. Because any lie, if only it is repeated often enough, becomes in time a proven fact.'

It was growing late; the jukebox played a song about a little girl who falls ill and flies away to heaven, and one of the strawberry blondes began to cry, silently, insistently, with her hands up over her eyes.

Leaning forward, Eddie sucked up the very last drops from the bottom of his Dr Pepper and, when he spoke again, he sounded sad and weary. 'If only folks would try to understand. If only they would open their eyes, cast aside their prejudice and fear, and start again from the beginning. Then they might see the light, that Death is really their friend, and they would rush to greet her.'

'They would?'

'Indeed they would.'

'What if they preferred to go on living?'

'Why should they? What's so sweet about life, that they should care to cling on? In almost every case, if they were honest, the end would come as a blessed release.'

'It comes of its own accord soon enough.'

'Why wait? What's the use in delaying until you're old and feeble, too decayed to enjoy it, and they lay you out in a darkened room, with nothing left to do but wait and pray – that isn't Death, it's dying, and I wouldn't cross the street to watch.'

One by one, the blondes put on their coats and went home. The glowlights grew dim, the chairs were piled on the tables and soon The Golden Slipper was deserted, except for the two men at the bar and an ancient black janitor, who commenced to sweep the floor.

Eventually, Eddie dropped his dice back into his overcoat pocket, straightened his hat brim and stood up to leave. 'It has been my pleasure,' he said. 'I hope I have proved of service.'

'I don't know what to say,' Seaton answered. 'You have shown me so much, opened up so many new vistas, all at once – I am confounded; I can hardly tell if I'm on my head or my heels.'

Eddie almost smiled and, as he turned to depart, he laid his hand on Seaton's shoulder, as if in solace and reassurance. But his face, when the Englishman looked up, was as blank and meaningless as ever, and his eyes were full of fog. 'Life pulls so strong,' said Seaton.

'Death pulls stronger,' replied the performer and, picking up his black suitcase, he went away to bed.

At ten o'clock on the following morning, when Eddie stepped out on to the sidewalk, Seaton was already waiting outside The Golden Slipper, seated at the wheel of a shiny red Lamborghini. 'Where are you going?' asked the Englishman.

'Montgomery, Alabama,' Eddie replied.

'On business?'

'Inside the industry,' said the performer, 'we call it a contract.'

Immediately, Seaton began to rev his motor, shattering the calm, and he drummed up his best dimpled smile. 'Hop in,' he said and Eddie, having gazed at him for some seconds without expression, bowed his head and consented.

For most of the day, the two men drove without speaking. Seaton wore a Magdalen scarf, twirled casually twice across his shoulder, and drove at a steady hundred. The Lamborghini howled like a jet, enclosed in a billowing cloud of yellow dust, and everywhere that it passed, people by the roadside flinched and stopped to stare. Meanwhile, Eddie sat with his eyes shut, perfect in repose, and his case lay tucked up in his lap, as fat and smug as a sleeping black cat.

When at last they reached the city limits, it was late afternoon. Seaton slammed on the brakes and shrieked to a halt, and Eddie opened his eyes, refreshed. 'I am indebted; you have been more than neighbourly,' he said, and he began to climb out on to the kerb. But before he could do so, Seaton had reached out and restrained him, a soft clammy hand on his wrist: 'Please,' said the Englishman. 'Don't run away so fast.'

'I have an appointment.'

'I know it, and I would not dream of delaying you,' Seaton said. 'It's just that I couldn't help wondering, I hope you wouldn't mind, but perhaps I might come along with you.

If I promised faithfully to be good, that is, and not get in the way and never make a sound. If I simply stayed in the background.'

'And what?'

'And watched.'

'But you watched in Tupelo.'

'I did; I did indeed; and I was overwhelmed. But I was placed so far away, I could not rightly see and I'm sure I missed so much. All the little details, those special finesses and nuances of style, in which Death was truly expressed. And also I wasn't prepared, I was taken by surprise. So naturally I was a trifle disconnected. But if I got another chance, if only I could see you perform once more, live and in close-up, I know that my confusion would be swept aside and I would truly understand.'

With his left foot in the car, his right foot on the kerb, Eddie stroked his chin and considered, while Seaton continued to tug at his wrist and plead with soggy eyes. 'You are requesting a special service,' said the professional. 'And specials cost money.'

'Five hundred dollars,' said Seaton.

'Drive,' said Eddie; and they drove.

Seaton had been in Montgomery before. But somehow, travelling with Eddie, everything looked different, and he found himself in a neighbourhood that he had never known existed, full of tenements, so high and so dark that passing among them was like descending into a pit.

Down here, the streets were full of black men in smoked glasses and little round hats. Women called obscenities from the doorways, young boys threw stones from fire escapes. Even on a hot afternoon, the sidewalks were plunged deep in shadow, the windows were ablaze with neon and, from far down in the basements, there came a remorseless rhythmic shuddering, which made the walls sweat and shake.

As soon as he entered this world, Seaton wound up his window as far as it would go, to keep out the smell, and he tried hard not to look. Just the same, there was a tingling, an odd empty aching in the pit of his stomach, and his face felt pinched and crumpled.

Cruising along beside the railroad tracks, the Lamborghini flowed past block after block of bars and honkytonks, fifty-cent dance halls, dekinking salons and magical mojo booths. Some men were brawling in alleys, while others lay face down in doorways. Still others sat on the kerb, staring, and did not focus on anything. 'What a most peculiar place,' Seaton said.

'Only because you aren't accustomed,' Eddie reassured him. 'Once you've gotten used to it, you'll take it all for granted.'

At a crossroads, they came to a broken-down brownstone, the Hotel Amsterdam, with smashed windows and no front door. 'Stop here, and wait,' said Eddie.

'Where are you going?' Seaton asked.

'I wish to be private. Before I perform, it is my custom to prepare myself, in calm and contemplation,' the professional told him and, getting out of the car, he disappeared into the coal-black chasm of the hotel doorway.

Stumbling in the dark, he made his way up three flights of stairs and came to a small blank room, twelve feet by ten. Inside, there was a bed, a table and chair, a washstand in the corner, and an old cracked mirror. The window was boarded up, a naked light bulb hung from the ceiling and Eddie lay down across the unmade bed, hands clasped loosely behind his head.

A small radio, produced from his overcoat pocket, played

softly beside his ear, sentimental torch songs from a long time ago, and for the next four hours he lay without moving, eyes open wide. Meanwhile, Seaton waited downstairs, surrounded by the men in smoked glasses and little round hats, who stared at him without blinking.

At first they were content to watch from a distance and wait; but gradually, lured by the gloss and glitter of the Lamborghini, which was so much like a shiny red spaceship, they crept up closer and closer. They ran their fingers along the paintwork, prodded the tyres with alligator shoes, studied the warp of their reflections in the hubcaps. Then they scrawled rude words in the dust on the fenders and pressed their noses flat against the windows, as though the Englishman were a rare pink fish from the tropics.

Upstairs in the Hotel Amsterdam, on the stroke of seven o'clock, Eddie rose and sat down in front of the mirror, his suitcase open on his knees and his overcoat unbuttoned, so that a silver crucifix could be seen at his throat. In reflection, he was dark and lean, of medium height and build, with regular features and no distinguishing marks, except perhaps for his hands, which were small and extraordinarily delicate, almost feminine, with thin pointed fingers and no lines whatever on the palms.

The radio played *Dardanella* and, one by one, the performer emptied out the contents of the case, the sum of his earthly possessions, arranging them in neat rows on the table, where he could study their image in the glass.

There was an early Victorian fowling piece, circa 1840, with gilt-embossed barrel; a spare pair of gloves; a clean white shirt and a clean black waistcoat; two Gilronan .32s and a snub-nosed De Quincey .38; a change of underwear, a plastic washbag and a tin of boot polish; trucidator, jugulator and Albanian occisor; dice, a gold tooth and a rabbit's foot; silencers (economy packs); colourless fluid in one vial, smelling of burnt almonds, and opaque crystals in another, smelling of old socks; a Gideons' Bible; a jar of old-fashioned mint candies; and a yellowed and moth-eaten snapshot of his mother, too blurred to be deciphered.

When all his trophies had been placed in their due order, and Eddie was content, he turned up his overcoat collar, held the Bible in his right hand and adjusted his hat brim to an angle of 13 degrees 30 minutes from the horizontal. Then he gazed directly into the mirror and for an instant, as he went still, the frame seemed to freeze, to turn into a photograph.

The radio played *Melancholy Baby*. All of a sudden, Eddie emerged from his reverie, his gloves grew tight as sausage skins and he put his possessions back into their proper place. Shutting his suitcase with a snap, he tucked it under his arm, turned away from the glass and went out on to the dark, foul-smelling stairs.

The walls were hot and damp, vermin ran between his feet. Ice-cold water dripped down the back of his neck and, in the recess of the second landing, he passed a tin-cup beggar and his performing monkey, who beat upon a drum and wore a red velvet fez with golden tassels.

Inside the Lamborghini, Seaton had reached two thousand three hundred and twenty-nine: 'Drive,' said Eddie; and they drove.

Dusk was falling and the neon sidewalks glowed brighter, more lurid than ever. Music blared from every window, there was a side-show at every corner. Blind men played the harmonica, chickens danced on hot plates, women in red dresses performed the signifying strut. The streets were ablaze with silks and satins in numberless different colours, so vivid that Seaton raised his hand to shade his eyes, and each time that the Lamborghini passed a patch of waste ground, the space was filled with a roaring bonfire, a holocaust of effigies and masques.

At the end of the seventh block, across the street from a storefront mission, there was a sign that read Sam's Soul Place. Inside, there was another room full of hats and smoked glasses, focused on nothing. The air was thick with the scent of exotic cheroots and a quartet of dudes was casting dice against a wall. Eddie sat down by the window and called for a bowl of collard greens and dumplings, polk salad, grits and beans. The Englishman had a glass of milk.

Outside the storefront mission, a large man and a small man engaged in furious argument. The large man tweaked the small man's nose. The small man punched the large man in the eye. The large man threw the small man smack into a concrete wall. The small man stuck a stiletto into the large man's ribs. Then both of them brought out their pearl-handled razors and, calmly, methodically, they carved each other into small pieces.

Eddie ate dumplings.

When the performance outside was ended and the two men had stopped twitching, Seaton stood up and made his way to the toilet, where he vomited. For some minutes, he remained locked up in the dark, shaking, with his head buried in both hands. Afterwards, as he began to recover, he struck a match and cut his initials into the door with a blunt penknife.

Back at the table, Eddie dabbed at his lips with a paper napkin and, looking grave, he pushed away his plate. 'That's what I mean by amateurs, and I am not surprised that you were sickened,' he said, as the bodies were removed. 'But now it's time to look on the other side of the coin. Come with me, and I will show you what true Death can be.'

Safe in the Lamborghini, they left the neon behind, veering off across the railroad tracks to find themselves in a neighbourhood of empty streets and towering apartment blocks, where the avenues were like canyons and every sound and tremor made an echo. The sidewalks were spotless, all the doors were locked and bolted. Everything was clean and ordered; passions had no place.

Round a certain corner, however, Seaton was confronted by a woman who did not belong. Fat and ageless, she was standing underneath a street lamp, in a sequin-spangled dress, sucking on a corn-cob. Butter glinted on her chin, the sequins danced like fireflies in the light and, behind her, there was a fire escape, which appeared to reach straight upward into infinity.

At Eddie's command Seaton stopped the car, and they dismounted. 'Climb,' said the performer; and they climbed.

They rose seventeen floors up the fire escape, Eddie zigzagging swiftly in the lead, a silent black phantom, and Seaton floundering half a flight behind. At the eighteenth floor, they halted.

Looking in through a lighted window, they saw a man sprawled upon a bed, with his shoes and socks kicked off, reading about prize fighters in a glossy magazine. A small pile of beer cans lay scattered across the carpet and the walls were plastered with pictures of naked starlets. Beside the man on his bed, there were several wads of bank notes, circled with elastic bands.

Light brown in colour, the man was still quite young and unused, with a long pink scar slashed down one cheek. There was an outsized diamond on his little finger, an opal in his tiepin, flashing gold inside his mouth, and he wore a gun in a fancy Mexican holster. Without any question, here was a hipster and, stretching, he yawned and wriggled his toes.

Outside the window, Eddie straightened his hat brim, raised his right hand and, though he seemed to tap quite gently, the glass broke. The man sat up straight and half turned his head, directly into the path of Eddie's eyes, which went translucent and began to dazzle, just as they had done in Tupelo, outside the Chinese laundry. Polite and unhurried, the performer smiled and his subject, who had started to rise and go for his holster, immediately sat down again. His hands fell to his sides, he simpered and a bullet passed cleanly, with a noise like a damp squib, through the centre of his forehead and into his brain.

His magazine fell fluttering to the floor, he lay down on his bed, among the bank notes, and Eddie set off back down the fire escape. But Seaton remained, staring in through the broken window, and tried to fix this frame for ever in his memory – pictures pinned on a wall, beer cans strewn at random on a scuffed green carpet, and a man asleep, faintly smiling, upon an unmade bed.

Far below, Eddie honked the car horn and the Englishman shook his head, shook his entire body, like a dog emerging from deep water. It was only when he left the window and started his descent that he found, with a sense of distant surprise, that he was shuddering, his legs were soaking wet and he was, he understood, weeping uncontrollably.

Ten hours later, Eddie and Seaton were eating breakfast beside a silvery lake, some twenty miles from Tuscaloosa, and they sat enshrouded on a vine-trellised balcony, overhanging the water, while they gorged themselves on waffles and maple syrup.

At dawn they had pulled in at a clapboard truck stop, just outside Magnolia City, and Seaton shut himself inside the backyard washroom. When he entered, he was soiled and shambling with red-rimmed eyes. Seven minutes later, when he reappeared, he had been changed back into a choirboy.

He shone from head to toe. His fingernails and teeth, his chukka boots and even the brass buttons on his blazer had all been freshly polished; his hair was slicked down flat with soapy water, lank and glutinous against his scalp; and every millimetre of his visible flesh had been scrubbed till it gleamed. Most dazzling of all, his tie was a riot of scarlet cricket bats and, just as he stepped out into the forecourt, pink and new, he was caught by the first thin rays of morning sunlight, which made him squint and smile uncertainly, as if for a prep-school photograph.

Now he ate waffles and the water sparkled beside him, the air was full of columbine and jasmine. Soon syrup began to ooze from the corners of his mouth, and he gestured vaguely out across the lake with his fork. 'Tell me,' he said.

'What about?' asked Eddie.

'Anything and everything – where you came from, who were your folks, how did you grow up, what formed you and guided you, how you first got involved in the industry.'

Eddie reached for the huckleberry jam and helped himself to more syrup. 'These here are mighty fine waffles,' he said.

In spite of his night's exertions, he looked as spruce and unflustered now as he'd been when he stepped forth from his room in the Hotel Amsterdam. Sunlight, sneaking in through the trellises, formed soft dapples on the crown of his hat and, in the morning brightness, with his plate piled high and his napkin tucked neatly into the neck of his overcoat, he might almost have passed for a juvenile.

For the next five minutes, Seaton did not speak, and it seemed that he must be pondering some deep problem, for his head was bowed and his fork lay idle in his hand. Absent-minded, he smeared his sticky fingers up and down his thighs, while one drop of syrup congealed and hung on his chin.

At last he seemed to reach a decision, and he lit a fat cigar. Dragging deep, he coughed three times on to the back of his hand and gazed past Eddie's left shoulder, straight into infinity. 'I hope you won't think I'm forward; I do not mean to presume,' he said. 'But I have a proposition.'

'What is it you desire?'

'Death,' said Seaton. 'And you.'

Far beyond the balcony, a lone white bird went wheeling and spinning on the water. At first it flew quite flat, skimming close above the surface, and gradually its plumage turned to silvery blue, merging with its background. Then all of a sudden it reared and flared into the sun, as though magicked from a conjurer's sleeve. Dazzling white, it swooped and swirled and circled, then dropped back down on to the water, just as suddenly as it had soared, and its radiance was extinguished in an instant. 'Permit me to elaborate,' said Seaton.

'Go right ahead.'

'I am by profession a salesman. To be precise, I trade in spectacles and TV entertainments, which I call images. Furthermore, I am most extremely successful, I have grossed many millions of dollars.'

'Yes?' said Eddie, with his mouth full.

'Therefore, performers are my specialty. I have been watching and marketing them half my life, ever since I got out of knee socks. And if there's one thing that I have learned to know when I see it, that thing is magic. Charisma, stardust, Secret Ingredient X – call it what you like, no man can define it but, once I have witnessed it, I can neither mistake nor forget it.'

'And I've got it?'

'You have indeed; you've got it in the absolute. From the very first moment I glimpsed you, looking down from my window, I was convinced. And everything that has passed between us since – our talk in The Golden Slipper, last night in Montgomery, your every word and gesture – has only served to render me more certain. You are a star. You were born to touch the skies.'

Eddie made no comment.

With a little sigh, he put down his knife and fork, wiped his lips and folded his napkin. Then he rose from the table, replete, and wandered down to the lakeside, where he collected a random sampling of pebbles and began to skim them across the smooth water.

Seaton stood close behind his shoulder, where even the softest murmur could not escape him, and puffed at his cigar, and watched. The performer drew back his arm and the pebbles hissed through the air, bouncing as they touched the waves. 'What is your proposition?' Eddie asked.

'I wish to become your manager,' Seaton replied. 'I want to take you away from here and carry you back to Los Angeles, where you rightfully belong; I want to package and promote you, launch a campaign and sell you clear across the nation; and I give you my guarantee, I will not rest content until I have made you into the greatest, best-loved and biggest-grossing image in creation.'

Eddie skimmed pebbles.

Raising his head, he looked out across the lake, at the pale blue mountains beyond, and tiny waves lapped at his boots, his hat brim was furled by gentle breezes. 'I'm sorry,' he said. 'Regrettably, I must decline your offer. I am happy as I am and, besides, I have already been contracted in Peoria, Illinois.'

'Who is your subject?'

'She is described as a faithless Jezebel.'

'And what, if I may ask, will be your reward?'

'One thousand dollars in cash,' said Eddie. 'Plus expenses, and the joy of a job well done.'

Behind the professional's back, Seaton blinked and shook his head, as if in disbelief. 'A thousand dollars,' he exclaimed. 'Why, goodness gracious, that's scarcely more than chicken feed.'

'It suffices to my needs.'

'But you're being most grossly exploited. If you came with me, you could earn a hundred times that much, no problem whatsoever. You could live in a penthouse, drive a pink Cadillac and surround yourself with starlets. Before a year was out, I promise you, you would have soared to the utmost peak of the industry, and the world would be your oyster.'

Eddie fingered his crucifix.

'These things do not concern me,' he said. 'Wealth and fame are baubles, and vulgar praise hurts worse than insults. My one and only care is Death herself and, like a doctor of medicine, I perform anywhere that she's required, regardless of the circumstance.'

'But that's just the point,' cried Seaton and, despite himself, his voice grew shrill and insistent. 'By underselling yourself, don't you see, you sell her short as well.'

On the point of letting loose another pebble, Eddie stayed his hand. He looked down into his open palm, where only a few stones survived, and his brow was furrowed: 'I don't understand,' he said.

'She was not made for this, and neither were you.'

'For what?'

'Obscurity,' said Seaton, puffing his cigar. 'You were not created to be a nonentity, to pass your life in shadows, stuck for ever in the same shallow rut, a thousand dollars here, another thousand there, always on the move, from town to B-feature town, with their squalid little rooms and squalid little subjects, until at last you're caught or grow too old or you simply disintegrate.'

'I have no complaints.'

'But what about Death? Skulking in this fashion, swathed in mediocrity, she has no chance to breathe. So long as you keep her buried in alleys and darkened doorways, where no one can see her clearly, all her beauties go for nothing and, whatever her potential, she's doomed to remain an outlaw.'

'Such is not my intention.'

'Then why don't you unleash her? Why not bring her out into the daylight and let the multitudes see her in action? Then everyone would have the chance to know and understand, not just mechanics and initiates but the whole wide world. And at last they might learn how to love her.'

Far away across the water, the white bird reappeared and once more went swooping and swirling, flashing like a switchblade against the sun. Eddie cast another stone, which sank without trace, and Seaton threw away his cigar: 'I have a dream,' said the Englishman.

'A dream?'

'I see a day when you become a celluloid god, and Death is enthroned as your bride. For the first time in history, with you and me in partnership, she is released from bondage, shorn of all restrictions. Just as you have always dreamed, she is universally cherished and desired, and no more fear exists.'

Eddie blew his nose.

'I don't pretend that it will be easy,' Seaton said. 'Prejudice, superstition and incomprehension always sink the deepest roots, and the habit of centuries is not overthrown at a whim. Without the slightest doubt, our road will be long and hard. Critics and politicians will abuse us, the law will hound us. But we shall not be deterred. No matter how we're obstructed, our purpose will not waver.'

For the second time, Eddie opened his palm and looked down at its contents. By now only two more pebbles remained, one flat and one round, so small and insignificant that they hardly seemed worth skimming. 'I have a dream,' said Seaton again, 'and my dreams do not fail to come true.'

'How can I be sure?'

'You can't,' said the Englishman candidly. 'In matters such as these, no certainty exists. Every move you make is clouded with doubt and risk, and you can only jump in the dark, hoping for the best. But if you don't jump, you can't expect to fly. And if you let your misgivings swamp you, if you turn your back on this dream and scuttle off to Peoria, Death will never be freed.'

Eddie skimmed a pebble.

The white bird hovered in the blue and, with the sweetest and most cherubic smile at his disposal, Seaton stepped up even closer behind the performer's back, to place a soft hand on his elbow. 'Come,' said the Englishman. 'If you care for her the way you claim, you have no choice. This is her great chance, her one true hope of redemption, and you're the only one who can bring her through. If you let this vision perish, you will have stabbed her in the back and she will never forgive you.'

Eddie watched his own reflection in the shallows, and the white bird dropped down upon the surface of the lake, where it sparkled once and was gone. 'Come,' said Seaton. 'Your destiny calls.'

Unclenching his fist, the performer released the last of the stones, which fell into a stagnant rock pool. Seaton extended his hand, Eddie shook it and they were partners. Then, turning their backs on the blue waters, they smiled into space with open mouths and vacant eyes, as if for a flash bulb, and they drove away to Hollywood.

2

One afternoon, shortly after his twenty-sixth birthday, Seaton was driving through the Hollywood Hills, heading nowhere in particular, when he passed a Spanish mansion behind a high electric fence and his eye was drawn to a gilded nameplate, which read Tierra de Ensueños: 'Land of Dreams,' said the Englishman, and he paid a quarter of a million dollars to live inside.

Originally built for Avril Orchid, the siren of the silent screen, the mansion had thirty-one rooms and everything in them was heart-shaped. There were heart-shaped windows, heart-shaped beds, heart-shaped mirrors and chandeliers. Even the grand pianos, the sunken baths and tiger-skin rugs were heart-shaped and, at the centre of a labyrinth of twisted corridors, there was a heart-shaped perfumed garden.

Here Seaton took his ease in a velveteen hammock, in the shade of a slumbrous fig tree, whose fruit hung down about his head in deep red crystals. He was surrounded by songbirds, alabaster cupids and a hundred different kinds of blossom. Moorish minarets soared far above him, wild animals ate crumbs from his hand. At his feet, a scented fountain played in a bowl full of silvery snowfish.

Nobody knew where he had come from, what his origins were, exactly how he had begun. But he had arrived in Los Angeles when he was twenty-one, already rich, and proceeded to make himself still richer. He owned rock groups, produced motion pictures, invested in real estate. He had five cars, three bodyguards and twenty-seven TV sets, and he put up the largest, most dazzling neon sign on the whole of Sunset Strip.

In due course he became twenty-five, and he began to grow stale. Deals no longer excited him; neither did anything else. So he grew his hair to his shoulders and lay motionless on Oriental cushions. He passed through a maze of analysts, clairvoyants and avatars, he was married and divorced and married again, and he was naughty in every way that he could think of. He yawned and played Russian roulette. At the end of everything, he was twenty-six.

It was at this moment that he drove past Tierra de Ensueños. That same day, he dismissed his wives and lovers and friends, sold off his corporations, disposed of all his possessions and, when he was stripped to his bare essentials, by which he meant himself and his money, he stretched out in the hammock and sucked on a fig.

Ever since the death of Avril Orchid, fifteen years before, the mansion had been deserted. The chandeliers were hung thick with cobwebs, the mirrors and ganymedes had lost their gilt, fungus sprouted from the walls, and the corridors were infested with vermin. The perfumed garden, where once there had been order, was now a teeming, sweating jungle, and Seaton was hemmed in by every form of flower, plant and creature that his imagination could create.

Padding along the galleries in Turkish slippers, the Englishman scrawled his initials in the dust, a thousand times repeated. Nobody came to see him, he never went beyond the gates. For the next four years, alone in this mausoleum, he lost himself in his collection of Wisden, the *Cricketers' Almanack*, and nothing else existed.

On the morning of his thirtieth birthday, he drove off into the heights of the Sierra Magdalena and stood at the edge of a precipice, poised above a thousand feet of nothingness. Vultures circled overhead, wolves waited underneath and Seaton hovered on the brink, imagining. But he did not jump. Instead, he was seized by a most terrible hunger, against which he was defenceless. Far away in the valley, a church bell rang, and he turned aside in defeat.

In the nearest roadhouse, he fed himself on charbroiled hamburgers and crinkle-cut French fries, tacos and enchiladas, hot pastrami on rye, lox and a double portion of Aztec Glory (strawberry, chocolate and pistachio ice, with whipped cream and Melba sauce, almond flakes, canned peaches and a maraschino cherry on top), and when he was quite satisfied, he drove home to Tierra de Ensueños, where he fell into a bottomless sleep.

The gardens ran riot.

There were catalpas and syringas and liquidambars, monkey trees and prickly pawpaws, Spanish clementians and scarlet kawligas, all flung together in madness, thronging and overspilling. Parakeets perched in the mimosa, mocking-birds scoffed from the depths of the tulip trees, silver foxes went whispering through the undergrowth. Above the sleeper's head, perganzas of gold and crimson and azure blue formed an impenetrable canopy, and he lay perfectly still.

At the end of three weeks, awaking from his dream, he

sat up straight and rubbed his eyes. He brushed his teeth, cut his fingernails, put on a clean white suit and made another excursion beyond the electric gates, out into the streets of the city, where he chose a random selection of families, purchased all rights to them and carried them off in a fleet of yellow taxis.

Back inside the mansion, he fed and clothed and warmed them, supplied them with every toy and diversion they desired, guaranteed their safety. He even redecorated their rooms, ripping out the velvets and heart-shaped mosaics and replacing them with formica, polyurethane, and grease-proof laminated Perspex. In return they had only to look at images.

From morning to night, they watched TV, and the mansion was filled with screens. There were pictures on every wall, round every corner, behind every door. When Seaton lay down to rest in his hammock, the flickering images lit up the minarets like a radiance of stars.

For a year, the Englishman was content to watch, observe the families' reactions, learn. Then he felt that he knew them by heart, and he began to manufacture images of his own.

Once again, he became successful and famous. In the next five seasons, he created a dozen different formulae and all of them topped the ratings. The garden was hung with gold awards, magazines blazoned him across their covers, journalists came queuing at his gates. But he did not let them in, for he had a horror of being photographed. Without his invisibility, like Samson shorn of his hair, he believed that he would lose his gifts, and it was his great ambition that, when he died, he should leave absolutely no record that he had ever existed.

Night after night he lay in his garden and dreamed, until at last he began to feel restless. He itched, he ached. Though the screens continued to flicker and burn, their pictures did not reach him. So he climbed inside his Lamborghini and drove away across America, to refresh himself.

He travelled across deserts and infinite plains, over snow-capped mountains, beside storm-whipped rivers. He lost himself in cities black as night, was stranded in the swamplands; slept in cheap motels, ate at corner drugstores, watched lovers through peepholes; was beaten up and robbed, got drunk and was thrown in a cell. But through it all he remained entirely passive, as though none of this were happening to himself, not in reality, but rather to a stand-in, clothed in his flesh. Thus he drove and watched without feeling and finally, in Tupelo, when he looked down from his bedroom window, Eddie was standing in the doorway of the Chinese laundry.

The partners came to the mansion together and sat down in the perfumed garden. Reptiles crawled at their feet, butterflies hung in clouds about their heads, the jungles were full of secret whisperings. 'I call it home,' said Seaton modestly. 'But do you know something strange?'

'What's that?'

'Apart from the families, who do not count, you are the first human being I have ever asked inside. In fact, you are the only one alive who can guess what these gardens are really like.'

Eddie rested on a cold stone love-seat, eyes downcast, while birds perched on his shoulders and small furry animals scampered up his legs, as though he were an inanimate object. 'I am honoured,' he said.

'Then let us begin.' And they entered a maze of dark, dank corridors, where the dust was so thick that their footsteps left no echo. Seaton shone a flashlight, lighting them through the shadows, and Eddie's lips were brushed by cold, wet tendrils, like seaweed.

Periodically, the Englishman opened doors and they came into bright, strip-lit oases, where the families sat and watched. In Room 13, the McGhees witnessed a garrotting; in 22, the Pottersons studied rape; in 5, the Carters gazed blankly at tear gas on the News. Everywhere that the partners entered, the screens were filled with carnage, perversion and excess, and Eddie averted his eyes, for he could not tolerate pain or any form of cruelty.

In due course, Seaton led him back into the sunlight and they arrived at a heart-shaped Chinese pagoda, lost in the depths of the wilderness, where they drank tea and ate chocolate biscuits.

Eddie rested silent, brooding, and every time he looked up, he saw the families reflected on the screens, watching bloodshed. 'This will be your audience,' Seaton told him. 'What do you think of them?'

'They are in love with mayhem.'

'Indeed they are; but you must not hold it against them. After all, they spend their whole lives as spectators. They exist through images, always at one remove, and can never experience for themselves. So naturally their taste runs to novelties, thrills, explosions. Anything that stirs their blood and makes them feel alive.'

'A man feels sick,' said Eddie.

'Of course he does,' said Seaton. 'And that is why we are here. To show a better way. To demonstrate that vulgar slaughter and bestiality can never lead to true fulfilment; and that the dignity of Death makes for a finer, deeper spectacle than any atrocity.'

They sat beside an ornamental fountain. Lemonade spurted from the mouths of nymphs and leaping dolphins, and Seaton trailed his fingers idly along the bronzed back of a triton: 'Of course, before our mission can succeed, there is one great obstacle that we must overcome.'

'Prejudice.'

'Just so.' And the Englishman heaved a sigh. 'If I were simply to unleash you, without preamble or context, no one would understand. Mistaking your true nature, they would cast you as a common hoodlum. However much you might secretly excite and move them, they would refuse to let themselves accept you, and you would be destroyed before you'd even begun.'

'Crucified,' said Eddie.

'Therefore, we must find an angle. We must devise a strategy, prepare our ground. Before the moment of final revelation, when Death is presented in all her glory, we must learn to use diplomacy, until our audience trusts us without question and will follow wherever we may lead.'

From a branch above his head, the Englishman plucked a handful of fat black grapes and began to suck on them, spitting out the pips into the lemonade fountain. 'Trust,' he said. 'That is the key to everything. The only path from private thrill to public acclamation.'

Eddie made no comment, and once more they went wandering through the mansion. Immersed in silent meditations, they lost themselves in the labyrinth and, as they drifted, Seaton flashed his flashlight on portrait after portrait of Avril Orchid, nude and clothed, posing by the poolside and on a tiger-skin rug, cuddling a baby cheetah, radiant on her wedding days, pensive in intimate close-up. Trapped in a hall of mirrors, she waved and pouted, she blew soft kisses. Stardust glittered in her hair, and her image was repeated to infinity.

In late afternoon, a blue teal flew down from the minarets and settled in the branches of Seaton's favourite fig tree. Its plumage, mingling with the dying sunlight, turned the fruit from red to deepest purple, glowing like precious stones, and the Englishman hid in his hammock.

Eddie rested in the shade of a mummified dwarf, with gilded eyes and sequins encrusted in its navel. Concealed behind his hat brim, he turned up his overcoat collar against the gathering dusk and, when he spoke, his voice was even softer and more remote than usual, as though lost in private reverie. 'I am reminded of a time when I was stranded in Miami Beach,' he said. 'My connection had run away with my fee and I was left without a dollar to my name, faced with destitution.'

'How did you cope?'

'I had no choice. For the first and last time in my career, I was forced to compromise and take a job outside the industry. Though it shamed me, I hired myself out as a bodyguard and went to work for a Cuban gambler.'

'What was he like?'

'He was paralysed by fear. The week before, he had received a threat against his life and now he could not move or control his limbs, he could hardly speak for shaking. All day long, he cowered in his wheelchair, smothered in shawls and blankets and patchwork quilts and, when he went to bed at night, he wept like a motherless child.'

'What was the outcome?'

'No assignment could have been easier. Late one evening, soon after I had joined him, I heard a scuffling outside the window and two young professionals came creeping through the shrubbery, guns in hand. Raising the blinds, I called their names and cancelled them, and they fell into a lily pond, where they sank. Then I collected my reward and got ready to move along.'

'Where did you go?'

'Nowhere,' said Eddie. 'The Cuban would not let me. Now that I had proved myself, it seemed that he could not rest or breathe freely unless I was close by his side. So he doubled and trebled my wages, showered me with gifts, filled my suitcase with the very finest equipment. And, like a fool, I submitted.'

When darkness fell, the partners arrived at a deserted ballroom, at the top of a sweeping marble stairway, and Eddie sat in the centre of the dance floor, beneath a crystal chandelier, which tinkled faintly in the draught.

Seaton prowled round him in circles, taking snapshots with a drugstore Polaroid. Frozen in reproduction, the performer was straight-backed and stiff, his suitcase on his knees, and he wore no expression at all.

'What happened next?' asked Seaton.

'I was trapped.'

'How come?'

'I was cut off from everything that I knew, all the places I belonged. My life was spent in yachts, limousines and casinos, when I was created to stand on street corners. Nothing felt natural, I could not relax. Before a month had passed, I knew I must either escape or perish. So in the end, to scare the Cuban off, I told him the truth, that I was not really a bodyguard and my true vocation was Death.'

'How did he react?'

'He was thrilled.'

'He was?'

'He drooled,' said the performer. 'No man could have feared Death more, yet he blushed bright pink with pleasure, his lips began to tremble and he could not stop asking questions.'

'How come he felt so free?'

'Because I had won his trust, just like you said. Because I was his servant and he knew that I would not harm him. So all his curiosity and pent-up hunger could spill out unrestrained. From that moment on, he never stopped pestering me for reminiscences and demonstrations. Soon he even began to give me contracts, to practise on his friends and associates. If I had not escaped in time, up and over his garden wall at midnight, he would have used me up entirely.'

Inside a baronial banquet hall, seated in two small pools of light, they dined at opposite ends of an interminable table. Eddie worked his way through three large helpings of ham hocks, collards and grits and did not speak again until he was replete. On the screens, guns blazed, blood flowed. The professional sipped Dr Pepper, and Seaton kept on taking snapshots.

On the first stroke of midnight, Eddie pushed aside his plate and got to his feet, ready for his bed. 'So you see,' he said, wiping the grease from his lips, 'when you speak about Death, everything depends on the subject's point of view. So long as he thinks of her as his enemy, she is the greatest monster that exists. But if he is persuaded that she is on his side, that her only purpose is to serve him, all his terrors disappear and he rushes to embrace her, as his very best friend and ally.'

'His protector,' said Seaton.

'That's right,' said the performer. 'His guardian angel.'

J Jones Dickerson, a grey man with a grey suit and a tight grey mouth, sucked jujubes and sat behind a large grey desk in a large grey office, secure beyond bullet-proof doors.

For the past fifteen years, he had been Commander in Chief at the American Bureau of Control. In this capacity, he was served by a host of agents, an all-embracing network of spies and lawmen. No one in the entire country, so it seemed, could meet or act without his knowledge, and his powers were almost limitless.

Now Seaton stood before him, all dimples, and smiled directly into his dead grey eyes. 'I bring you a story so bizarre,' said the Englishman, 'I am almost ashamed to tell you.'

'Well?' said J Jones Dickerson.

'About a month ago, I was relaxing at my home, on a sleepy Sunday afternoon, when a young man knocked on my door. He was a stranger but he seemed polite and clean, he had the sweetest smile, and I liked him at first sight.'

'And?'

'He said he wanted my advice. So I asked him in for tea and cucumber sandwiches, and he told me that he dealt in Death. Apparently, he was blessed with a God-given genius, a miraculous gift for every form of elimination. But he was not a criminal, and he shrank from squandering his abilities in evil. On the contrary, he was a law-abiding American, patriotic to a degree, and his one great ambition was to serve his native land.'

'So?'

'The only trouble was, he did not know where to start. He was just a kid off the streets, green and friendless, and though he believed that he possessed a sacred destiny, he felt helpless to pursue it. Therefore, he had come to me, to seek my help and guidance.'

'And?'

'I will be frank with you. At first, when he told me this tale, I was inclined to scoff. I thought that he must be some crank or practical jokester, and I sniffed at his claims of genius. Still, he had such honest eyes, his smile was so pure and dazzling, and I did not wish to seem ungracious. So I asked him to give me a demonstration. And he did.'

'And?'

'I was thunderstruck,' said Seaton. 'Everything that he had claimed was justified, a hundred times over. In all my life, I was never so moved or mesmerised by any performer before.'

J Jones Dickerson yawned.

On his desk, there was a framed photograph of his wife and children, at which he stared unseeingly. His hands lay slackly in his lap, grey on grey, and nothing moved but his jaws, which never ceased to suck. 'And?' he said.

'Experience has taught me caution; I did not betray my excitement. Instead, I arranged to go with him into the San Fernando Valley, where he had some contracts to fulfil, and watch him under actual combat conditions, live and with the chips down.'

'And?'

'He surpassed himself. Truly, he seemed superhuman. Speed, imagination, versatility, nerve – you name it, he possessed it, and he appeared to be infallible. By the time I had witnessed him in three separate performances, under three separate circumstances, using three separate techniques, I had no hesitation in judging that this young man, scarcely more than a boy, was absolutely and indisputably the greatest exponent of his art that the world has ever known.'

'And?'

'So I signed him to a five-year contract and vowed that he would have the chance he dreamed of, to serve and fight for

Right. But when I got down to brass tacks and drew up our plan of campaign, I saw that we were faced with the gravest obstacles. Convention was all against us; so was the law and the full weight of the Establishment. Therefore, to have any hope of success, we had to secure some help.'

'So?'

'What we needed was a guardian. Someone of wisdom and experience, compassion and great influence, who would appreciate our purpose and sympathise with our difficulties, and who would take us under his wing.'

'And?'

'Naturally, I thought of you.'

J Jones Dickerson sighed.

His office was surrounded by guards. They were hiding behind the walls, lurking in the corridors, peeping through the peepholes. Underneath J Jones Dickerson's desk there was a button and, if he pressed it, they would all come running. For a moment, his forefinger itched and hovered. Then it drew back again, and he helped himself to another jujube. 'And?' he said.

'I thought perhaps that the young man's dream might touch you and you would consent to be his friend.'

'Why?'

'Because both of you love your country, and both of you know that she is menaced by alien elements, dedicated to treason and disruption. Fanatics and conspirators, weirdos, dope fiends and perverts – Un-Americans, in a nutshell, who will not rest satisfied until they have brought her to her knees.'

'And?'

'And doubtless this is a situation that grieves you sore, and you would rejoice to see such elements crushed. But that is easier said than done. Unfortunately, it is not possible to destroy the offenders out of hand, as they deserve, for the majority have only broken the spirit, not the letter, of the law. So your hands are tied with red tape and the Bureau is forced to stand by, impotent, while everything that it loves best is defiled and dragged down in the mire.'

'Well?'

'But what if a private citizen arose, unhampered by bureaucracy, and decided to take matters into his own hands? What if he sought out these cankers and cancelled them, and America was purged of her poisons? Would you take offence? Would you call him a murderer and try to stop him? Or would you simply call him Providence?'

'And?' said J Jones Dickerson.

'And smile on him,' said Seaton.

The Englishman stood by the window and looked down into the street. Directly underneath, thirty-one floors below, a uniformed guard stood stiffly to attention. If Seaton had possessed a jujube, he could have spat it out and watched it fall, straight and true, eight hundred feet on to the centre of the guard's crew-cut scalp, splitting him in two. But he had no jujubes, not of his own, and J Jones Dickerson did not give him one.

Behind his grey desk, the Commander doodled blank faces on his blotting pad and suddenly, for no reason he could think of, he saw himself running down an alley, aged eight, throwing stones through darkened windows. 'And?' he said.

'Naturally, any support that you might give us would be tacit, the Bureau would never be mentioned by name and there would be no question of payment,' Seaton said. 'As far as the young man himself is concerned, idealist and dreamer that he is, the labour would be its own reward and any other fee would demean him.'

'But?'

'But just conceivably, if we gave you satisfaction, you would not scorn to act as our fairy godmother. Your generosity and brotherhood might be stirred, and you would honour us with something more precious than all the gold in Fort Knox.'

'Which is?'

'Protection.'

'And?'

'Just that – you might grant us shelter, so that we wouldn't be plagued by snoopers or interfering lawmen, who did not understand the sanctity of our mission and treated us like criminals.'

'And?'

'Then the young man would be free to follow his destiny unimpaired, and every one of us would reap the benefits – you, me, the Bureau and, most of all, America herself.'

J Jones Dickerson allowed his eyes to close, imagining, and he saw himself in a high-school boys' room, scrawling rude words on the walls. His mouth ceased to suck, his tongue slipped out between his grey lips. 'And?' he said.

'There is nothing more,' said Seaton. 'Our future lies in your hands.'

For a few seconds, the Commander was perfectly still. Then his eyelids trembled and he fumbled inside his trouser pocket. The Englishman was standing very close beside him, making him sweat, and he pulled out a half-emptied packet of candies. 'What do you say?' said Seaton.

'Have a jujube,' replied J Jones Dickerson.

In Tierra de Ensueños, Eddie shut himself away in a small, dark box room in the attic, where he stretched out on the bed and stared at the ceiling. The radio played *Dancing in the Dark* and he found an old gilt mirror in a cupboard, so cracked and scarred that it rendered him almost invisible, a faintest phantasmal shadow. Nightingales and whippoorwills sang sweetly in the eaves, and he passed his nights in calm self-contemplation, pursuing his own mirage.

Every morning, from nine to twelve, he trained in Manny Kaplan's gym downtown. A man in a black uniform, with a shiny peaked cap and red frogging on his shoulders, drove him down the hill in a limousine, disappearing into the smog, and Seaton came along as well, just for the ride.

The gymnasium was high and clear, an empty white gallery, as impersonal as an abattoir. It smelled of embrocation and abstinence, a stale sour scent that stung the eyes and dried out the throat, like chlorine. Entering, Eddie would remove his hat and coat, rub the soles of his shiny boots with resin, spit into his black leather palms, jog and shuffle on the spot. Sometimes he went so far as to strip off his gloves or loosen his belt a notch. Beyond that he would not go, however, for every form of nakedness, even his own, repelled him.

Seaton had hired him a personal trainer, a crabbed old scarface named Mantequilla Wickham, thirty years a veteran, revered throughout the industry, though he was holed and gouged like a crater of the moon. In spats and fedora, with his back against the wall, his hands might be a trifle shaky these days, his joints a hint arthritic, but his eyes were still remorseless, his mouth a vice, and what he did not know about Death only a corpse could have told.

Mantequilla did not speak but spat out his instructions, like tiny plugs of tobacco, through a hole in his lower lip. Rapping time on the floor with a silver-topped cane, he was merciless; and Eddie skipped rope, vaulted over wooden horses, drove himself through round after round of press-ups, trunk curls, abdominal stretches. Medicine balls were hurled into his flanks and belly, ropes cut his hands, dust choked him. His clean white shirt and tight black vest were soaked in sweat, and his eyes filled with blood.

The doors were locked, tarpaulins placed over the windows, every crack and chink of light extinguished, until the performer was cloaked in total darkness, so profound that he could not even make out the glint of his own crucifix. A projector whirred, a shadow ran across a doorway, and he whirled and fired and fired again. Phantom knives flew at his back and he flung himself sideways, backward, flat on his face. His feet hissed and scuffed on the canvas, iron weights crashed down from the ceiling. Mantequilla spat, and he was trapped and bound by lassos. Images cornered and crushed him, he blazed from the hip and they were gone. A crystal ball crashed into his face, he shattered it in a hundred fragments. Mantequilla spat and Eddie was motionless. He stood in pitch blackness, waiting.

Beneath the gymnasium windows, there was a Mexicali street market. The sidewalks spilled over with watermelons and ripe avocados, tacos stalls, hot tamales. Fat women scrimmaged for bargains, and skinny young dudes, with greased-back hair and pencil moustaches, pared their nails with switchblades. Seaton waited at the corner, in the back of the long black limousine, and watched through smoked-glass windows.

At the sound of gunfire, nobody screamed and nobody ran. A gaggle of small children, playing touch football with an iceberg lettuce, paused for a moment to look up at the blacked-out windows and moved off round the corner. The women paid and picked up their baskets, the stallholders turned away, the dudes slouched off into basements. Curtains were drawn, radios stopped playing and doors slammed far away. Eddie whirled and fired and fired again, and the block was deserted.

Only Seaton was left. Snug inside the limousine, nestling in Turkish tapestry cushions, he consulted Wisden on Victor Trumper, for the golden summer of 1902. Stray cats prowled among the stalls, papers flapped idly in the gutters. Promptly at noon, the man in the black uniform brought out egg and tomato sandwiches, Dundee cake and jasmine tea in a thermos. Then Seaton lay back like a plump pink cat, purring. Nothing moved in the market and the only sound was gunfire.

Mort Mossbacher was Programme Director at HBLF, the number one network in the nation, and had collaborated with Seaton in all of the Englishman's most successful images. Inside the medium, he was a mogul second to none, and his subordinates called him The Man. Yet he suffered severely from haemorrhoids and often cried out in his sleep, his toupee blew off in high winds and there was almost always a gap of white, hairless shin to be seen between his socks and his trouser cuffs.

Throughout their long association, Seaton had never once invited him inside the mansion gates. But now Mossbacher suddenly received a summons, and he found himself in a velvet viewing theatre, high among the minarets.

Resplendent in a white tuxedo, Seaton smoked a fat cigar and quaffed champagne from a silver goblet, and he put his arm around Mort Mossbacher's shoulders. 'I have a new performer. I believe you're going to like him,' Seaton said.

'What is his angle?'

'Watch, and I will show you.'

A screen was projected on to the ceiling, the lights were

dimmed. Seaton clapped his hands, and Eddie was revealed in medium close-up, silhouetted in left profile, dark and brooding against a pale dawn sky.

The performer stood motionless in a swamp of seaweed, while the waters lapped at his shiny black boots, and he faced out towards the horizon. The shore was cold and grey and desolate. Then Seaton clapped his hands again and immediately the water turned bright blue, the sand became mellow gold. Sunlight sparkled on the waves and, as the first rays caught his face, awakening him, Eddie began to turn his head towards the cameras, until he was gazing directly into the lens. His eyes seemed to fill the entire screen.

He started walking, coming straight towards the viewers. His face was absolutely still and his eyes never blinked. Shaded by the angle of his hat brim, they were both tender and unreachable, and he almost smiled.

Mort Mossbacher began to sweat. His heart burned and he reached inside his pocket, in search of a yellow pill. But before he could find one, Eddie had produced a gun and shot him lovingly through the centre of his forehead, an illusion so vivid that he actually seemed to feel the bullet rip through his skull, his blood spurt, all his life drain away.

He slumped back in his seat and went limp. Once again, Seaton clapped his hands, and Eddie put away his smoking gun, turned his back, returned to the water's edge. The sunshine was extinguished, the shore grew bleak again. Silhouetted in left profile, dark and brooding, Eddie faced out towards the horizon.

The screen went blank, the lights were rekindled. Seaton poured himself another glass of champagne, and Mort Mossbacher did not move. Eyes closed, mouth open, his arms hung loosely by his sides. For almost a minute, there was silence. Then the Englishman struck a match. 'What do you think?' he asked.

'He's got something,' replied the Director faintly.

'That is the understatement of the century,' Seaton cried. 'I have been showing this same sequence to my families and let me tell you, the response has been absolutely electric. They have been dumbstruck, staggered, spellbound. In all the years that they have lived here, I don't believe that I have ever seen them so stirred by any new image before.'

'He certainly has impact.'

'Impact? He's magic. In my opinion, he possesses the very greatest gift that any artist can ever be blessed with.'

'Which is?'

'Sensation,' said the Englishman. 'He has the power to make people feel.'

Three weeks passed, and every day followed an identical pattern. In the mornings, Mantequilla spat in the dark and Eddie fired from the hip; in the afternoons, the performer posed for the cameras; and at night, alone in his attic bedroom, he sat motionless in front of the mirror. Meanwhile, Seaton went strolling through his gardens with J Jones Dickerson and Mort Mossbacher, their heads bent close in consultation.

As the days went by, all that Eddie ever did was rehearse, and he began to grow restless. It was almost two months since he had made his last completion, the longest layoff that he'd had in years, and the inactivity brought him out in a rash.

Descending from his room, he tracked Seaton down to his hammock and confronted him squarely: 'I am not happy,' said Eddie.

'How come?'

'I am kept too long in idleness,' the performer told him.

'If this doesn't end soon, I will lose everything.'

'Why should you?'

'Death will not be kept waiting. If her blessing is wasted, she will withdraw it and, once she is gone, no professional can ever win her back. Therefore, I must keep hard at work. Training is all very well, kept in its proper place, but there is no substitute for the reality. Without it, a man goes soft, his touch and timing desert him and he forgets what he was created for. Before he knows what's happened, he has lost his vocation altogether and is only fit for killing.'

After dark, the partners drank hot toddies by the fireside and a dry wind hissed in the chimney, the windows rattled, the floorboards creaked and sighed. The mansion stretched out interminably on every side, full of draughts and indecipherable echoes, and Eddie was troubled by a persistent itch in the small of his back, which he couldn't quite reach to scratch: 'Besides,' he said, 'I don't feel right inside.'

'What's the matter?'

'I cannot rightly say. So long as I stay downtown, in the gym or on the streets, I'm fine. But as soon as I come back through these gates, the moment I set foot in the gardens, I turn sour and listless and my limbs are weighted down with lead. Maybe it's the air, maybe I'm just homesick. But whatever the cause, when I wake up in the night, there is the strangest taste in my mouth.'

'Perhaps there's something wrong with your regime,' Seaton said.

'How could there be? I follow the same discipline that I've always done. I eat nothing but honest home cooking, I do not drink or smoke, I have no truck with women and I sleep eight hours every night. I am clean.'

'And yet?'

'Inside this house,' said Eddie, 'I feel soiled.'

The Englishman looked blank and asked no more questions. But long after midnight, when Eddie had gone upstairs to bed, he continued to sit by the fire, staring into the embers. The screens were dead, the families were all asleep. Lost birds flew into the windows, and Seaton was utterly alone.

First thing in the morning, he called for J Jones Dickerson and Mort Mossbacher, and the three of them reclined in an arbour full of pink and yellow roses. Watching from his attic, Eddie could not hear what they were saying, but they sported carnations and drank repeatedly from the lemonade fountain. For an hour, they laughed with their mouths wide open and scattered petals every which way. When at last they arose, however, they shook hands formally and, suddenly, all of them looked most solemn.

Three days later, as Seaton lolled in the back of the black limousine, surrounded by chickpeas, *guacamole* and red hot peppers, a scrofulous youth in blue jeans came sauntering through the market and ambled down the block, passing underneath the blackened gymnasium windows.

Between a pawnshop and a seafood store, he came to a large brick wall, every inch of which was covered with scrawled obscenities, propaganda slogans, love plights and catchwords. Inside the gym, behind the tarpaulins, there was a rattle of machine-gun fire and the youth paused for a moment, idly scratching his rump, as he scanned the collected graffiti. Then he reached inside his back pocket and, while the Englishman watched through smoked-glass windows, he pulled out a stick of yellow chalk.

Upstairs, Eddie threw nine knives in the space of 3.78 seconds, to form a perfect heart on the wall. Mantequilla spat and in large, clumsy lettering, obliterating half a dozen previous declarations at a single scrawl, the youth wrote:

KARL ROSEN IS AN UNAMERICAN.

Seen in long shot, early in the morning, Popular Park was a wasteland. Three tramps were asleep on sacking and one old lady walked her dog. A soft rain fell on shrivelled trees and, in the distance, there were high black tenements with tiny windows.

From one of these windows, on the sixth floor, came a faint and intermittent dazzle, like Morse code spelled out on a scrap of broken mirror. Inside there was a small bare room, with just a bed, a table and rickety chair, and Eddie stood with his back to the cameras, flicking dice.

On the other side of town, meanwhile, Karl Rosen yawned. Rising from slumber, he stretched and shook himself. Then he sat on the edge of his bed, bare feet dangling, and his long black hair fell forward in a tangle across his face.

He was a mischief-maker; disturbance was his profession. He organised marches and mass rallies, he made speeches about revolution, he was photographed with machine guns. He waved his fist and shook his hair and swore. Three times already, he had been arrested and brought to trial; three times, on different technicalities, he had won an acquittal.

Such feats had made him heroic. His public appearances filled football stadiums and amusement parks, his books and manifestos were bibles, and a hundred thousand posters, stuck up in lofts and cellars across the country, showed him brooding and defiant, in beard and beret, behind a barbed-wire barricade.

In celebration of his latest acquittal, he undertook

a nationwide tour, declaiming at rallies in every major city, and so it was that he had come to Chicago, where he commandeered a duplex overlooking the lake and turned it into his operational headquarters. He had the front door painted red, pulled down all the blinds and installed a target range. Men with rifles and steel-capped boots patrolled the corridors, there were hand grenades in the icebox. Underneath the guerrilla's bedroom window, a gaggle of teenage girls kept vigil through the night.

On the day appointed for his appearance, fans and sympathisers began to assemble from breakfast onward. At first in twos and threes, then in a continuous stream, they converged from all over the city, and by noon Popular Park was filled to overflowing.

The crowd was dressed in anoraks and badges and dirtied-down sneakers, they carried banners and chanted slogans. Police encircled them and helicopters hovered overhead, cameras weaved and burrowed among them like electronic ferrets. Electric music blared, and the black mass of the tenements was almost forgotten.

At the sixth-floor window, a shadow appeared, a dark watching shape, barely visible behind the glass. In close-up, this shape was revealed as a black slouch hat, drawn low across a single opaque eye, steady and unblinking.

After lunch, Karl Rosen put on his army boots, his combat jacket, his beret. He kissed his wife and children goodbye and was driven away in a jeep, closely followed by a convoy of other jeeps, flanked in turn by a troupe of motorcycle outriders. There was a bodyguard to his left, a bodyguard to his right, a bodyguard in front and a bodyguard behind, and Karl sat snug in a bullet-proof vest.

By now the crowd had reached forty thousand and, right

at the farthest extreme of the park, raised high on a wooden platform, where they were half hidden behind a rampart of microphones, men in beards and berets had already begun to make speeches.

When Karl Rosen came into sight, he stood up in the back of his jeep and raised his right arm above his head, his fist tightly clenched. Instantly, forty thousand fists shot up in response, like so many TV aerials, and the chanting rose to a crescendo. The outriders revved their engines, the police fingered their batons. Karl Rosen's black hair blew out behind him in a slipstream.

In the sixth-floor bedroom, Eddie opened up his suitcase and crouched down by the window, focused in left profile. His image was repeated endlessly; his eyes, his hands, his silhouette. Under the blazing arc lights, he crossed himself, and Karl Rosen, stately, most solemn, ascended the platform.

He took up his station behind the microphones. Seen from the tenements, he looked frail and undernourished and for almost a minute he waited without speaking, while the chanting broke in wave after wave upon his bowed head. When he raised his hand for silence and the tumult was hushed, everything went still. 'Peace,' said Karl Rosen, and instantly his eyes were snuffed out, like candles, in giant close-up.

The guerrilla fell over backwards. As he did so, his feet got entangled with the microphone wires and the entire system came crashing down on top of him, almost burying him. Eddie gazed directly into the lens and, for a second, his eyes caught fire. Then they dimmed again and he was gone.

From the park below, there arose a formless muttering and growling, like bubbling in a cauldron. At first impact, the crowd had been paralysed but now they began to crane their necks and shout. The bodyguards drew their guns, the lieutenants sprang to their fallen leader's side. A single volcanic scream, pre-recorded, soared high and clear above the hubbub, in ultimate grief and terror, and in this instant the sound was cut, the image froze.

The final frame, in medium close-up, showed Karl Rosen flat on his back. You could see the soles of his army boots and his beret, which lay by his side, just an inch from his clutching fingers; you could see the foreshortened rise of his torso and the petrified faces of his aides, suspended above him. The lone scream reverberated in pure silence and, printed neatly across the centre of the screen, two words appeared:

KING DEATH.

3

The first reviews were most disappointing. Out of three hundred and seventy-three publications which gave the Rosen completion headlines and/or editorials, not a single one proved sympathetic, and the vast majority were downright rude. Nobody understood and nobody was impressed. Nobody even recognised the artistry of execution, the sheer virtuosity of both performance and production. Instead, there was a unanimous howl of outrage, and Eddie himself was described as an assassin.

In Tierra de Ensueños, the morning afterwards, he sat beside the swimming pool, with his head bowed and his hat pulled low across his eyes, and employed his jugulator to whittle at a switch of elm, carving holes for a penny whistle. The shavings flew over his shoulder, to float on the chlorine-green waters, and even in medium long shot, judging by the speed and severity of his strokes, it was plain that he was distressed.

Front pages stuck to his feet, twined themselves about his shins, and everywhere he looked, he saw himself referred to as a psychopath, a canker and an animal. He felt trapped and kicked out his ankles, to free himself. But the more he fretted, the tighter the newsprint clung.

Meanwhile, Seaton was sunning himself in his hammock, clad in a tartan swimsuit. His belly slopped loosely over his waistband and, sipping at a Pimms, he worked his way serenely through the whole massive pile of clippings.

Dutiful, he went tut-tut at every insult and wrinkled up his nose at each fresh tirade. Nevertheless, he did not stop smiling and, when at last he arrived at the bottom of the pile, he merely shrugged and spread wide his hands: 'Not to worry,' he said. 'Rome was not built in a day, and big oaks from little acorns grow. We've known all along that we would meet with folly and injustice, at least to begin with, and Death would not triumph without a long, hard fight.'

'They call me a killer,' Eddie said.

'I noticed that, and I'm not surprised that you take it amiss. Still, we mustn't lose our sense of proportion. They're only expressing a conditioned reflex, a built-in sales resistance. Nothing that patience and perseverance won't put right. The day will come, I promise you, when many of these self-same hysterics will be numbered among your staunchest adherents.'

Eddie was not consoled. Even though Seaton had warned him in advance, he was profoundly shocked and hurt. Constructive criticism was one thing, and he had no objection to civilised debate. But this was something else entirely – brutish and foul-mouthed abuse – and he burned inside for shame.

Seaton, sorrowing to see him so cast down, poured him a Dr Pepper; but the performer left it untouched, and the jugulator flashed and hissed like a serpent's tongue: 'They say that I'm a disease and I'm mentally deformed,' he said. 'One of them even calls me godless.'

'Take no notice,' Seaton told him. 'Critics are buffoons, they always have been, they always will be, and you mustn't let them upset you. Besides, they are irrelevant. When it comes to selling images, only one thing matters. John Q Public. Mister Average.'

'He hates me, too.'

'How do you know?'

'This morning, while I was brushing my teeth, Jerry McGhee was on the monitor and he called me something I will not repeat. Furthermore, his wife and daughter agreed with him.'

'Is that so?'

'You know I do not lie.'

'Then all I can say is splendid,' Seaton cried. 'If they call you names of such a nature, it proves that they must have watched. And what is far more important, they must have been deeply stirred.'

This was very true. Indeed, when Jerry first witnessed the Karl Rosen completion, his knees had turned to jelly and he almost purged his bowels. 'Sweet Jesus Christ,' he muttered and turned his face to the wall, while his wife Martha knelt down on the floor and was sick into a green plastic bucket.

The same sort of reaction was repeated throughout the mansion; without exception, the residents were startled, shaken, thrown into disarray. Nonetheless, though they were sickened, they were also fascinated. When the instant replay came up, they did not stop watching.

Beside the pool, reflected in a dozen screens, Karl Rosen raised his hand for silence and his eyes disappeared, first the left, then the right. In slow motion, he described a graceful backward parabola, weightless as a spacewalker. He floated and looped, he drifted to earth like a leaf. When he went still, his toes pointed straight up to heaven.

After a moment's interval, the same sequence began all over again. Eddie raised his half-finished whistle to his lips and blew a few notes, shrill and discordant. The lizards basking in the sun were startled and scuttled off into the shadows, and all the songbirds were silenced. 'I don't belong here; I'm lost,' Eddie said.

'Please don't despair,' said Seaton. 'At this stage of the game, believe me, love and hate are meaningless. Your only need is to make an impact, establish your name and image, as you are already doing. Afterwards, adulation comes automatically.'

But Eddie was not listening. For a moment, all he could think of was Tupelo, where he had felt at home and no one had dared call him names. When he shut his eyes, he felt again the heat and torpor of the sidewalks, the seclusion of the darkened doorway, the ever-changing glowlights inside The Golden Slipper, and his heart was caught up by strange currents, which made him want to hide.

Although it was not complete, he dropped the whistle into his overcoat pocket, and he put away the jugulator in his suitcase. He disappeared inside the mansion, lost himself in the labyrinth, and the only trace that was left of him was a pool full of shavings.

That same night, when Tierra de Ensueños was sleeping, he packed his suitcase, knotted his sheets and secured them to the bedpost, swung his left leg across the window sill and prepared to make good his escape.

A full moon gleamed among the minarets, lighting his way, and the gardens were flooded by a silvery radiance. Just before he began his descent, Eddie looked down and saw a young doe drinking from a fountain, directly beneath his window.

As it gazed at its own reflection, bathed in moonlight, it could almost have passed for Bambi. So pure did it appear, indeed, that the whole garden was transformed. All sense of decay and corruption disappeared. The undergrowths were silenced, there were no more whisperings or hidden scurryings. So long as the fawn went on drinking, Tierra de Ensueños was lulled into innocence, stillness, peace.

Hovering on the brink of his window sill, with one leg out and one leg in, Eddie watched for a long time without moving. Then at last he drew back, put down his suitcase and, instead of running, he lay down on his bed, where he soon fell fast asleep.

First thing next morning, he went back into training.

Clearly, after Karl Rosen, it was not feasible to venture downtown any more, so Eddie rigged up an impromptu gym behind the greenhouses and threw himself fiercely, almost fanatically, into his work. Mantequilla spat in the petunia patch and the performer jumped through blazing hoops, flung himself through windows, shot from the hip until his trigger finger was raw and bleeding. Meanwhile, the Englishman consulted endlessly in the maze with J Jones Dickerson and Mort Mossbacher.

Outside the mansion gates, the police searched high and low but King Death could not be found. For almost a week, both he and Karl Rosen kept a firm grip on the front pages. Then other sensations took their place and they quickly receded into the background.

At the same time, the families slipped back into their familiar apathy. Fresh images overlaid the gutted sockets of the Un-American's eyes, the perfection of Eddie's left profile. Everything returned to normal.

Jerry McGhee struck up a casual liaison with Sarah Carter, Tom Potterson came down with mumps, Barney Brannigan made himself sick on applejack. The orchids bloomed and the catalpas died, and the screens never ceased to flicker.

Eddie stood by his window, lay on his bed, sat in front of his mirror. The radio played *Love For Sale* and, at the end of the fifth week, suitcase in hand, he descended from the attic and was driven away across America, in search of Jade Carney, the singer, idol and pervert.

He travelled to Dallas, immured behind smoked-glass windows, and felt as though he were cruising in a space capsule, divorced from weight and time. Though the limousine sped at a hundred miles an hour, it was not he but the landscape outside that seemed to move, flashing past like a series of back-projected sets in a film, while Eddie himself never stirred.

Wild ponies went galloping through the redwoods, waterfalls burst and exploded far below. On the far horizon, across an infinity of wheat fields, there was a cowboy on an unblemished white horse. Wires hummed, distant lights flared up in the dark. A vulture circled high overhead and, when Eddie awoke, the sky was full of thick black smoke. The prairies were transformed into factories, the factories into oil fields. Monstrous red ovens glowed in the night and the limousine was deluged with writhing fireballs. In the morning, the plains were full of cattle. At dusk, Eddie slept beside a deep dark river.

In Dallas, Jade Carney sniffed crystals in his dressing room and made up his eyes with golden glitterdust. Then he began to brush out his corn-yellow hair, one hundred strokes with the left hand, one hundred strokes with the right.

Jade, whose father had been a postal worker in Hoboken, had a mouth like a shiny red mailbox and a slipping and sliding, squirming and slithering pink electric tongue. Onstage, he moved his legs so fast that they blurred and dissolved like pages in a flicker book and, when young girls screamed at him, he would stick out his buttocks, stick out his electric tongue, entice and goad and tease, until they were driven past endurance and stormed the stage in delirium, at which point the guards would swing their batons, blood would flow and Jade would disappear.

Now, alone in his dressing room, waiting to be unleashed, he puckered his lips and painted them bright scarlet. From the auditorium, there came an incessant high-pitched screaming, unvarying, inhuman.

Though the noise was deafening, Jade remained quite separate and did not seem to notice. Fists hammered at his door, despairing voices cried out his name, screams and electronic feedback meshed together into a single apocalyptic howl – he blew himself a kiss, studying his lips in the mirror, and reached again for the crystals.

Fluttering his eyelashes, he bent his head to sniff and, as he did so, a shadow fell across the glass. Without any sound or preparation, Eddie appeared behind the singer's back and their heads moved close together, their cheeks almost touched.

So thickly was Jade painted, so masklike was his face, that it wasn't easy, even in full-screen close-up, to guess at his real feelings. For the first few seconds, he opened and shut his bright mouth, possibly in protest. But no words came out, only faintest gurglings, which might have meant almost anything, and soon even these were silenced. Then Eddie held him close, soothing him and petting him, coaxing him like a groom with a nervous colt, and, as if of their own accord, Jade's limbs relaxed.

Now the din and confusion vanished, all mess and hysteria gone for ever, and nothing remained but Jade and the performer, his touch so firm yet gentle, his eyes so full of light. With a little sigh, the singer shut his eyes and, when Eddie whispered in his ear, he must have heard something amusing. At any rate, he smiled and stuck out the tip of his pink tongue and, abandoning himself entirely, he let himself drift down into sleep, where he was safe.

Having rendered Jade Carney, Eddie drove back to the mansion and shut himself inside his bedroom. For three days and nights, he lay on his back, sleeping, flicking dice and playing *The Battle Hymn of the Republic* on a beat-up old harmonica. He neither read his reviews nor watched his performance on the screens, and he was content.

When at last he returned to the perfumed garden, he discovered Seaton lounging in the shade of the fig tree, with his mouth full of ripe red flesh. 'Dear boy,' said the Englishman. 'You were magnificent.'

'I'm glad you liked it.'

'Liked it? I was overcome. Even by your own standards, it was a *tour de force* beyond words, and this time, make no mistake, you have truly put the cat among the pigeons. At a single stroke, you have become a superstar. Every paper in the country is full of you, the networks plug you hourly. As for the families, they talk of nothing else.'

'Do they still hate me?'

'They do not know,' said Seaton. 'They hate you and they are drawn to you, they are shocked and overawed, and they can't forget you. Just like myself, when I first saw you, they are flung into hopeless confusion.'

Eddie asked no more questions; now that he had recovered from the shock of his first reviews, the details of his progress no longer intrigued him. On the contrary, all this fuss and hysteria was an embarrassment. By nature, he was discreet and retiring, a born ascetic, and bright lights hurt his eyes.

In particular, he was disturbed by this new name, King Death, which made him think of all-in wrestlers – cheap, loud and exhibitionist, everything that Death herself would most despise. So he hurried back inside his attic, where vulgarities could not reach him, and there he waited, emerging only to train, until it was time for the next completion.

He cultivated geraniums in a window box, he played on his harmonica, he carved two small notches on the bedpost with his occisor. At dead of night, when nothing moved or made a sound, he fingered his crucifix in the dark and was transported back to Tupelo, to the doorway of the Chinese laundry.

At last, when another month had elapsed, Seaton tapped lightly on the door and he was released. Pausing only to pick up his suitcase, he set out towards Milwaukee, where he met with Ahmed Abdul Fakir.

Ahmed Abdul, formerly known as Leroy Jefferson, was eighty-six inches tall, played basketball for the Cleveland Juggernauts, and in his spare time preached Islam. He faced east at sunset, he yearned for Ethiopia, he carried guns underneath his caftan, and every time he passed a lawman, he spat in the dust. When he appeared on the Marvin Quincey Show, he referred to Uncle Sam as a honky racist pigfucker.

Accordingly, on the following evening, just as he was rising to the basket, he felt a sudden pain in the back of his neck, which did not destroy him instantly but left him paralysed. For a moment, there was an illusion that he had simply congealed and was hanging in mid air, suspended by invisible wires. Then he unfurled and gently swooned upon the court, where he stretched out flat on his back, a stricken black giraffe.

Viewer response was overwhelming.

As relayed by HBLF, Ahmed Abdul achieved an audience rating of 63.27 per cent across the nation, which made him the number one spectacle of the entire season. Wherever he was shown, in bars or coffee shops or supermarts, excited crowds assembled and women screamed, men started fights. Three senators, seven congressmen and thirteen clerics made speeches, and the police posted notices on every blank wall they could find, in which King Death was valued at a hundred thousand dollars, dead or alive.

Meanwhile, in Tierra de Ensueños, buzzers buzzed and bleepers bleeped in chorus, sounding forth with an eagerness and insistency not equalled for many long months, and their mingled song rang out in the Englishman's ears like electronic church bells, joyful and triumphant.

Sarah Carter festooned her windows with strings of garlic, to keep the performer at bay, and big Jim Haggard took to sleeping with a loaded pistol underneath his pillow. On the first night alone, Seaton replayed the completion sixteen times; Barney Brannigan watched them all.

Another month passed by.

Once again, King Death faded from the headlines. But this time his memory remained undimmed. In just three renditions, he had created such a profound impression that no amount of strikes, air crashes or South American revolutions could erase him. Through all the years that the families had spent watching, no other image had ever reached them so deeply, had caused their hearts to beat so hard or their stomachs to lurch so strangely, and even while he was languishing in abeyance, they dreamed of him nightly.

For thirty-three days, Eddie stared at the ceiling and, on the thirty-fourth, he travelled to Boston, where he introduced himself to Mayor Claude O'Hannigan, the homosexual.

On the evening that the King arrived, Mayor Claude was special guest of honour at a Gala Trans-sexual Funfest and made his speech in a scarlet satin dress, peroxide wig and frilly garters. Afterwards, when the shrieks and cheering died down, he returned to his hotel and entered an empty elevator.

Halfway between the twenty-third and twenty-fourth floors, the mechanism jammed and the lights went out, leaving him stranded in pitch blackness. He bit his lip, he held his breath, he tried not to whimper. Then somebody struck a match and he found himself gazing into the strangest blank eyes, which lured him irresistibly. As if of their own accord, his eyelashes fluttered, his red lips parted and one of his shoulder straps slipped. 'Love me,' whispered Mayor Claude, and his throat was slit in a kiss.

Yet another month elapsed, and then came Walter 'Big Walt' Grodzinski, the Trotskyite labour leader from Pittsburgh, consumed in one of his own blast furnaces; then Preston Pitts, the chemical mystic; and then Dr Reuben Mark, the Harvard militant.

Now King Death had appeared seven times in so many months, and his works had been witnessed by the best part of one hundred and fifty million citizens. His name had become universal, his image inescapable. According to the ratings, he was the hottest property in all America.

At HBLF headquarters, six secretaries and six stenographers in slate-grey uniforms laboured five days a week to cope with his mail and file his reviews, no matter how unkind. After each performance, the switchboards would be jammed solid for twenty-four hours.

By this time, the King had received official recognition. Even as the last fragments of Big Walt Grodzinski glimmered and died in the background, Attorney General Flaherty called an emergency press conference and named the professional Public Enemy Number One, with an adjusted valuation of half a million dollars.

For a performer still in his first season, this was a distinction quite without parallel. But soon he achieved an even greater landmark, something so tremendous that, when Eddie returned to the mansion after Reuben Mark, Seaton opened wide his arms and clasped him to his bosom: 'Words fail me,' said the Englishman.

'Why? What has happened?'

'Mr President himself has responded. Last night, when he got the news about the Doctor, he made an unscheduled appearance on HBLF and spoke of you to the nation, as a major domestic issue.'

'Was he rude?'

'Indeed he was. In less than ten minutes, he denounced you with fifty-three adjectives, thirty-seven nouns, eighteen verbs and twenty-six adverbs. His cheeks went grey, there were traces of froth at the corners of his mouth, his voice grew hoarse with passion. Without exaggeration, I have never known him wax so wrathful about anything.'

'And that makes you happy?'

'It overwhelms me,' Seaton said, blowing his nose. 'To think that a man of his position should be so deeply stirred, his imagination so devoured, all in the space of a few short months, that passion overwhelms him and he shouts it from the rooftops – it almost exceeds my dreams.'

'I do my best; no man can do more,' Eddie told him, and once more the performer escaped into his attic.

Still, he did not feel at peace. The longer he spent in Tierra de Ensueños, the less its climate seemed to suit his blood, and he was afflicted by an ever-increasing lethargy. He lost his appetite, his senses were clouded by a ceaseless buzzing in his ears, and his limbs were weighed down by a most peculiar drowsiness, which no amount of sleep could dissipate.

Each day passed like the one before. Mechanical as a sleep-walker, Eddie wandered through the corridors, looked down from his window, trained behind the greenhouses, tended his geraniums, put out breadcrumbs for the orioles, rummaged in his suitcase, studied his reflection, threw knives, twirled lassos and yawned. From time to time, when he could not avoid it, he suffered himself to be posed in left profile, silhouetted against a technorama sunset. But mostly he lay on his back, eyes wide open, and dreamed of sidewalks.

Down below, Seaton ambled through the gardens, sniffing contentedly at the roses. These were carefree, sunlit passages in his life, and there were moments when he almost felt like new.

But the families grew restless.

King Death had become a habit; they felt flat without him. After completions, all other images seemed empty and used up, hopelessly artificial. To while away the time, they thumbed through magazines, stared at the screens, studied their horoscopes. But nothing could hold their attention or take their minds off the King. They still called him names but he alone could release them, could actually make them *feel*, and even though they knew that they were wrong to do so, they yearned for his return.

Facing the mirror, Eddie brought out his occisor and carved an eighth notch on the bedpost. Thirty-six hours later, in San Francisco, the pornographer Cal McCracklin was drowned in a cesspit.

On a hill overlooking the city, McCracklin's works were gathered together into a gigantic bonfire, arranged in the shape of a cross. Eddie lit the blue touch paper and instantly, courtesy of HBLF, a great flame swept the nation. In medium close-up framed against the blazing cross, the performer adjusted his hat and raised his right hand, as if to take his solemn oath, pledging himself till Death.

His flesh was incandescent, his eyes shone like candles at an altar. In Tierra de Ensueños, the fire leaped high in the deserted galleries, refracted through a hundred mirrors and screens, and the families were blinded by the glare. Even in reflection, the heat made them sweat, smoke got in their eyes, they could hardly breathe. Safe and snug in their compartments, they burned.

On the first anniversary of Karl Rosen, Seaton organised a small celebration and the partners dined together by candlelight, seated at opposite ends of the banquet hall.

They sat in two pools of light, so far apart that neither could guess the other's expression. In one, the Englishman appeared in a white dinner jacket, patent pumps and a velvet bow tie, and fed himself on asparagus and lobster, roast quail and strawberry trifle; in the other, his uniform unchanging, Eddie consumed a bowl of black-eyed peas.

In the absence of any conversation, the screens performed a selection of highlights from the past year's works and, when the sequence was over, Seaton rose to his feet, raising his glass in a toast. 'To us,' he said.

'To Death,' replied the professional.

Afterwards in the library, over brandy and Dr Pepper, they listened to the wind howl in the chimney, hiss in the corridors, rattle at the windows, and both of them were borne away on different journeys, Eddie to the wastelands of Mississippi, Seaton back to the cricket grounds of England.

Meanwhile, on the monitor, Jerry McGhee, Charley Mitchell and Barney Brannigan were revealed in the pool room, drinking cold Coors, and, as was their custom, they talked about King Death.

Seaton paid no attention. By this time, discussions of the King were ten a penny, and he snuggled deep into his armchair, feet up in front of the fire, dreaming contentedly of Trumper and SF Barnes, 1903–4.

Ten minutes went by in perfect peace, and he was just on the verge of dozing off, when suddenly one remark detached itself from the background mumble and hit him between the eyes: 'Facts is facts,' said Jerry McGhee. 'The guy is still a killer.'

On the surface, this remark was nothing untoward. It had been made many thousands of times before, both inside and outside the mansion, and Seaton had always shrugged it off. But this time, for some odd reason, perhaps because he was dreaming of cricket, his tolerance snapped.

Furious, he pulled himself upright in the armchair, snatched his feet from in front of the comforting fire, and shut off the monitors with a thump of his clenched fist. 'Ingrates,' he said. 'Bare-faced hypocrites.'

'They still seem confused,' said Eddie.

'I have tried to be patient. God knows, I've done my best

to understand. When the first reviews came out and you were downcast, it was I who told you to be philosophic and wait without rancour until the tide turned, believing deep in my heart that Right must out in the end. But a full year has passed, still they persist in the same inanities, and I have reached the end of my tether.'

'They mean no harm; they just don't know any better.'

'Then it's time that they learned. Week after week, month after month, they have had an unparalleled chance to learn and comprehend and, if they haven't seen the light by now, they ought to be ashamed.'

'They have no guidance.'

'The plain fact is they're using you. They gobble up everything that you offer them, wallow in your sensations, come alive through your magic, live out all their dreams and most secret imaginings. And then, the moment that you're gone, they turn around and call you a killer.'

'I bear no grudge.'

'They simply don't deserve you. Spoiled brats that they are, they take you for granted and think they can treat you like dirt. And yet, if ever they lost you, how soon they'd change their tune!'

Midnight struck. At once, Eddie stood up and prepared to leave. By candlelight, his features seemed to dissolve and reform continually, and his eyes glowed green and gold, as though he were a Persian cat. 'Folks are strange,' he said. 'They never miss their water until the well runs dry.'

'That being the case,' replied the Englishman, 'I believe that we're due for a drought.'

Three days later, a stranger in a black overcoat, black gloves and a black slouch hat booked into a seedy backroads motel, somewhere on the fringes of Bakersfield, and shut himself in his room.

The desk clerk recognised him straightaway, called the police and, within fifteen minutes, the motel was surrounded by a hundred lawmen, armed to the teeth, who moved in as warily as if they were tracking a yeti. When at last they reached the stranger's door, they took a deep breath and broke it down without knocking.

Inside, the man in black was stretched out idly on his bed with his shoes and socks off, watching his own image on Channel 5. Looking up at the intruders, he gave no sign of surprise or dismay but simply put his boots back on and, rising, presented his wrists to be handcuffed. 'No comment,' he said, and his eyes were hidden behind a pair of big black shades.

When they brought him back to Bakersfield headquarters, the lawmen placed him in a white room without windows and tried to make him suffer. They tied him to a hard-backed chair, took away his hat and gloves and coat, exploded flashbulbs in his face. Then they asked him hundreds and thousands of questions. 'No comment,' said the stranger.

Attorney General Flaherty arrived from Washington, exultant, and with a single sweep of his arm, he flung aside the all-concealing shades. Underneath, he found a face without distinction of any kind. The flesh was pallid, the lips unfirm, the eyes dull and asexual. Clearly, removed from the magic of the cameras, King Death looked just like anyone else.

For a moment, Flaherty felt the clammiest touch on the back of his neck. Somehow, he had assumed that the King must be special, full of strangeness and mystique, and this absolute normality upset him worse than any deformity. Still, he was too professional to let his disappointment show.

Without a word or sign, he rescued the broken shades from underneath a desk and dusted them, and the prisoner was led away to a cell.

When the news of his capture was released, the first reaction was simply one of shock. King Death had performed so many times without being caught, had displayed such uncanny gifts for escaping, that the public had come to think of him as intangible, like some kind of comic-strip Superman, who could appear and vanish at will, ride the wind, transmogrify himself into any shape that he desired. Yet here he was, for no good reason, with no appropriate drama, trapped like any other mortal: 'Say what you like,' said Jerry McGhee. 'It's a bit of a letdown.'

'I guess he got tired,' said Mildred Potterson.

'And who could blame him?' said big Jim Haggard. 'All alone on the highway, no place to call his home, not a friend in the world, not even a change of clothes, and a hundred thousand lawmen on his trail, like hounds out of hell – no wonder he grew discouraged.'

'Just the same,' said Jerry McGhee. 'It isn't much of an ending.'

This sense of anticlimax was increased by the trial itself. Televised live, it opened to ratings of 79.83 per cent and the expectation of most stupendous dramas. As things turned out, however, there were no thrills or treats of any kind.

Two hundred witnesses came forward in turn, each naming the prisoner as King Death. The prosecution thundered, the cameras rolled, the judge banged away with his gavel. But the man in black made not the slightest response. From first to last, he only said No Comment, even when he was found guilty and sentenced to nine hundred and ninety-nine years in prison. Unguessable behind his cracked and cellophaned shades, he simply reached in his overcoat pocket and brought out his dice, flicking them lightly across the top of the dock.

For his final close-up, he appeared in iron handcuffs. Guards gripped him by the elbows and flung him into the back of an armoured van. Steel doors slammed in his face, the key was turned in the lock. For a split second, the blank eye was visible beyond the bars, signifying nothing. Then the wagon turned the corner, and King Death was gone for ever.

'Nine hundred and ninety-nine years,' said Jerry McGhee. 'By the time he gets paroled, we'll all be dead and buried.'

For the first time, the families began to grasp what the situation really meant. So far, they had viewed the capture and trial as a spectacle, one more performance, though sadly substandard. But now that the show was over, and King Death was buried in San Quentin, they were left with the cold realities – no more completions, no more eyes at the window.

They had been hopelessly spoiled. Under the King's regime, sensation had become a habit, and they felt lost without it. However hard HBLF and the other networks might try to fill the vacuum, swamping them with new and gleaming images, they would accept no substitutes, and they refused to be consoled.

Three months passed, and they turned mean and sour. They drank too much, they bickered and sulked. There was continuous quarrelling and a succession of brawls. Deprived of any other outlet, they spent their energies in smashing mirrors, shooting songbirds, scrawling obscenities on the mansion walls.

At Thanksgiving, in an orgy of vengeance, they attacked

the screens with brickbats and hammers, flung them bodily from the balconies, burned them on bonfires. But the following morning, when they awoke, they found that the mangled images had all been restored to their places, as bright and inescapable as ever.

It was Jerry McGhee who finally broke the spell.

On a golden evening, rising from his couch, where he had yawned and festered all through the afternoon, he went to his window and, for the first time in sixty-three days, he raised the blinds. Immediately, the room was flooded with dazzling sunlight. 'It isn't fair,' he said.

'What isn't?' said Martha, half-asleep.

'To lock him away like this. To chain him in a dungeon for all time,' said Jerry. 'And what in hell's name for? Truthfully, when you get right down to cases, what was his crime?'

'Twelve networked killings,' said Barney Brannigan.

'But who were his victims? Only Commies and creeps, and traitors, and alien perverts, who deserved everything that they got.'

'True enough,' said Charley Mitchell. 'They was scum.'

'Un-Americans,' said Jerry, simply. 'They should have been swept up years ago and flushed away like vermin, back into the sewers, where they rightfully belonged.'

'But they weren't,' said Mildred Potterson.

'Of course they weren't – they were pampered and spoonfed, coddled like pet poodles, and they spread their poison everywhere, while the law stood by and picked its nose.'

Far away on the second balcony, Seaton sat in company with Mort Mossbacher and J Jones Dickerson. Together they watched and listened, and the Englishman dipped his fingers deep inside a jar of homemade curds: 'And then came King

Death,' said Jerry McGhee. 'And it turned him sick to his stomach.'

'What did?' asked his wife.

'The treachery,' said Jerry. 'He saw his country betrayed and degraded, everything that he loved being dragged in the gutters, and in the end he exploded.'

'A man sees red; it's only natural,' said big Jim Haggard.

'He was driven to desperate measures,' said Jerry. 'Maddened with rage and shame, he tackled the whole evil bunch single-handed and vowed not to quit until the land was freed from snakes. Maybe he went too far, maybe he stepped a mite out of line. But good God almighty, even if he did, that's no cause to destroy him.'

'Because he meant it for the best,' said Sarah Carter.

'He did it for America,' said Billy Mace.

'And that means us,' said Jerry McGhee.

Up in the balcony, Seaton withdrew his fingers from the jar of curds and, one by one, he licked them clean. The Director and Commander went back to their offices, and Seaton curled up like a cat in his hammock, snug and invisible. When morning came, he clapped his hands, and James Link Foley appeared in medium close-up, seated in a small sordid room, eating grits from a rolled-up newspaper.

The floor was covered with magazines and dirty pictures, there were unwashed socks in the sink, plates and empty bottles lay piled on every available surface. As for Foley himself, a hairy man in a sweatshirt and decomposing shorts, he had grease on his hands, grease on his chin, grease smeared on his belly and, when his rest was disturbed by a gentle tapping on his door, his instant response was to belch.

Three years before, when his name was Ronnie Cisco, this man had been convicted of the murder and sexual mutilation of five small children in Santa Monica. After only seven months in captivity, however, he had broken out and run away, and ever since, try as they might, the police had found no trace of him.

In actual fact, he had taken refuge in Guadalajara, moved onward to Caracas and Montevideo, undergone a series of comprehensive plastic surgeries and hidden for many months down a coal hole. Finally, when the heat had died down, he ventured back to Pittsburgh and there he fashioned a whole new life, in which he was perfectly clean and godly.

The only place where his former self survived was in this room, where no one else ever entered. Here he wallowed in filth like a hippo. Pornography, slime and half-eaten food enclosed him in a womb, and he felt free.

Because of this, when the knocking began at his door, it seemed like a blasphemous intrusion and he ignored it. But the tapping, though gentle, proved relentless, and in the end he could not resist it.

Mumbling obscenities, Foley waded to the door and opened up three inches. Immediately, he was startled by a blaze of machine-gun fire, which drove him irresistibly backward, ploughing through the mire like a tank, until he reached the opposite wall. For a few seconds he remained semi-standing, jouncing and jiggling like a demented jellybean. Then the firing ceased, and he lay down on the floor, with his face in a tub of ketchup.

When the smoke had cleared and the last echo died away, King Death was standing in the doorway, almost smiling.

'He's back,' said Jerry McGhee.

'He can't be,' said Billy Mace.

'But he is,' said Charley Mitchell.

High above Times Square, to celebrate the miracle, there appeared an all-seeing neon eye and a giant monogrammed trademark, **KD**, etched in golden glitterdust. Within a few minutes, a crowd of several thousands had gathered underneath and were gazing upward, silent and awed, as if at a flying saucer.

Attorney General Flaherty flew west to San Quentin and peeked through the peephole at the prisoner, who was playing solitaire and smiling. His big black shades had been confiscated, his uniform exchanged for a suit of arrowed denims and, without these props, all resemblance to King Death ended. Shorn of image, he might have passed for almost any American.

Flaherty bit his hands, the captive was set free; at the same time, Eddie was released from his attic, where he had been locked up for one hundred and twenty-seven days, with only his suitcase and mirror for company.

He had suffered considerably. Indeed, he would gladly have swapped places with his other self in San Quentin, for Tierra de Ensueños had come to oppress him far worse than chains or bars could ever do. Cut off from America, he couldn't sleep, couldn't eat, could hardly bear to watch his own reflection and, the moment he shut his eyes, in search of repose, he was stricken by visions of hubcaps, cottonfields and skin-tight sequinned dresses, water-melon stands and glowlights, craps, pigs' knuckles and Wednesday nights at the Assembly of God – all those things that had made him and were now lost.

He was too proud to complain. No matter what his deprivations, dignity and professionalism demanded that he bear them in silence and bury the hurt within. Nonetheless, when at last he was unleashed and sent back to work, he felt as though he were surfacing from a bottomless black pit.

As he stepped down from his bedroom, blinking in the unaccustomed light, all his frustration, constriction, pent-up resentment and yearning gathered together in a wild and most ferocious combustion of energies, in which he trained until he dropped, broke down doors with his skull, demolished brick walls with flying kung-fu feet; and doubtless this was one of the reasons why his rendering of James Link Foley proved so physical, so extreme in violence and vengeance.

There was another reason, however, every bit as important, and that was his personal distaste for the subject, who was everything that had made Death feared and hated. 'Vicious, animal, dirty, diseased,' said Eddie gently. 'It's people like him, maniacs and misfits, who've caused all our troubles. If it weren't for them, the industry would never have been degraded or made abhorrent, there would be no prejudice or misunderstanding, and professionals like me would not be branded as butchers.'

'Amateurs,' said Seaton.

'They poison everything they touch.'

'So you deny them true Death.'

'Because they haven't earned her; because they wouldn't know how to savour her. Brute slaughter is all they know, the only language they can understand. So slaughter is what I give them.'

Sick at heart, the professional went away to the gymnasium, where he burned himself into forgetfulness. But long after he was gone, Seaton continued to brood on his words and their implications and, as a result, King Death underwent a crucial shift of emphasis. Instead of hunting revolutionaries, freaks and Un-Americans in general, as in the past, he began to concentrate specifically on the enemies of Death. Child murderers, bomb throwers, mad axemen, sex maniacs – all those who offended against the industry, therefore against all mankind, and yet, for whatever reason, went unpunished.

In terms of salesmanship, this change made everything much simpler. With subjects like Karl Rosen or Ahmed Abdul Fakir, there had been room for argument. However much they might be loathed by the masses, they had commanded a strong minority support, which naturally kicked up a fuss when they were completed. But who would weep for a Foley? Who could deny that he was better off defunct, or that America was a finer, cleaner place without him? In such a case as this, only a fool or fanatic would speak of murder.

The last barriers collapsed; any reservations the audience might still have felt were swept aside in a flood tide of righteousness and rage: 'Vengeance is ours,' said Jerry McGhee.

So Death was launched on her second phase. Apart from being a spectacle, a dazzling entertainment, she also became a crusade.

Stern-faced, remorseless, Eddie set out once more in the black limousine and this time, instead of a gift, he brought retribution. The Mafioso Vito Pavese was splattered all over his penthouse carpet; Ulysses Grant Majeski, the dope peddler, had his arm pumped full of rat poison; the Satanist Joachim van Sallust was sacrificed at the foot of his own unclean altar; and with each new deliverance, support for the King increased.

To the families, watching from the mansion, it seemed almost sacrilegious that such an artist could still be officially known as Public Enemy Number One. By any standards, he was performing a very great service; and yet the critics continued to revile him, the law pursued him as avidly as ever: 'A man befriends his homeland,' said Jerry McGhee, 'and this is his reward.'

'Vitriol,' said big Jim Haggard.

'When he ought to be draped with honours,' said Jerry. 'At the very least, he has earned a presidential pardon, though the Good Lord knows he's worth a whole lot more.'

'Like a congressional citation,' said Barney Brannigan.

'Or an Oscar,' said Mildred Potterson.

Still the law remained obstinate. Live on HBLF, Flaherty claimed that no man could be allowed to place himself above the rules, whatever the temptations or excuses, or else the nation must inevitably tumble into anarchy, chaos, apocalypse.

Mr President agreed with him. So did 37 senators, 147 congressmen, 356 editors, and 622 priests. According to the pollsters, however, 62.55 per cent of the general public felt otherwise.

So King Death arrived at his second anniversary, and it seemed that he had reached an impasse. Authority would not give way, neither would he, and it was obvious to his followers that if he was ever to receive his just deserts, the time had come for them to speak out: 'If we don't stand up for ourselves,' said Jerry McGhee, 'we might as well give in.'

'No good relying on justice,' said Tom Potterson.

'Useless to put our faith in prayer,' said Betsy Mitchell.

'Our only hope is action,' said Jerry McGhee.

So a new and solemn movement took shape, a sort of underground resistance, starting in Orange County, then spreading right across the country, and its members called themselves the King Death Loyalists.

One night, Eddie woke up sweating from the strangest dream, in which he had been standing by the open door of the conservatory, bathed in moonlight, when a shaggy golden lion came ambling towards him through the undergrowth, its smiling mouth just visible above the orchids, and sat down at his feet.

Though its hands and feet were animal, there was no fur on its face and it wore a silken leash around its throat. Eddie gave it a sugar lump and it licked his black glove in gratitude. After a moment, they embraced.

Instantly, Eddie was filled with a sense of deepest contentment and, picking up the leash, he began to lead the lion through the gardens, pointing out the various beauties and curiosities as they went. Moonlight cleared their path and turned everything to silver. Then Eddie became aware that the lion was bleeding from many hidden wounds and was, in fact, dying. But its blood was also silver, and quite transparent, and he was not disturbed.

Wherever they turned, their images were repeated in water, which dazzled and distracted them, and they escaped inside the mansion. A door slammed distantly behind them, the candles flickered and went out. Excited by the darkness, the lion chuckled, very, soft and low, and Eddie gave it another sugar lump. Alone, together, invisible, they went walking in the labyrinth.

When he awakened, the performer felt oddly disturbed, almost as if he had befouled himself in his sleep. From earliest infancy, he had been self-contained, and any form of feeling or vulnerability offended him deeply. So imagine his embarrassment at such stuff as this – moonlight, silver blood, half-human lions and most peculiar kisses. Not only was it tasteless, undignified, girlish; what was much more important, it was unprofessional.

When he came to breakfast, the performer's eyes were dark with remorse; Seaton, on the other hand, was jubilant. Sunning himself on the patio, he kept reading and re-reading a telex from Arkansas, which he brandished triumphantly in Eddie's sorrowing face.

Apparently, the night before, just about the same time that the professional was being accosted by the lion, a group of fifty citizens in Helena had formed themselves into a torchlight procession and marched together to the steps of City Hall, where they bared their heads and displayed a hand-painted banner, simply saying KING DEATH, and there they had remained for almost an hour, motionless and hushed.

Eddie was profoundly moved. In a flash, his dream was forgotten, and he raised his hand to shade his eyes, he buried his mouth in the depths of his overcoat collar: 'A man feels humble,' he said.

'I bet he does,' said Seaton.

'Humble, and proud, and also a mite ashamed.'

'Why ashamed?'

'Because he did not have faith,' said the King. 'Because he thought he was alone, nobody cared or understood, and all his efforts fell on barren ground. But now he knows better, and he only wishes that he'd had more trust.'

From these small beginnings, Loyalism spread fast and could not be contained. All over America, secret cells sprang up. At midnight, men marched through the deserted streets, their steel-capped boots scrunching rhythmically on the pavement and, every time they passed an image of King Death, they saluted.

Posters and placards appeared by the hundreds of

thousands, and bumper stickers, lapel buttons, sloganised balloons. A password was devised, namely Death, and a secret handclasp. And in fifty states, majorettes pranced and twirled to a brand new anthem, entitled *The Shadow Knows*.

In Corpus Christi, Texas, an unofficial KD Day was declared, a public holiday, with carnivals and rodeos, beauty queens, fireworks and free ice cream for the children. Meanwhile, in Tierra de Ensueños, the Englishman ate hot buttered crab with his fingers.

Awash in grease, he breathed in long and deep, as though inhaling a rare, elusive and most exotic perfume. 'Fans,' he said.

'I call them friends,' replied the performer stiffly, for fans were a vulgarity, and he travelled to Cincinnati, where he rendered the sex fiend Ringo Bullett.

From now on, each morning's paper seemed to carry some fresh tale of devotion and sacrifice. The harder the authorities tried to clamp down, the faster the movement spread, and there were a number of bitter clashes.

In Syracuse, New York, police broke up a procession with tear gas and truncheons. Thirteen marchers were taken to the hospital, twenty-two arrested and severely punished. Even so, they remained unrepentant, and they were pictured with heads held high, grinning, on the courthouse steps.

Sighing, Seaton spread a slice of Melba toast with Patum Pepperium and brushed his fingers across his eyes. 'These men need our help,' he said. 'They have suffered in our cause and we must not sit idly by, like pampered pashas, while they do all the work and take all the knocks. They have carried the weight long enough. Now it's our turn.'

'What do you propose?' asked Eddie.

'Sponsorship,' said the Englishman. 'The time has come

to go to their aid. Undoubtedly, they must be in dire need of funds and guidance. And we will not fail them.'

Having once decided to act, he wasted no more time. Within a week, he had recruited a force of one hundred publicists, whom he christened King Death Kouncillors, and he sent them out into every corner of the nation, to help spread the good word.

As soon as a Kouncillor arrived in a new town, he located the nearest Loyalist cell and whispered the password. He shook hands, slapped backs and distributed a suitcase full of posters and stickers, badges and glossy photographs. He read out a personal message from the King, donated a satchel full of dollars and, if the atmosphere seemed right, delivered a short sharp lecture on Death herself, her meaning and true purpose. Finally, he showed a selection of 16-mm films, in which the performer waved from a balcony, bared his head beneath a star-spangled banner, knelt to pray in a tiny whitewashed chapel, revealed his face through a stained-glass window.

Having won the members' confidence, the Kouncillor now got down to serious business. From each cell, he chose a nucleus of lieutenants, men to be relied upon in a crisis, and with their help he embarked on a phase of rigorous training. A formal hierarchy of officials was established, meetings properly ordered, all information filed, rowdy and dilettante elements ruthlessly weeded out. At the end, only the truest believers survived.

Each of those who remained was rewarded with his own private uniform, which consisted of a long black overcoat, black hat, black gloves and shiny black boots. They were taught how to march and how to salute and how to stand completely motionless. They were given pamphlets to study, autographed pictures to place beneath their pillows. They were indoctrinated, drilled, flattered with military rankings. Whenever their spirits showed any signs of flagging, they were revived with treats, such as dictaphones and sten guns.

By these methods, within a few short months, a close-knit and fully operational network was built up, nationwide, incorporating more than three hundred chapters and fifty thousand members.

King Death was booming as never before; he had become an institution, an integral part of everyday living, like toothpaste; and his image, serving as an icon, gazed down blankly from a million bedroom walls.

Yet, for all his triumphs, Eddie could not be satisfied; officially he was still a killer. Stuck upstairs in his attic, there were times when he believed that pardon would never come at all, that he would never again walk the streets or breathe the city air in freedom. At such moments, all the love and adulation of the Loyalists became a mockery, which only served to tighten the screws of his confinement, and the name King Death was a curse.

One afternoon, when he felt especially low, he went to visit Seaton in the Chinese pagoda, where the Englishman was nibbling at a packet of chocolate fingers. 'What's the use?' said the performer. 'My ratings might reach a hundred per cent, the whole of America might give me their support, and still I would not be legalised. I have not forgotten my friends, and I am most truly grateful. But they cannot achieve the impossible – no matter how they try, regardless of all my services rendered, I am doomed to remain an outlaw.'

'Do not despair,' Seaton told him.

'How can I help it?'

'The law cannot touch you. If only you knew your own

strength, you would understand that you have soared far above it, where no one and nothing can reach you. Officials may still abuse you and pretend to chase you; but believe me, they dare not harm you. If they ever caught you, even if you were served to them upon a silver platter, they could no longer take advantage. For if they did, as they well know, they would set off such a holocaust of rage and sacred vengeance that every part of the nation would catch fire, and they themselves would be the first to be consumed in the blaze.'

The floor of the pagoda was carpeted wall-to-wall with unopened fan mail; peacocks and mockingbirds waded knee-deep in a sea of glossy photographs, and Seaton helped himself to another chocolate finger: 'In plain point of fact, you are omnipotent,' he said.

'How can you be so certain?' Eddie asked.

'If you don't believe me,' said Seaton, 'I will prove it.'

Sure enough, before another two weeks were out, he staged a practical demonstration. Taking Independence Day as his cue, he instructed that every able-bodied Loyalist make his way to Washington, complete with uniform, and when they were all assembled and darkness fell, they marched together to the Pentagon.

The result was a full-scale army, more than a hundred thousand strong, and they set out to the sound of muffled drums, their way illumined by a myriad of flickering torches. Ten deep they marched, a procession that stretched for almost three miles, and one of them, indistinguishable from all the rest, was King Death himself.

When the Loyalists were half a mile from their goal, they were confronted by the National Guard, who lined up across the concourse, guns at the ready. Immediately, the marchers halted and knelt, humbly removing their slouch hats, and only their leader was left standing, an open target for anyone who cared to destroy him. He made no speeches and gave no signal. In medium close-up, he simply stood to attention, staring straight ahead, and he waited to be captured, shot down, annihilated or whatever else might befall. His head was high, his features frozen. From a distance, he might have been an effigy.

From the depths of the Loyalist ranks, faintly at first, then with increasing fervour, there now arose the strains of *The Battle Hymn of the Republic*. The muffled drumming grew steadily louder, the torches were stilled, the kneeling marchers laid their pistols at rest upon the ground. Music filled the night and, silhouetted in left profile, King Death saluted.

For a full minute, he remained unprotected, and his silhouette was framed by a star-spangled banner, flying proud and free. Across the nation, he was watched by 89.67 per cent of all Americans. But nobody shot him, and nobody tried to seize him. Just as Seaton had said, he was inviolable and only the cameras dared touch him. Creeping in relentlessly, they devoured the flag, his uniform, his face. Then only his eyes were left, filling the whole screen.

When the minute of observance was over, the army rose to its feet and Eddie was instantly swallowed up again. *The Battle Hymn* soared to a crescendo, and he was just one of the multitude. Wheeling, the Loyalists began to march away.

The performance was complete.

4

To celebrate his freedom, King Death embarked on a journey through America. Seaton created a private train for him, called the Deliverance Special. The Stars and Stripes flew proudly from the smokestack, a golden eye and a monogrammed **KD** were emblazoned on each carriage and, all along its route, the tracks were strewn with fresh-cut roses.

In the first carriage Eddie lay alone, in a skid-row bedroom; in the second, surrounded by gilt and cut crystal, came the Englishman; in the third the Kouncillors and publicists; in the fourth the assistant directors, executive producers, cameramen and scriptwriters; in the fifth the accountants; in the sixth the journalists; in the seventh the wardrobe mistress, stills photographer, hairdresser, make-up artist and grips; in the eighth Mantequilla Wickham and the stand-ins, extras and sparring partners; in the ninth the stenographers; in the tenth the caterers, chambermaids and messenger boys; and in the eleventh, visible only to Eddie, a shaggy golden lion.

For ninety days this cavalcade passed back and forth across

the nation without a rest, describing such a labyrinthine network of loops and vaults, zigzags, circumferences and sudden detours that by the end it seemed there was not a single city, township or even whistle stop that had not been included.

Six or ten or a dozen times a day, the Special would pause at a different station, always to be greeted by the same demonstration. Brass bands played, civic dignitaries paraded, majorettes pranced. In the middle of the platform, flanked by a military guard, a banner of scarlet blooms spelled out WELCOME.

The crowds were held back behind steel-mesh fences, while the publicists fed them with souvenir badges and streamers, flung over the wires like cream buns at the zoo. Touts sold autographs and spurious relics, the loudspeaker exploded with a roar of pre-recorded gunfire. Behind the fence, the fans clawed and scrabbled, and the band played *God Bless America*.

Occasionally, Eddie would show his face beyond his window. Then cheerleaders in bobbysocks and high school sweaters chanted 'King Death, KD, King Death, KD,' and all the young girls began to scream and stretch out their imploring hands. Mothers held up their babies to be blessed, cripples threw away their crutches, the blind pretended to see. One minute passed, and the Special rolled on.

On board the train, time passed in a vacuum. Blurred by repetition, landscapes lost all meaning and reality, became no more than a series of slides, flashed upon the screen at random, to create an illusion of change. Mountain ranges and valleys, cities and rivers and flatlands – all were reduced to picture postcards and, like the limousine before it, the Special became a time machine, a compression chamber, in which the only reminder of motion was the rhythm of the wheels, the ceaseless buckle and sway below.

The inhabitants played cards, read paperbacks, stared out through the windows. They fell asleep in the Chicago stockyards and woke up again in the midst of the Georgia peach orchards. They browsed through the funny papers and soused themselves on lukewarm beer. They witnessed the Golden Gate, Niagara Falls, the Great Grand Coolee Dam. They yawned, they scratched themselves, they played strip poker. The bands played *Chattanooga Choo-Choo* and they fell asleep in the Rockies, they woke up beside the wide Missouri.

There were images of fall in New England, harvest time in Kansas, and the flies were murderous in Alabama. Grizzly bears and wildcats roamed across the tracks in Colorado and a man in an old blue suit flung himself beneath the wheels. There was a heat wave along the Gulf of Mexico. In Idaho, the temperature touched twelve below freezing and the snow was piled high as a house.

City after city passed by, dark and all-engulfing as tunnels. Black men in little round hats shook their fists and mouthed obscenities, young girls in ribbons shamelessly offered up their bodies. First the sky turned deep purple, then it burst into flame. The windows were blinded by the belch of factories, soot fell like rain. Turning his face to the wall, Eddie shut his eyes and, when he woke up, he was lost in a sea of pale-gold wheat.

At last, on the evening of the ninetieth day, the Special arrived at Los Angeles and halted. The travellers dispersed, the cameras were dismantled. All that was left was debris.

Cigarette stubs and plastic containers, half-eaten sandwiches, scrunched-up newspapers and dirty underclothes formed a rich, decomposing carpet underfoot. Windows were blurred with grime, gilded monograms chipped and rusted. The Stars and Stripes hung limp and dejected from the prow, and the all-seeing eyes were dimmed. Of the spotless, virgin train that had first set out, so full of hopes, hardly a trace survived.

Seaton was not distressed. Seated in the midst of the rubble, clad in a maroon velvet dressing gown with deep blue cuffs and collar, he seemed oblivious of the surrounding filth. His hair was all awry, his eyes black and heavy with fatigue, he reached for a nearby plastic cup, greasy and stained with lipstick, and filled it to the brim with tepid champagne.

He quaffed, he smacked his lips. Drinking off the cup at a single draught, he flung the dregs through the window and dipped his hand deep inside a bag of KD marbles, which were designed to look like golden eyeballs. As Eddie watched, he gathered a generous fistful, rattled them in his palm and held them up against the light: 'Now we come to the best part of all,' he said.

'Death,' said Eddie.

'Money,' said Seaton.

And he scooted the eyeballs down the carriage, one by one, careering and clacking wildly along the aisles, until they reached the open doorway and flew into space.

Overnight, America was swamped with produce.

There were KD wallpapers, KD canned peaches, KD golf clubs and charm bracelets, KD bubble gums, KD lipsticks and powder puffs, KD percolators, KD gas masks; KD lawn mowers, Bermuda shorts, diaries, electric guitars, washing machines, bubble baths and breakfast cereals; Golden Eye ballpoints and T-shirts, tennis rackets, motor cycles, jukeboxes, videos; Deliverance Special train sets; hats and gloves and overcoats, black suitcases and pre-scarred mirrors; motels and hamburger heavens; record companies, car rental services, real estate developments; bobbysocks, toy guns, heart-shaped lockets, loofahs, soda pops, holsters, garden gnomes, clocks and watches, fluffy bedroom slippers, sweet cigarettes, diapers, silhouettes and profiles, ketchups, jellies, jockey shorts and undershirts, comics, lampshades, sanitary napkins, bibles, TV dinners, dice, kewpie dolls, coffee mugs, fortune cookies and margarines; gymnasiums and funeral parlours; drugstores, laundromats, dance instruction centres; and a thousand-acre Disneyland in Santa Monica, called 'King Death's All-America'.

In the first year of trading alone, the turnover amounted to almost one hundred million dollars: 'A mere bagatelle,' said Seaton modestly. 'No more than a drop in the ocean, compared to the long-term potentials.'

Commerce was not his only concern. In the intervals between making profits, he found time to sponsor a series of charitable organisations, among them the KD Save the Children Fund, the KD Campaign to Keep America Clean, the KD Library of Death and fifty KD Valhalla Retirement Homes, one in each state, for aged or ailing professionals. In years to come, God willing, there would also be schools and colleges, orphanages, crematoriums, perhaps a football franchise and one day, who could tell, a chain of KD temples.

Meanwhile, Eddie himself was paraded on a non-stop round of public engagements. He launched battleships, shook hands with senators and governors, dined at the White House. He threw the season's first slider at Yankee Stadium and took the salute at West Point. On Christmas Eve, live from Tierra de Ensueños, he stood at his attic window and waved, and viewers voted him American of the Year.

And yet, in spite of all these honours, he was not at peace, for he still felt trapped.

While he was outlawed, he had believed that pardon would alter everything, that he would be truly released, but this had not proved to be the case. On the contrary, now that he was universally loved and idolised, he found himself more constrained than ever.

Wherever he went, he was mobbed. The moment that he ventured out into the open, the very instant that his foot touched a sidewalk, he was engulfed by fans and, even though he called them his friends, they tore his clothes off, ripped at his flesh, tried to gouge out his eyes. If they had not been forcibly prevented, their adoration would have destroyed him outright.

As a result, he was forced to live behind smoked glass. Henceforth, whether inside the mansion, on board the Deliverance Special or sunk in the cushions of the black limousine, he was separated from reality by an impenetrable screen, and he could never touch or be touched.

In a sense, King Death had made him redundant. Image had taken him over so completely that his own secret self, which he called Eddie, had lost all relevance. Alone in his attic, he might continue to eat and sleep and defecate, watch, dream and yearn. But he had no meaning or function. Unless Seaton clapped and the cameras rolled, he did not truly exist.

He tried not to be embittered. Plighted to Death as he was, committed through and through, he knew that her needs must always come before his own and he was thankful to be sacrificed in her service. Nonetheless, he could not help but feel claustrophobic, displaced, and the golden lion haunted him nightly.

Prowling through the tangled undergrowth, sneaking up behind him as he slept, it purred and whispered and sighed, murmuring sweet nothings, and the professional found himself drawn into the strangest and most disturbing caresses. Hand in paw, he abandoned himself to the labyrinth, the echoes, the never-ending mirrors, and gradually he was led deep underground.

Far below the mansion, in a grotto hung with pink and emerald stalactites, he came upon a limpid pool, where the waters were as thick and smooth as molasses. The lion relieved him of his uniform and he slid beneath the surface. Immediately, his limbs grew lax and impossibly heavy, and he could make no movement. Floating on his back, he drifted off downstream and felt that he was drowning in golden syrup.

At the first light of dawn, awakening in a swamp of cold sweat, Eddie crept downstairs on tiptoe, climbed inside the black limousine and was driven away to Tupelo.

He was not running away; professional pride forbade him from betraying his trust, to shirk his destiny in flight. But he wished to say farewell. One last time, he yearned to touch the sidewalk, lurk in the shadows, breathe in the carbonised air that had made him.

Though he gave no outward sign, this pilgrimage passed in great anxiety, in case he should find that his past had been changed or obliterated, and by the time he entered the city limits and arrived upon the block where he was born, his fingers were tightly twined in the chain of his silver crucifix, his hat was pulled down right across his eyes.

He need not have worried. The moment he opened his window and let the air flood in, he knew that everything was just the same as always: the afternoon heat, the drowsiness, the slow decay; the smell of bacon grease and collards; the dust, and the music playing far away; the beat-up Chevrolet parked outside the pool hall; the faded colours, the sweat-damp walls; even the busted neon S on the sign outside The Golden Slipper.

Down on the corner, the neighbourhood dudes were slouched against a wall of one hundred graffiti, shooting craps. Most of them were dressed in the style of King Death but, when the performer passed among them, they gave no sign of recognition. They did not shriek or riot, like everybody else, but stared him up and down, impassive, and he did the same in return. They spat upon the sidewalk, so did he. Two small girls in pigtails were sucking popsicles on a fire escape, a radio was playing *Honky-Tonk Angels* behind a scarlet door. Eddie moved along.

Slow as a creeping shadow, savouring every inch, he travelled down the block, past the pool hall, past The Golden Slipper. Across the street, upstairs in The Playtime Inn, he was aware that someone was watching him from behind a lace-curtained window.

Beneath a street-lamp, he paused and rested. With eyes half-shut, he sensed the pavement hot and sticky beneath his boots, the silken dresses flashing pink and gold and silver in the depths of the saloon. Sweat trickled down the back of his neck, and his throat was sandpaper dry.

A fat blue fly settled on the tip of his nose, distracting him, and he set his face towards the Chinese laundry, where he hoped to spend a few last minutes in solitude, out of the heat and glare, waiting for a stranger.

However, when he reached the doorway and looked inside, he found that his place was already occupied. Lost in the shadows, which had once been his own, there stood a man in a trench coat.

So profound were the shadows that Eddie could not make out any details of it. The shiny tips of the man's shoes protruded just a fraction into the light and, from the ease and certainty of their stance, there could be no doubt that this was their established territory, their professional pitch, which no one else might share.

Eddie was powerless. Though his mouth was filled with bile, he could only bow his head and accept the facts. He did not belong here, this was no longer his rightful home. In becoming King Death, an image, he had lost his place for ever.

His limousine was waiting at the corner, and he disappeared inside. Expressionless, he rolled up the windows as tight as they would go, to shut out all sound and smell of the sidewalk, and he turned back towards the mansion, Tierra de Ensueños, which owned him.

'We have come a long way,' said Seaton.

'We certainly have,' said Mort Mossbacher.

'From a single grain of sand, we have built a mighty mountain. Though our path was strewn with numberless obstacles and setbacks, which others might have found insurmountable, we battled on regardless. Deep down in our hearts, we knew that God was on our side. Therefore we would not take No for an answer, and our faith never faltered.'

'And?' said J Jones Dickerson.

'And now we are rewarded. Truth and justice stand triumphant and, naturally, our hearts are swelled with pride.'

'But?' said J Jones Dickerson.

'But pride is not the same as smugness and, just because we have performed a miracle, we must not grow complacent.

Our duties are not finished, the saga is by no means complete. When the first flush of jubilation fades, we will see that freedom is not an ending, but a fresh beginning, and far from resting on our laurels, still greater tasks await us.'

J Jones Dickerson looked at Mort Mossbacher, and Mort Mossbacher looked at J Jones Dickerson, and neither of them spoke. Side by side on a cold stone banquette, they sucked their jujubes in silence.

Seaton was buried in his hammock and all that was visible above the rim was the soft swell of his belly, the tips of his stockinged toes, the lazy curl of his cigar smoke. Underneath the surface, however, the Englishman was beaming. Pomegranates, passion fruit and figs were scattered across his lap in wild profusion; his Wisden lay open at Gregory, McDonald and F.E Woolley (Lords, 1921). Beatific, he munched on a Hershey bar.

For a time, he was content to muse and enjoy his invisibility, while his associates were kept waiting down below. Then he sat up straight and fixed them with his softest, blandest smile. 'I have a dream,' he said.

'And?' said J Jones Dickerson.

'I call it democracy.'

'What does it mean?' asked Mort Mossbacher.

'In the simplest terms, it means that Death steps down from her pedestal and is made universal, so that all men may share in her. Until this moment, if she has had a fault, it's been a certain taint of elitism. Her televised subjects have all been famous, rich or in some sense glamorous. Meanwhile, Mister Average has been left out in the cold.'

'He has not complained,' said Mort Mossbacher.

'That is beside the point – injustice is injustice, even if no one notices, and the time has come to restore the balance.

Death was not created for snobbery or false distinction; she belongs to each of us equally. In the words of the King himself, she is the birthright of every true American, regardless of colour, class or creed.'

'And?' said J Jones Dickerson.

'And that inheritance must be observed,' said Seaton sternly, sucking on a nectarine. 'So long as she was outlawed, there was an excuse for keeping her rationed. But now that she is free, her largesse requires no restrictions. Everyone who desires her must receive his or her rightful turn.'

Once again, J Jones Dickerson looked at Mort Mossbacher, and Mort Mossbacher looked at J Jones Dickerson. Mangoes, oleanders and crystalline chandrasekhars formed a technorama canopy above their heads, hemming them in, and everywhere they turned, they found themselves surrounded by unknown animals, staring at them through the undergrowth.

Upstairs in the attic, the radio played the *Long Gone Lonesome Blues* and Eddie began to dress. He put on a new shirt, a new waistcoat, a pair of spotless new gloves. Dutiful, he presented his profile at the window: 'I have a dream,' said Seaton again. 'To be precise, I call it *Meet the King.*'

'Well?' said J Jones Dickerson.

'I picture King Death on board the Deliverance Special, ceaselessly moving back and forth across the nation, and as he travels, he smiles, he waves, he keeps tender watch on his homeland. At the end of each week, he pulls in at a resting place, dismounts and shakes hands with a chosen American, live on HBLF. Then he returns straightaway to his carriage, and once more the Special rolls on.'

'What American?' asked Mort Mossbacher.

'Any American,' replied the Englishman. 'Anyone and

everyone who cares to apply. All requests will be sifted and carefully considered, and the honour each week will go to the subject deemed most worthy.'

'But what if no one applies?'

'That is not possible,' said Seaton, spitting out a peach pip. 'You have seen for yourselves how the King is feted and pursued. Every time that he so much as shows his silhouette behind a window, the multitudes go berserk. So just imagine how they would feel if they had the chance to meet him in person, to look in his eyes and share his deepest secrets, while the whole nation watched.'

'They would be excited,' Mort Mossbacher admitted.

'Excited? They would be ecstatic; they would be thrilled beyond their wildest dreams. For such a moment, they would sell their very souls.'

'Yes,' said the Commander, 'but what if they get frightened?'

'Why should they? How could they fear that their King would do them harm? Has he not proved his love and protection a hundred times, and do they not trust him absolutely? Wherever he leads, whatever he proposes, they will follow without question.'

'And?' said J Jones Dickerson.

'And rightly so,' said Seaton. 'For he will give them stardom, which is the greatest thrill of all, and then they will be fulfilled.'

'Are you sure?'

'Of course I'm sure. They will come flocking in their thousands and their millions, and our only problem will be to hold the demand at bay. Before the first year is out, I give you my word, *Meet the King* will be established as the greatest, best-loved and biggest-grossing spectacle that man has ever seen, in the history of the world and show business.'

Far above, the performer watered his geraniums and watched. His suitcase was already packed, his hat and coat were waiting by the door. Down the hill in the smog-bound valley, the Deliverance Special gleamed brand new, primed and hissing at its platform. 'I have a dream; a vision of Death unconfined,' said the Englishman.

'And?' said J Jones Dickerson.

'I call it America.'

Trumpets sounded a fanfare and Jerry McGhee stepped out from behind a green velvet curtain. With eyes downcast, he began to walk very slowly down a long sweeping stairway, and everybody cheered.

When he reached the bottom, he was received by a man in a tuxedo, who pumped his hand and slapped his back. Long blonde girls with long blonde legs kissed him on the cheek, a battery of cameras pinned him against a shimmering screen. Everywhere that he looked, he saw white flashing teeth.

The man in the tuxedo began to talk very fast, grinning and gesticulating, words and movements that Jerry did not understand. The noise and dazzle bewildered him; the blaze of the arc lights made him dizzy. Trapped in giant close-up, he could not remember why he was here, and his only clear sensation was the need to empty his bladder.

On board a magic roundabout, hung with a myriad of twinkling fairy lights, he was presented with a candyfloss pink Cadillac, a holiday home in Nassau, fifty thousand dollars in bonds and a hundred shares in King Death Consolidates, and after each donation, there was another flourish of trumpets, a redoubled roar of applause. Sweat dripped into his eyes, half-blinding him, and soft fingers tugged at his sleeve. Not wishing to seem ungracious, he opened his mouth and tried to smile, and when his vision cleared, he found himself surrounded by family and friends.

Martha was holding his hand, looking elsewhere; Charley Mitchell, Barney Brannigan and big Jim Haggard were smoking cigars and smiling past his shoulder. Cornered, Jerry blinked and looked vacant, as if they were strangers.

His daughter Sharon flung her arms around his neck and made his cheek wet with tears. Everybody stamped and shouted and whistled, and the fanfares rose to a crescendo. Then Jerry bowed his head and was led away by the long blonde girls, out of the light into darkness. The cheering died away, and he was on his own.

At first, he thought that he must have fainted, or perhaps that he was already complete. But then he felt a gentle purring underneath him, a distant swishing and hum, and he understood that he was seated in the back of a black limousine, passing through the night streets of the city, on his way to *Meet the King.*

All of a sudden, he felt sick.

His stomach lurched and clenched, his mouth was filled with acid. When the limousine slowed at a junction he tried to unwind the windows, tried to open the doors. But the windows were jammed, all the doors were locked. So he knew that he was powerless, and at last he believed that this was a true story.

Originally, when he had sent in his application, he had done so out of bravado, simply because Barney Brannigan had dared him to. He had not dreamed that he might really be chosen or, if he was, that anything serious would come of it. The King was so olympian, so remote and absolute – the thought of ever meeting him, of receiving his touch in person, was more than Jerry could conceive.

Even when his name was drawn from the black slouch hat, his imagination stayed frozen. Seeing his picture in the papers, his image transmitted on HBLF, he dismissed it all as a pantomime, some kind of mirage, which would dissolve at any moment, and he neither thought nor felt.

Within this charade, he had become a seven-day celebrity. He had been flown away in a private aeroplane, lodged in a penthouse, photographed with senators and movie stars, gorged on caviar, soused on champagne, showered with treats and symbols of every description. Wherever he appeared, people asked him for his autograph; each time he glanced at a screen, he saw his own reflection; and twenty-four hours a day, sleeping or awake, he had been cushioned by milling, jabbering crowds.

But now he was alone. For the first time since his ascension, he was removed from noise and light and all diversions, and there was no space left for evasion. Inside this limousine, King Death was inescapable, and Jerry trembled. Like any other fan about to meet his idol, he was overwhelmed by shyness and a sense of most abject unworthiness, and he curled up tight like a foetus.

Just then, the limousine drew to a halt outside Central Station and the doors were flung open. One of the blondes took his hand, gentle but not to be resisted, and she drew him forth on to the sidewalk, into another onslaught of flash bulbs and blinding lights. Jerry winced, shied, threw up his hands to shelter his eyes. Stumbling, he appeared to genuflect, and everybody cheered.

He tried to speak. Though his words made no sound, swamped by fanfares and applause, he explained that there must be some mistake, that he was not adequate, that he had a weak heart. But the cameras did not stop rolling, the blondes went right on smiling. No matter what he said, the cheering never faltered.

When at last there was silence, he found himself in the middle of the station concourse, alone once more, lost in a maze of fancy mosaic tiling. In aerial long shot, he looked exceedingly small and helpless, and the concourse seemed infinite.

There were cameras everywhere, on the roof, on the balustrades, lurking in every doorway, and Jerry was powerless to resist them. For a moment, he made as if to start running. Then his shoulders sagged and he sank to his knees.

Nervousness had caused him to sweat and his Brylcreemed hair had come unslicked, flopping forward over his eyes. As he knelt, he shivered and twitched, and he bit at his lips until they bled.

One by one, the cameras crept out of their holes. Slowly, stealthily, they closed in from every direction, circling their subject like wolves around firelight, and Jerry was too weakened to struggle. He was blinded by the brightness, dizzied by the heat, and his mind went blank. But when the cameras had come so near that they were almost touching him, he produced a steel-toothed comb from his back trouser pocket and began to brush the hair out of his eyes. Methodically, with infinite care, he constructed a smooth wavy pompadour, and it glistened in the arc lights.

Solemn music began to play. The lighting went soft and rosy pink, the cameras drew back respectfully and, just as Jerry was perfecting the final lock, a long dark shadow passed across his face.

King Death presented his left profile.

Stretching out his right hand, he placed it about three

inches above the subject's bowed head, as if in absolution, and Jerry went still. The comb slipped from his fingers, the unfinished lock curled back across his forehead and, though he did not wish to, he raised his face towards the light, the soft-focus radiance, that streamed from Eddie's eyes.

Then King Death almost smiled.

And Jerry melted.

Like fudge exposed to the sun, he went all soft and sticky, and he did not feel anything. He existed, no more than that, and he was at home.

He opened his mouth, he closed his eyes. Head back, throat upraised, he offered himself without shame or the least regret. Once again, a shadow passed across his face and, as it did so, he remembered that he still owed Barney Brannigan five dollars for his entry fee, a debt which would not now be repaid. In the final close-up, this thought caused him to smile.

Death embarked upon her golden age.

Enshrined aboard the Deliverance Special, the King toured the nation without rest and, everywhere that he passed, his subjects knelt at his feet. Fireworks lit up the sky, cannonades and church bells rang out together. The multitudes bayed in adulation, and the performer gave them his blessing, far away behind smoked glass.

His trademark was everywhere. According to *The Wall Street Journal*, three thousand six hundred and sixty-two products carried the King's endorsement, his image appeared on fifty-four thousand eight hundred and thirty-three billboards, and he commanded more than five million Loyalists. Death was a billion-dollar industry, many times over, and if a man walked from Cape Cod to Seattle, crossing America in an unswerving line, it was estimated that he would pass the monogram **KD**, on the average, once in every 3.227 miles.

Just as Seaton had predicted, *Meet the King* broke all records.

At the very beginning, it's true, the new format was received with a certain reserve and nervousness, and most of the early entries came from undesirables. But the doubts were quickly resolved. When the viewers saw how ecstatic the meetings proved, just how deeply the subjects were pleased and moved, all their inhibitions crumbled. They thought of the thrill, they thought of the stardom, they thought of the whole nation watching. Eddie stretched out his hand, and they rushed to take their turn.

Each performance was different. Location, mood and technique were all tailored to the subject's own personality, and Eddie never looked or acted the same way twice running. Sometimes he was tender and sometimes terrible, sometimes seductive, sometimes evangelical, sometimes all these things at once: 'Whatever the subject truly desires, deep down in his most secret dreams, that is what I give him,' said the King.

From now on, Death proceeded in unbroken splendour and tranquillity, and no more traumas marred the even rhythm of her days. She was a universal fun fair, a never-ending Mardi Gras. Wherever she went, she brought release, and comfort, and life.

Five years passed, and gradually the performer turned into a deity. So long as he watched over the multitudes, they felt safe and free, and they relied on him absolutely. Hallowed by repetition, his every move took on the weight of scripture. He was all-seeing, all-knowing. His face at the window belonged to a father confessor.

Success had not changed him.

Even though he had become a godhead, he did not cease to be humble. He did not grow too big to say Please and Thank You, and he raised his hat every time he met a lady. He still did not smoke or drink alcoholic liquors, he had no truck with naked women, he said his prayers on his knees every night. Above all, he never wavered in his sense of gratitude. 'I owe it all to my friends,' said King Death. 'Everything I am today, America has made me.'

Nothing lasts for ever. One morning, shortly after the unveiling, Eddie was sitting in the attic and watching his reflection in the mirror, when all of a sudden he noticed a grey hair above his left ear.

Downstairs in the perfumed garden, Seaton was bowling leg breaks and googlies against the gymnasium wall. Profoundly disturbed, the performer fingered his crucifix and stood deep in shadow, so that his face was made invisible. 'I'm getting older,' he said.

'What's wrong with that?' asked the Englishman.

'It isn't natural,' Eddie replied. 'Leastways, it never happened before.'

This was perfectly true. Throughout his career, he had been ageless, and his image had shifted from moment to moment, according to circumstances and the needs of his subjects. But now, when he glimpsed himself in the goldfish pond, his reflection was fixed and inescapable – he had become a man in middle age, well-preserved but weary, with faint lines around his eyes, a slight but unmistakable thickening at his waist, a certain sluggishness of touch and tread.

That night, as he lay in bed, he found that he could not breathe. His lungs were choked with pollen and the scents of dead flowers, his skull burst with unremembered songs.

Across the room, the shaggy lion was curled up beyond the mirror, quietly licking its paws, and Eddie coughed up orchids, butterflies, packets of rotting leaves.

He felt as though his blood had ceased to flow, had congealed and curdled in his veins. The radio played *Smoke Gets in Your Eyes*, and he dragged himself to the window, desperate for air.

Opening his suitcase, he laid out the contents by moonlight. But when he began to polish his pearl-handled pistols, something small and dark and shiny flew down from the minarets and brushed, ice-cold, against his upraised throat. Then he sank to his knees, just like one of his own subjects.

For five years, ever since his farewell journey to Tupelo, he had been holding this moment at bay. He had cut off all memories, drowned all yearnings, abandoned himself utterly to Death. On the train, in this attic, even in the act of completion itself, he had made himself a blank, insensate.

His only weakness lay in sleep. Every night, as soon as he shut his eyes, the lion came creeping to his side and tempted him with marzipan, liquorice, scented jasmine twirls. It whispered in his ear, nibbled at his fingers, nuzzled in his groin. On the flimsiest of pretexts, it coaxed him from the sanctuary of his bedroom and lured him down into the labyrinth, where it deserted him in the darkest, most twisted corridors.

In self-defence, Eddie forced himself to remain awake, fifty, eighty, a hundred hours at a stretch. But in the end even this did not work. Casting aside all modesty and secrecy, the lion took to visiting him in broad daylight, and nothing that Eddie could do would make it disappear.

Thereafter, they became inseparable. Month after month, year after year, they travelled side by side and the lion never ceased its insinuations. Wherever Eddie moved, it lay in wait, simpering and fawning. It fluttered its eyelashes, mocked him in his most solemn moments. Even when he was in the very act of completion, it laid its lips close against his ear and whispered indecent suggestions, with a tongue that tickled and quivered like an aspen leaf.

Eddie had put up a most stern resistance. Whatever he felt inside, he gave no outward sign and his eyes remained as empty, as opaque and inhuman as ever. He took shelter in his dice, his suitcase, the angle of his hat brim; he hid himself in his reflection. Somehow or other, he endured.

But now the struggle was ended. In the instant that he discovered the grey hair, the performer knew that he was defeated, and when morning came, there was dirt beneath his fingernails, a tiny yellow spot on his chin.

Despairing, he hastened away to the gymnasium, to lose himself in gunsmoke. A dry wind stirred the oleanders, hyenas cackled in the shrubbery, the swimming pool was full of moths. Mantequilla spat behind the pagoda, and Eddie whirled and fired and fired again.

And he missed.

For the first time ever, when he blazed from the hip, his bullets did not automatically find their target. Nine out of ten were flawless. But the tenth flew out through the window and slaughtered a hummingbird.

The professional hung his head and went in search of Seaton, who was hard at work in the library, pouring over a sheaf of yellowed documents, by the dwindling light of an oil lamp.

Of late, the Englishman's involvement with King Death had greatly diminished. His dream had been fulfilled, the image was complete. There were no more great mountains left for him to climb and day-to-day business bored him. So he handed over all his practical duties to a team of subordinates, and he sank into semi-retirement.

Henceforth, he did not move beyond the gates of the mansion. Shuffling through the gardens in his velveteen slippers, he affected pince-nez and snuff, and he decided to dedicate the rest of his life to scholarship. Without the slightest regret, he turned his back on the screens, forgot all about the families and set out to create the definitive statistical record, once and for all time, of cricket's golden age, 1895–1914.

Inside the library, he buried himself beneath a vast, collapsing mountain of press clippings, scorecards and decomposing Wisdens. Here he laboured far through the night, compiling charts and graphs without end, for all the world like an astrologer or alchemist, a keeper of secret mysteries, and he lived entirely through Trumper, Ranji and CB Fry, just as he had once lived through Death.

Entering this sanctum, Eddie felt like an intruder and took off his hat in deference. He cleared himself a small space among the archives and Seaton looked up at him absent-mindedly, lost in tender reveries of Jessop at The Oval, 1902. 'I am finished,' said the performer.

'How come?'

'I have lost my gift.'

At this, Seaton removed his pince-nez and pushed aside his papers. In an instant, the scholar was changed back into a manager, and once again he became a fallen choirboy. 'Explain yourself,' he said.

'I'm all used up. My resources are exhausted, and the time has come for me to make my ending.'

'But that cannot be,' said the Englishman.

'Why can't it?'

'Death is still in need of you. If you desert her now, she will fall to pieces, and everything that you have achieved together will be destroyed.'

'You exaggerate.'

'I only wish that I did. But I know the way that images work. The moment that your back is turned, I give you my guarantee, all hell will be unleashed.'

'In what respect?'

'Your public would despair. Over the years, you have become such a habit, such a deep-down addiction, that they would be completely lost without you. They would have no outlet, no means of release. All their passions and hungers would be bottled up inside, to fester and turn sick. And in their panic, they would reach out blindly for substitutes.'

'Substitutes?'

'Other professionals,' Seaton said. 'In the circumstances, the networks would have no choice but to replace you, rig up some new line in performers and completions, or else there would be a national explosion.'

'Having retired myself, I could not object,' said Eddie, grave but magnanimous.

'That's typical of your big heart. But sometimes generosity can be misplaced. The world is full of cheapness and deceit. And if you were no longer on hand to protect her, true Death would surely perish.'

'How come?'

'She would be vulgarised, perverted, betrayed. A hundred to one, her new practitioners would not share your own high principles and would sell her straight down the river. In pursuit of ratings and a fast buck, they would forget her real meaning and riddle her with gimmicks. Without you to rescue her, she would be raped of all dignity and honour, and in no time she would be reduced to a freak show.'

'Just like before King Death,' Eddie said, downcast.

'Exactly. She would be overrun by thugs and opportunists, blood-crazed amateurs, and before you knew what had happened, she would be right back where she started, drowning in the sewers.'

A second grey hair had appeared above the performer's ear. Sick at heart, he sensed that Seaton was right, and he turned his face towards the outer darkness, beyond the guttering oil lamp: 'I'm tired,' he said.

'But you must go on regardless.'

'I am no longer worthy.'

'But Death cannot let you go.'

Eddie did not argue; silently, he accepted his duty and went on his way. But it was all that he could do to drag himself back inside his attic, where he slumped face down across his bed and promptly fell into a deep, drugged slumber, filled with scorpions.

When he woke up, it was night again and he discovered that the lion had chewed up his coat, his hat and his black gloves while he slept.

5

Another year went past and King Death proceeded in unbroken triumph. He rode the Deliverance Special, he travelled the nation, he presented his profile at the window. His revenues and ratings had never been higher, and America was content.

At the end of each week, he made his ritual completion, just as if nothing was changed. Though his work no longer brought him joy or fulfilment, he went through the familiar motions and nobody seemed to notice any difference.

Then one day, without warning, his magic deserted him. In the stockyards of Chicago, his subject knelt at his feet, ready for absolution. But when the moment of intermingling came, nothing happened. Eddie's eyes did not sparkle or grow incandescent; the subject was not transfigured. Instead, he suddenly turned green and looked seasick, and he tried to scramble to his feet. He raised his hands to cover his face, he made a noise like gargling. In wild panic, he grabbed hold of Eddie's knees, almost toppling him, and the performer was forced to shoot him blindly, once, twice, three times, before he would let go.

Back on board the Special, Eddie looked into the mirror and saw only flabbiness, squalor, decay. Death had abandoned him, once and for ever, and when he took out his gun, to shoot the dead eyes of his image, his hand was shaking so badly that he could hardly squeeze the trigger.

From now on, completion became a nightmare. Each rendition seemed worse, more botched and sordid than the one before. However hard he tried, his eyes refused to function and his subjects would not surrender. Instead of swooning in ecstasy, they cowered, screamed, befouled themselves. When he reached out his hand, to bring them beatitude, they bit it.

Eddie could not rest, could not find a moment's peace. As soon as he closed his eyes, even for a few seconds, the lion came creeping up behind him and licked him in his private places.

Gradually, he began to fall into disrepair. His uniform was stained and frayed, he no longer cleaned his equipment, and he wiped his nose on his sleeve. There was a three-day stubble on his chin, his eyes were red-rimmed and sunken. Finally, he took to alcohol.

Alone in his skid-row bedroom, as the Special rolled relentlessly across the flatlands of Ohio and Missouri, he slugged directly from the bottle and did not stop until he was sick. His grease paint and make-up ran, melted by cold sweat. Mascara and rouge got into his eyes, and his suitcase burst open in his hand, scattering its treasures all over the floor.

He lapsed into semi-consciousness and found himself in an infinite desert, where the lion knelt in prayer. Blood flowed from its open mouth and spread across the sand in a translucent lake. Its lips were soft as swansdown, they tasted of vanilla essence. Sighing, it lay down in its blood and whispered, and Eddie crept helplessly into its embrace.

When he came round, his hair was so grey that he was forced to blacken it with boot polish. He had developed jowls and halitosis, he had to wear a corset and, with every week that passed, his completions grew more distressing.

Now that his subjects had learned to struggle, tenderness and dignity were no longer possible, and he dispatched them like a butcher. Blood splashed his hands and uniform; bodies collapsed in poses of grotesque distortion, with gaping mouths and eyes full of loathing. Sometimes, so fiercely did they resist him that the performer was not able to finish them cleanly, and they continued to writhe and blubber, twitching like maimed animals.

The sun rose in Colorado and set in North Dakota, rose again in Maine and set in Mississippi. Outside his window, the brass bands still played, the majorettes pranced, the crowds cried out his name in worship. But Eddie did not hear them, was aware of nothing beyond his bedroom. All day long, he stared out through the smoked glass, sightless. America passed by him in a blur, and his face was wet with tears.

Serene in the next compartment, Seaton lived only for cricket, and Death never crossed his mind. From time to time, in the middle of the night, he was awakened by a sudden burst of gunfire, and a ravaged, distorted profile showed itself at his window, mouthing obscenities. A bottle smashed against the wall, Eddie ground his fist in the shattered glass, blood seeped underneath the door. But Seaton gave no sign of recognition, his face did not move. Rolling over to face the wall, he took refuge in thoughts of Lords and went straight back to sleep.

Periodically, the Special came to a halt and the partners

stopped off for a few days in Tierra de Ensueños, to refresh themselves.

During the last few years, the perfumed garden had been left to moulder and was completely overrun by weeds. Vermin had taken over the labyrinth, the windows were blotted out by ivy. One by one, the roses had withered and died, and the whole mansion stank of rot.

For the most part, Eddie kept to his attic, Seaton to his library, and their paths did not cross. One afternoon, however, when the performer was too drunk to resist, the lion lured him out into the gardens and they lost themselves in the suffocating jungles.

The paths were so overgrown as to be almost impassable, and Eddie had to carve his way through with a scimitar. Hyenas cackled in the monkey trees, reptiles basked and grinned in the stagnant ponds. Pouring sweat, Eddie waded knee-deep through a fetid swamp, which sucked him down like quicksand, and every time that he paused to catch his breath, the lion sniggered behind his back.

At last, arriving at the pagoda, he came into a small space of sunlight, filled with orchids and pink flamingos, where Seaton sat huddled in his Bath chair, reading Wisden.

Eddie stood with lowered head, shuffling, swaying, like a bull just before it falls to its knees. His eyes were bloodshot, there was a loud buzzing in his ears and, after a few seconds, he spat out a slug of yellow rheum, which landed with a splat at Seaton's feet.

The Englishman looked up from his studies and saw a tramp, a stumbling skid-row bum, with matted hair and holes in his boots. 'Good afternoon,' said Seaton. 'Can I help you?'

'It is your fault. You are the one to blame.'

'I'm afraid that I don't understand.'

'Everything that used to be pure and true has been perverted, and you have turned me into scum. Just to keep yourself amused, you have taken God's own beauty and covered it with filth.'

'I am sorry,' said the Englishman. 'I meant it for the best.'

The sun beat down hot and hard, and the lion drank deeply from a fountain, to cool itself. Refreshed, it reached up and whispered in Eddie's ear, and the performer picked Seaton up by the throat.

Mechanically, without any sign of passion, the Englishman was shaken back and forth, like a rag doll with half its stuffing spilled, until he went blue and began to gurgle. His eyes rolled up, he stuck out his tongue; in a few more seconds, he would have been defunct. But Eddie was too weary, too heartsick and drained to make the effort. When the crucial moment arrived, he was paralysed by loathing and shame, and his hands went limp.

Next day, the Special embarked on yet another journey and King Death resumed his vigil beyond the window. The Stars and Stripes flew proudly from the smokestack, the golden eyes gleamed and sparkled. On the screen, everything looked brand new.

Inside his bedroom, Eddie drank, sweated, cursed. When the train slowed down at its first stop, and the band began to play, he exposed himself indecently and shouted out a stream of blasphemies. But he was too far away, the smoked glass was too thick – the crowds could not hear or truly see him. All that they recognised was his silhouette, which was flawless, and they cheered as loud as ever.

Though Eddie himself was crumpling, King Death remained immaculate.

The cameras were omnipotent. They could create any truth that they chose and, even when the performer was reduced to a shambles, they kept his image perfect.

Once a week, he was led out from his refuge and pumped full of sedatives. Paint restored his profile, perfumes masked his smell, soft focus soothed his trembling. Viewed from a suitable distance and angle, buried in deep enough shadow, he hardly seemed altered at all.

At every stage, he was cushioned and camouflaged. Slow motion turned pain and panic into a dreamlike floating, and any hint of squalor was exorcised on the cutting-room floor. When the moment came for completion, Mantequilla spat out his instructions on to cue cards and Eddie performed by numbers, like a sleepwalker, hardly knowing what he rendered.

By all these strategems, Death was able to preserve her surface gloss and there were no ugly scenes or scandals. But her spirit, her power of inner exaltation – that could not be faked. Gradually, by imperceptible shifts, she ceased to be a sacrament. Though she looked and sounded the same as ever, she lost the secret of sensation.

The uniform, the golden eye, the face beyond the window – all the old rituals and symbols were unchanged. But they had lost their power. Little by little, they turned into formalities, dry-boned observances, and the watchers were not fulfilled.

Inside Tierra de Ensueños, the families grew fretful and uneasy. For as long as they could remember, King Death had watched over them and kept them satisfied. He had provided for their every hunger, they had yearned for nothing more. But now the spell was broken. For no reason that they could identify, his image failed to release them.

Deprived of sensation, they became resentful. After all

these years of contentment, they were filled with doubt, mistrust, unspecified dread, and they began to disintegrate. Martha McGhee kept bursting into tears, for no particular cause. The mansion was swept by epidemics. Charley Mitchell got drunk and broke all his windows. Brawls broke out, and big Jim Haggard lost three of his front teeth.

With every week, as the Special passed through the nation, the crowds grew more sullen. They didn't shout or wave, they no longer scrabbled at the fences. Even when Eddie appeared in silhouette, they did not react in any way. Faces set, they simply stood and stared.

Still, they did not complain out loud. King Death had been absolute for so long, the country owed him so much. To rise up against him now would have seemed like sacrilege, a treason.

So the cavalcade continued. Each Friday evening, just as though the golden age had never ended, the families tuned in to HBLF and the performer was put through his routine. The fanfares sounded, the subjects were deluged with prizes, the long blonde girls flashed their teeth. Propped up in left profile, King Death went through the familiar motions, and nobody dared to hiss.

On the last Sunday before Advent, King Death got off the train in Abilene and performed inside a Pentecostal church. By his own recent standards, the completion went quite smoothly. There was no struggle or mess, and the subject knelt down meekly before the altar, expiring with outstretched arms.

The candles flickered, the long blonde girls sprinkled incense, the organist played *Steal Away*. The producers shook hands with the cameramen, and the grips swapped jokes with the extras. Turning away from the arc lights, which hurt his eyes, Eddie mopped his brow, adjusted his hat brim and shuffled off down the aisle. Nobody noticed him go.

Far away, beyond a pair of embossed bronze doors, there was a small chink of sunlight and the lion led him through the shadows, stumbling, groping in the darkness, until they reached it and found themselves in the street outside.

Dulled by sedatives, dazzled by the sudden brightness, Eddie stood with hunched shoulders and waited to be mobbed. But nobody screamed, nobody tried to touch him. The street was almost deserted, and nothing moved.

It was a mild and aimless afternoon; a slow, sleepy Sunday. After a few moments, since no one made any move to prevent him, Eddie turned his face towards the sun and started walking. The sidewalk beneath his feet was scarred and broken, full of cracks, and he drifted past a laundromat, on past a junk shop and a wholesale fruiterer, while the lion ambled behind.

He moved in a daze, not knowing where he was, not watching where he was going, and soon he put his foot into one of the cracks, slightly jarring his ankle. Puzzled, he stopped and looked down, to see what had caused the trouble, and gradually, like a man awakening from a bottomless sleep, he grew aware of his surroundings.

He saw the sidewalk. He saw the grass growing up between the cracks and the faded marks of hopscotch. He saw the laundromat, the junk shop, the mission on the corner. He saw stray cats among the garbage cans, broken glass and candy wrappers in the gutters, a faded green door, a hand-painted sign for furniture. All at once, he could see everything.

Slowly, he drew his toe out of the crack; then, with utmost caution, as if testing unfathomed waters, he dipped it back in again. Deliberately, he scuffed his heel against the rim, savoured the roughness against his sole, and he heard a door slam in an alley. Far away, the organist was playing *Just A Closer Walk With Thee*. A foghorn sounded on the river. The lion purred behind his back. Growing reckless, Eddie wriggled his toes up and down inside his black boot, then wriggled them round in circles and suddenly, the last thing that he had ever expected, he found that he was laughing.

Someone was cooking collards and chicken dumplings in a room above his head. Up the alley, a radio was playing the lowdown blues, and Eddie felt for his gun. Behind his back, the lion shuffled and sniffed, and the performer gave a cry, an animal roar of release, as he whirled and fired and fired again, blazing wildly from the hip.

Shot three times through the heart, the lion lay down upon the sidewalk. Resting its head on its paws, it smiled serenely and wagged its tail, it nuzzled for the last time in Eddie's blackleather palm and, as its lifeblood flowed away, it began to change its shape. Its golden coat was turned into skin, its whiskers shrivelled and died, its body shrank to less than half its former size. Twitching, it snickered in triumph, and it was not a lion at all. When at last its blood stopped flowing, and it went still, it was revealed as a small human child, aged seven, who had walked five miles through the dust and heat, to ask King Death for his autograph.

'A child. An innocent baby,' said Martha McGhee.

'Gunned down without mercy,' said big Jim Haggard.

'Our trust has been betrayed,' said Charley Mitchell. 'We have been taken for a ride.'

When Eddie's malfeasance was first discovered, HBLF had done its best to cover up. The parents were given compensation, all the witnesses paid off, the child himself disposed of without trace. Mumbling incoherently, the performer was locked up again in his compartment. Then the Special moved on, and the matter was considered closed.

But one spectator had been overlooked. At the time of the shooting, Seaton had been stationed across the street, looking down from an upstairs window. Half-hidden behind a curtain, he watched everything that had happened, recording the details on a drugstore Polaroid and, when the prints were developed, he sent out copies to five hundred newspapers, networks and magazines.

The response was instant and absolute. Within an hour of receipt, the child had been splashed across every screen and front page in the nation, and the King was destroyed for ever.

All the resentments, doubts and buried lusts of the past months burst to the surface at once and exploded. The ties of faith and habit were swept aside, every inhibition collapsed. Reflected in the child's still face, America saw her own lost self and, in the instant of recognition, she was released from her bondage, she woke from her long dream.

Her first thought was for vengeance.

When the Deliverance Special pulled in at San Antonio, its next scheduled stop, it was received with stones and broken bottles. Hissing and howling, the crowds charged the fences and in no time, since the guards made no real effort to stop them, they were swarming all over the platform. The brass band was routed, the majorettes sent shrieking for sanctuary, firebrands flung through the carriage windows. A posse stormed the engine and gouged out the golden eye. Kouncillors were dragged from their beds, to be kicked and beaten unconscious. Looters rampaged through the compartments with brickbats, iron bars, cans of kerosene, and they did not rest satisfied until the entire train had been reduced to rubble.

Two nooses were slung from the station beams, but no trace could be found of either Seaton or the performer. Apparently, they had vanished into nothingness and, though America was combed inch by inch, they were never seen again.

Cheated of their prime targets, the avengers were forced to make do with minnows. Anyone who had ever been associated with Death, in whatever capacity, was systematically rounded up and purged. J Jones Dickerson caught a plane to Guatemala and did not return. Mort Mossbacher hanged himself from a clothes hook. Kouncillors were tried, live on HBLF, and sent to jail by the hundred. Publicists were tarred and feathered, long blonde girls tied to streetlamps with shaven skulls. Even rank-and-file Loyalists found themselves informed against, fired from their jobs, shunned by their friends, deserted by their wives and families.

In every city, monstrous bonfires consumed KD posters and propaganda. His supermarkets were stripped bare, his old films destroyed. All his industries changed their names, and it became a federal offence even to possess his photograph.

Just one month after the King had fallen, if a stranger had arrived in America for the first time, he would have found no visible sign that Death had ever existed.

Inside the mansion, when the families looked back on their years of residence, everything seemed hopelessly blurred. They could not remember why they had come here, what had made them watch the performer in the first place or how they had ever been induced to think of him as their friend: 'We must have been brainwashed,' said Charley Mitchell.

'Duped,' said Sarah Carter. 'We were cheated and bamboozled, until we didn't know what we were buying.

Otherwise, we would never have played along.'

'We would have recoiled in horror,' said Mildred Potterson. 'If only we had known, if we'd had the faintest idea of what was going on or what it really meant, we would have run a mile.'

'But we didn't understand,' said Billy Mace. 'We were victims of a conspiracy, and we didn't have a clue.'

'Perhaps we were gullible. Looking back, perhaps we were foolish to be taken in,' said Tom Potterson. 'But we meant no harm.'

'It wasn't our fault,' said Martha McGhee.

'Honest to God,' said big Jim Haggard, 'we were innocent.'

By this time, Tierra de Ensuenos had fallen completely into ruin and there was no point in remaining any longer. So they packed their bags and went back to their previous existences. They took new jobs, made new friends, moved into new apartments, and their lives drifted off in different directions. Soon there was nothing left to connect them, and their years together in the mansion lost all meaning, became no more than a mirage.

Meanwhile, beyond the barbed-wire fences, everything withered and rotted and crumbled. Inside the perfumed garden, the animals perished of starvation, the pools and fountains dried up, the jungle slowly choked itself to death. The labyrinth was blocked by landfalls and, one by one, the heart-shaped follies turned to dust. Then nothing moved or made a sound. The mansion was complete, and only the screens survived.

On a rainy February morning, just outside Tupelo city limits, Seaton stopped the car and passed a hand across his eyes, to wipe away the weariness. He had been driving throughout the night, all the way from Memphis, and now that he had finally arrived, his only sensations were of damp and grime.

For a few minutes, the partners sat in silence, lulled by the swishing of the windscreen wipers and the gentle murmur of country music on the radio. Then Eddie took out his trucidator and began to pick at his teeth.

He was greatly altered. Now that he had ceased to be an image, he no longer suffered and he had reverted to his former self. His hands had stopped shaking, his jowls and grey hair had vanished. In place of his uniform, he wore jeans, a windbreaker and a red-checked workshirt, and his face was placid, ageless, completely neutral.

From time to time, as he picked at his teeth, passers-by would glance in casually through the window. But none of them stopped or gave him a second look. Without his uniform, he looked just like anyone else, and nobody knew him.

Rain fell steadily, the windows were streaked with mud and wet sand. The car radio played a song about honky-tonk angels and Seaton rested his head upon the steering wheel, exhausted. 'Do you hate me?' he asked.

'Why should I?'

'Because I betrayed the King.'

'You made him,' said Eddie, indifferent. 'It was also your right to destroy him. When I was ill, it's true that I abhorred you and wanted you to be punished. But that lies in the past. I am cured again, the saga is concluded. What would be the point in vengeance now?'

Across the street, workmen in overalls were working on a giant billboard, which had once been a showplace for Death, sticking up a slogan for Coca-Cola: 'It was the only way,' Seaton said.

'For what?'

'To reach an ending. To be freed.'

Eddie made no comment. Snapping shut the trucidator, he put it back in his pocket and replaced it with a wad of gum. His jaws chomped in a steady rhythm and, opening the morning paper across his knees, he buried himself in the funny papers.

Inside his suitcase, there was only dirty underwear, a selection of comics, three packs of playing cards, two cans of shaving cream and a half-eaten Hershey bar. Of all his armoury, he had only retained one pistol, a Gilronan .32, which lay snug and warm against his heart.

Seaton's tie, Wykhamist, was slewed round beneath his right ear. His blazer was stained with slopped whisky, there was a smudge of soot on his nose and, when he tried to smile, he had no dimples left. 'What will become of you?' he asked.

'Who can tell?' Eddie said. 'I might take a job at The Golden Slipper. I might hustle in the pool hall or drive a truck or become a lawman. Or I might just stand in a doorway and watch.'

'Where will you live?'

'There was a girl, her name was Marie, she had a home down by the railroad tracks. Perhaps she has gotten married and left. But if she is still free, I will ask to make her mine.'

'And give up the profession?'

'My race is run,' said Eddie simply. 'I have enjoyed a fair span, I've got no complaints. Now it's time for someone else to take a turn. Death is bigger than any one performer, she will not perish without me. Professionals come and go but she survives for ever. No matter how she may be persecuted and abused, she is indestructible and you can bet that some day she will rise again, stronger and greater than ever.'

On the radio, the deejay spoke of hair oil, of second-hand cars and chicken coops. Damp steamed up the glass, seeped through the cracks in the bodywork. Tupelo was full of puddles, and Seaton felt numb.

'And what about yourself?' Eddie asked.

'I am trapped,' replied the Englishman. 'There is nowhere I can go, nothing left for me to do. All my documents and records, all the trappings of my life, are lost in Tierra de Ensueños, and I am too old to make a new start. Truthfully, I believe that I am finished.'

'Finished,' said Eddie. 'But not complete.'

'No. Not complete.'

'That is a waste.'

'Do you honestly think so?'

'Of course I do,' said the performer. 'It's time you were released. Even though you may have sinned, I know that Death forgives you and wants you to be fulfilled.'

'Perhaps she thinks that I don't deserve her.'

'Not her. Her heart is much too big to carry grudges. Everything that happened was inevitable, she knows that. Whatever your errors, she understands that you have always yearned for her, right from the moment you first saw her, and even though I am now in official retirement, she would not wish me to leave before you had received your just reward.'

Reaching inside his breast pocket, Eddie brought out the Gilronan and laid it in his lap. The radio played *Tumbling Tumbleweeds*, and Seaton wiped his wet palms on his thighs. 'Are you sure?' he said.

'I would not mislead you,' the professional replied. 'I know Death inside out, and I understand the way her mind works, just as though it were my own. Believe me, she is waiting to embrace you.'

When Seaton looked out through the window, he could see only drizzle and mist. His eyes stung, there was egg on his lapel, he wanted to go to the toilet. 'What must I do?' he asked.

'Just look into my eyes,' Eddie said. 'Then you will find everything that you require, everything that you have been looking for.'

So Seaton blew his nose, straightened his tie, patted down his rumpled hair, and he turned to face the performer. Eddie picked up the Gilronan, and their eyes met. But the Englishman's vision was blurred, his pupils seemed full of fog. Search as he might, the only image that came back to him was his own pale reflection, distant and distorted. 'Is that all?' he asked.

'More or less,' said Eddie.

And the professional pulled the trigger.

There was a bang. Then Seaton twitched and sighed, and he leaned back against the door, with a small red hole in the centre of his forehead. The windscreen wipers swished, the deejay spoke of Dr Pepper and Saturday night dances. Blood flowed, and Eddie stepped outside into the wet.

Shivering, he turned up his overcoat collar. As soon as he felt the open air, he realised that he was hungry, had been hungry for a very long time. So he tucked his suitcase under his arm and set off into town, to find himself some food.

PRAISE FOR NIK COHN

'A thrilling, inspirational read'
– *Guardian*

'Set the template for a whole new style of rock journalism, informed,
irreverent, passionate and polemical'
– *Choice Magazine*

'The book to read if you want to get some idea of the original primal
energy of pop music. Loads of unfounded, biased assertions that almost
always turn out to be right. Absolutely essential'
– Jarvis Cocker, *Guardian*

'Cohn was the first writer authentically to capture the raucous
vitality of pop music'
– *Sunday Telegraph*

BY NIK COHN

I Am Still the Greatest Says Johnny Angelo (1967)
Awopbopaloobop Alopbamboom (1970)
Market (1970)
Today There are No Gentlemen (1971)
Arfur: Teenage Pinball Queen (1973)
King Death (1975)
Rock Dreams (1974)
Ball the Wall: Nik Cohn in the Age of Rock (1989)
The Heart of the World (1992)
Need (1997)
God Given Months (1997)
Yes We Have No: Adventures in the Other England (1999)
20th Century Dreams (1999)
Soljas (2002)
Triksta: Life and Death and New Orleans Rap (2005)

I AM STILL THE GREATEST SAYS JOHNNY ANGELO

NIK COHN

NOEXIT2

This edition published in 2017 by No Exit Press,
an imprint of Oldcastle Books Ltd, P O Box 394,
Harpenden, AL5 1XJ
noexit.co.uk

A CIP catalogue record for this book is available from the British Library.

This is a work of fiction. Names, characters, places, and incidents either are
the product of the author's imagination or are used fictitiously, and any
resemblance to actual persons, living or dead, businesses, companies, events
or locales is entirely coincidental.

ISBN
978–1–84344-897-6 (print – double edition)
978-1-84344-982-9 (epub)
978-1-84344-983-6 (kindle)
978-1-84344-984-3 (pdf)

2 4 6 8 10 9 7 5 3 1

Typeset in 13.25pt Sabon
by Avocet Typeset, Somerton, Somerset TA11 6RT

Printed in Great Britain by Clays Ltd, St Ives plc

For more information about Crime Fiction go to @crimetimeuk

TO ELVIS AND JESSE,
THE PRESLEY TWINS; AND
FRANNY MAE LIPTON

TO JILL

I AM STILL THE GREATEST SAYS JOHNNY ANGELO

INTRODUCTION

I Am Still The Greatest Says Johnny Angelo was my second novel, written when I was nineteen and published at twenty-one. It was my attempt to create a rock 'n' roll myth, raw and wild and over the top, inspired in large part by meeting P J Proby.

Proby, for those who weren't around in 1965, was a big, swaggering Texan who burst on the British pop scene like John Wayne storming Iwo Jima – if you can imagine the Duke in a blue velvet boiler suit with silver buckles on his shoes and an 18th Century page-boy bob. For a brief spell, he was all the rage, but his prodigious gifts as a singer and showman were outweighed by an even greater gift for self-sabotage, and he quickly imploded.

The first time we met, he was still riding high. I was then covering the pop scene for *The Observer* and went to interview him at a hotel near Regent's Park. It was a sunny afternoon outdoors but the curtains of the suite were drawn and Proby sat hunched in semi-darkness, wearing only sky-blue knickers and a grubby T-shirt, as he downed

bourbon and coke by the tumblerful. Publicists and other flunkies bumbled about, trying to pump up the master's spirits, but he wasn't having any. All the world was against him, he claimed. He was surrounded by back-stabbers and conspirators. Nobody saw his true greatness, or treated him with due reverence. 'I am an artist and should be exempt from bullshit,' he said.

All through the afternoon he talked and talked, while I sat scribbling at his feet. He told epic tales of childhood traumas, of Hollywood nights and cutting demos for Elvis, of crazed drunken orgies, of cheating women and thieving women and women who cut up his heart for sport. Eventually, the stories blurred one into another, their twists and turns so byzantine, their language both so filthy and so grandiose, that in the end I lost track of them, and nothing was left but the sound of his bourbon-soaked Texas drawl.

I'd never met anyone like him. The darkened room, the obscenity, the madness – Proby scared me quite a bit but thrilled me even more. By the time I stumbled back onto the street, and daylight, I knew I'd been handed the bones of a book.

That isn't to say that Johnny Angelo is simply P J Proby with a few cosmetic details changed. What Proby provided was a springboard. The rest was all my own imagining.

I became obsessed with the notion of rock stars as self-made gods. Reinvention, a word that's become so cheapened it now covers anything from spiritual armageddon to getting a nose job, was still comparatively fresh then. The great transforming power of rock, I saw, was to let you throw off the identity you were born with, whatever drab and gutless existence was meant to lie in store, and make yourself into anything you had the nerve to conceive. Thus Elvis, white-

trash mamma's boy, curled his lip and swivelled his hips, and bingo! became a messiah. Thus Phil Spector, born to have sand kicked in his face, the class wimp with the bad skin and worse hair, became a teen millionaire. Thus John Lennon, Mick Jagger, Pete Townshend, and, in the years yet to come, David Bowie, Marc Bolan, Boy George, Prince. Thus P J Proby. And, of course, Johnny Angelo.

Truth be told, I'd have killed to possess the same power myself. Just grant me five minutes of heroic madness, down on my knees in a blue-velvet jumpsuit, with the bass pumping and trumpets braying and all the young girls screaming, melting in puddles at my feet, and I would have sworn off writing in a heartbeat. But no. The closest I could get was to sit in my North London bedsit with a toilet that didn't flush and a damp stain the shape of Winston Churchill's profile on the ceiling above my head, and pound out *I Am Still The Greatest*.

At root, the book was an act of vengeance – against the world and its unfairness, but even more against myself. It's filled with narcissistic self-loathing, a revelling in excess for excess's sake. When it was first published, some critics called it sick, and I took this as high praise.

'Sick' was not the only brickbat thrown. Rock wasn't generally regarded as a fit subject for a serious novel in 1967 and *I Am Still The Greatest* got thoroughly trashed by the mainstream. At the same time, it attracted an underground following, and more than its fair share of imitators.

This influence has never died out; on the contrary, it has grown with time. Over the years, the virgin turf that Johnny Angelo staked out has been worked and reworked, in a slew of other novels, as well as concept albums and films. Quite a few stinkers have resulted, but I've mostly felt flattered anyway.

The homage that would have meant most to Johnny himself, though, didn't come to my attention till a couple of years ago, when I happened into a huddled little bookshop in Westport, County Mayo. On the top shelf, safely out of reach of children, was a small selection of porn. A row of paperbacks with raunchy covers leered down at me. Their author? Johnny Angelo.

Nik Cohn, 2003

Part One

THE WALL

At the age of four, Johnny owned a red suit, a bright red suit. It had tight red trousers that tapered gently to the ankle, and a chunky-cut jacket, low-hung to below the waist, which was given added style by its bulky shoulder-padding. Attached was a matching red hood and, on top of this hood, there was a brilliant white pompom.

Again, the whiteness of the pompom was echoed by a white scarf, twirled once, twirled twice around his neck and then slung casually over his left shoulder to trail half way down his back.

At the far end of his mother's back yard, there was a high brick wall, ten foot high by thirty foot long with a thickness of nine inches across the top. It was a crumbling and weatherbeaten wall. And one day Johnny did a catwalk on top of it.

He climbed the wall in his red suit. He climbed it painfully, by centimetres and millimetres, inching up and falling back again, crawling up it by his fingertips. Twice he fell back to the bottom again. On the third attempt, he made it.

His head appeared over the top, the shrewd fat face of a baby, puckered with concentration and framed by the big red hood with the white pompom.

It was a very windy day. His mother was hanging out washing in the yard below, sheets and blankets that were caught by the wind and billowed up in her face. And the wind blew grit in Johnny's eyes, but he pulled himself up by his shoulders, until first his left knee and then his right were wedged solidly on top of the wall. Then he stood up and dusted himself.

He looked around. He had never been so high in his life. His mother was working in the yard below and Johnny shot her down with his forefinger. Then he did the catwalk.

His knees were stiff and his back was straight, his head was held high, his eyes looked straight ahead. His red suit shone.

He marched from one end of the wall to the other, then back again, then back once more. He marched stiffly, in the style of the Nazis, his leg held rigid at knee and hip. His white scarf billowed behind him in the wind.

Mrs Canning from 23 was the first to see him. She was washing her windows and she saw him on the wall, a child aged four, fat and squat, very solemn. She threw up her window and yelled at him. 'Johnny! Johnny! Come down off that wall!'

Johnny took no notice. He turned once more at the end of the wall and began the slow march back. His mother looked up and saw him. Then everyone knew and windows were raised all along the street. *Come down, Johnny, come down. Come down off that wall.* But Johnny didn't.

He kept on walking still. Once his foot slipped, a brick broke from the wall and fell and split in two. Johnny Angelo

marched from one end of the wall to the other in his bright red suit. He looked tiny and he had a very long way to fall. His mother began to weep.

Then Mr Stein from 34 came down in his shirtsleeves and tried to climb the wall. He was too heavy, he couldn't make it. Then the other people arrived and stood in the yard, shouting instructions. And Johnny walked above their heads and wouldn't come down.

They stood in clusters and watched him. The whole street was awake. A ladder was placed against the wall and Mr Parkes from 8 began to ascend. But the wood was rotten, a rung gave way and Mr Parkes fell heavily, turning his ankle.

Johnny Angelo wasn't reachable.

At the age of four, he walked the wall and everyone watched. His white scarf was whipped by the wind, his red suit gleamed and, when he was bored, he swung his legs over the side, glanced once at the crowd below and shinned down to the ground.

Then they all went home to tea.

THE ATTIC

Mrs Angelo was forty-one years of age. She was thin and tired and grey-faced. She coughed in the mornings and gasped for breath and stopped to hold her side halfway up a flight of stairs. Johnny Angelo didn't like her: she smelled of exhaustion.

She wore a white housecoat that was stained to grey and brown. It was frayed at the hem and almost worn through at the elbow. She wore it in the kitchen when she read the paper. She was wearing it in the morning when Johnny went out to school and she was still wearing it when he came home in the late afternoon.

Her home fell into disrepair. There was a front room and a back room. The back room was the centre of everything. It was the kitchen and the washroom and the dining-room. Johnny slept in it with his two sisters while his mother and his father slept in the front room, which was the best room. Then there was the back yard and there was also an attic, where Johnny Angelo was alone.

When he was six, he began to be disgusted.

The brown paint peeled off the back room walls and nothing was done to put it right. Johnny was ashamed to return from school. The beds weren't made, the sink was stacked with dirty washing, the drains were blocked. There was a sad sick smell everywhere.

His father was a silent man who worked in the docks. He used to spend all his spare time in his allotment and not come home until dark. Then he sat in an armchair and didn't speak.

Johnny's mother woke up coughing. He heard her scuffle in the front room, gasping for breath. When she came through into the back room, her flesh was grey and her hair hung all in rats' tails about her neck. She lit a cigarette. The milkman knocked on the door, his mother turned a blank face towards the noise. The tap was running. Then Johnny Angelo rolled over and turned against the wall.

The same thing, day after day. The exact same faces and expressions, the same walls – Johnny Angelo was bored and he walked the wall in his bright red suit.

He was sent to bed at seven.

His sisters, who were older, played card games on the kitchen table. Johnny lay in his bed, pretending to be asleep, but his eyes were open.

Inside the front room, his mother was talking to his father but his father didn't reply. The door was closed: light came through the cracks.

Each time a card hit the table, there was a slapping sound. Johnny Angelo waited for it. Five seconds passed and a card hit, slap. Then the two sisters watched each other across the table and Johnny waited. In between each slap, there was a silence and then another card hit, slap, and then another, slap, and the sisters watched each other

and there was silence and Johnny watched from beneath the bedclothes.

Then his sisters saw him and were angry: *'Johnny, go to sleep.'*

'Johnny, you are watching.'

'Johnny, I will tell.'

At the age of six, that's when Johnny Angelo retreated to the attic upstairs.

It was dirty, dank and damp, ten foot by seven. The roof slanted in on him and the attic was filled with discards of every description, with thrown-out clothes and books and broken toys. Rain came in through the roof, the skylight rattled in its frame. Everything smelled of dust and Johnny sat cross-legged on the floor, counting. This was his personal property.

He climbed up to his attic by rope ladder and drew it up behind him. He drilled a peephole in the trapdoor and squatted on the attic floor, his eye to the hole, watching.

He saw the people who came to visit. He heard his mother coughing, he knew his father was sitting in the armchair. Then he watched his sisters playing cards, he watched the cards slap on the table and he heard his sisters singing.

His mother shouted when his dinner was cooked. Johnny, come and eat. Come down. But Johnny stayed where he was and didn't come down.

He turned into a jackdaw.

He stole anything that he came across and hoarded it in his attic. Books, caps, football boots. Toy cars, comics, badges, popcorn, spanners, socks and saucepans. Each item sorted and catalogued, as follows: one dumdum thirty-eight; one cowboy hat; three spotted handkerchiefs; one hundred bangbang caps; one Dan Dare mask, flawed.

He filed everything, stored them in order, then gloated on them in the secrecy of his attic. What did he want? He wanted more.

In particular, he wanted turnip watches. Big flat turnips with umpteen hands. When he opened them up, it was like dissecting a frog, there was so much to notice, to study and compare. Hands that turned fast and hands that turned slowly, the ticking of engines, the whirring of motors. And the miniscule cogs that interwove that twined and drew apart, over and over. Then he closed them up again and the fronts were smooth and smug, very fat and it was a comforting thing, a turnip, to jiggle in his hand. To look at in the attic. To keep as a pet.

When he had collected twenty watches, Johnny Angelo took them all to pieces and, using the very best parts of each, he manufactured a turnip of his own design. It had five hands and they all went round at different speeds. They kept their own time, they moved in private cycles, 11 or 18 or 29 hours to their day.

In this style, Johnny made his speeds the way he wanted them, he retreated inside a secret place and, when he was eight years old, he went thieving in the market.

He was tall for his age, pretty and he had soft gold hair that fell across his eyes. His eyes were big and black. He fluttered his lashes, bit his lip and old gentlemen adored him.

In the Sunday morning markets, he cruised. Fruit markets and flower markets and fish markets. There were winkles and eels and cockles and whelks. Canaries and mockingbirds and nightingales. Fields of yellow silk and the stalls all thrown together in a heap, everything mingled, where the market flowed on like a river. Then Johnny Angelo turned around and turnips winked at him from everywhere he looked,

sitting all snug inside their pockets. His hand snaked out and plucked them one by one. Round and smooth and sleek and warm, they nestled like white mice in the palm of his hand.

Back inside his attic, he had a mirror in a gilded frame. He set it up against the slanting roof, jammed between the ceiling and the floor. Then he studied himself.

The skylight rattled in its sockets, rats skittered in the walls. And Johnny Angelo had a black Gladstone bag, inside which there jingled a dozen assorted turnips of varying description.

For instance, he selected a golden watch with silver engravings and he held it flat in his right hand. He smiled in the mirror, he frowned, he winked. Or he chose a heavy silver turnip with a false compartment for photographs and a sepia snapshot of a man with curled moustaches, then he placed it in his breast pocket so that the winder just peeped out coyly over the top. He looked soulful. He turned down the corners of his mouth and he drooped his nostrils. He sat cross-legged and watched himself. His mother was calling him for tea. He sat with his back to the mirror and sneaked glances at himself over his shoulder. He had golden hair and golden flesh: he was considered beautiful. He had many watches all laid out in a row.

His tea was burned. The back room was filled with smoke and the windows were steamed over. Johnny's father sat in the armchair and didn't speak. This man had worked in the docks for twenty-eight years. When he reached retiring age, he would be given a silver turnip watch.

At seven o'clock, directly after he'd finished his tea, Johnny was sent to bed. Motorbikes were revving up in the streets outside. His sisters were playing dominoes at the kitchen table, his mother was sitting by the fire with her eyes shut.

The fire was on her face; fire and shadow, sound and silence. The dominoes rattled on the board and Johnny's eyes were opening and shutting. The back room was very dark and he folded his knees into his belly. His eyes were opening and shutting all the time.

When he woke up, it was three in the morning and everything was still. Johnny rose up and climbed into his attic. Then he picked out five of his very finest turnips and arranged them in a line before the mirror. Then he sat down cross-legged behind them.

Johnny Angelo and a row of five watches: it made him happy and he sat watching for a very long time. He thought it was something quite beautiful and he wanted to keep it for ever, to trap it in his hand.

So he went out and stole a camera. At four o'clock in the morning he hurled a brick through a shop window and listened to the crash of falling glass. No one came. Johnny reached his hand through the hole and picked out the best-looking camera in the shop. He enjoyed this. He liked in particular the shattering of the glass, the jagged circle of the hole and the silence that surrounded him. And he walked home with his camera tucked openly under his arm, straight down the centre of the empty High Street.

Almost at dawn, he took pictures of his own reflection. Pictures of the five watches in a row and him sitting cross-legged behind them, pictures of him smiling and pictures of him looking sad. Pictures of Johnny Angelo.

THE DOCTOR

Johnny Angelo was not a person who changed. From the time of his birth, he hated squalor, sickness and ugliness of every kind and he lived for style.

To the last degree he was fastidious. Already at the age of nine he did not tolerate his mother's nylon stockings lying unwashed on a chair, nor his father's stale tobacco, nor his sisters' sanitary towels all crumpled in the trashcan. All of these things repelled him and drove him deep inside his attic.

He wasn't like a child. He didn't cry and he didn't get excited. Instead, he passed his time in solitude and he wore a watch with live hands and he lived through days of 7 or 18 or 29 hours, according to his mood.

For a long while, he lived inside his bright red suit with the flowing white scarf and the white pompom on top of the hood. Even after he'd grown too big for it, he kept it in his attic and took pictures of its reflection. But rats nibbled it while he was gone, moths caused it to disintegrate. One day, he picked it up and it fell to pieces in his hands. He took the remnants out on to the neighbourhood bombsite and he

buried it in a hole. His beautiful red suit, he folded it neatly and wrapped it in tissue paper and covered it over with earth. Then he went away.

When he returned inside the back room, his sisters were there, playing snap. Johnny Angelo lay in his bed and turned to the wall but his eyes remained open, he kept thinking of his bright red suit, buried in a bombsite. Of course, his sisters guessed. Their cards slapped against the kitchen table, they talked at him: *'Johnny, I can see you.'*

'Johnny, I know.'

In school, Johnny Angelo was given a new uniform – his blazer was a deep wine colour and there was a yellow dragon emblazoned on his breast pocket. Also, he had a matching wine-coloured cap, complete with yellow bands and his socks were black, with wine and yellow stripes.

He stayed by himself. During break, he stood in some empty corner of the playground and was always the last to troop back inside the classroom. Not that he was shy: he cared about dignity, that's all, and he had no wish to fraternise.

Similarly, he refused to undress in public. On the afternoon when everyone played football, he wouldn't get changed, wouldn't take his pants down. Simply, he thought it unbefitting and he sat without moving until all the rest were fitted out in their sky-blue shirts and silver studdings. His teacher called him names, the other boys snickered:

'Johnny, who d'you think you're kidding?'

'Johnny, we can see you.'

'Chicken Johnny Angelo.'

Still, he sat in front of his locker and wouldn't budge. One true thing about him, he was stubborn at least and prideful and he never changed his mind. Even when his teacher got

mad and hit him, he didn't cry and didn't smile but sat without moving and wouldn't be budged.

For this reason, he was disliked. When he walked into morning assembly, for instance, everyone laughed behind their hands and pointed. On Johnny's back, someone had pinned a notice and the following message: *kick me says Johnny Angelo.*

Johnny Angelo says kick me: he stood in some empty corner of the playground and, as soon as school was out, he went home to his attic.

Halfway down Mafeking Street, he met for the first time with the Doctor. It was mid-October and leaves swirled around their ankles. Straightaway, Johnny's life was changed.

The Doctor was a man of middle-age, with yellowed flesh and yellowed eyes. Each night, he went walking through the neighbourhoods of the city and he stood in the shadows. On the dark side of the street, he would wait beneath a gaslamp and he wore a long black overcoat, a black slouch hat.

Because of this, his reputation was sinister and he was known variously as Doctor Sax, Doctor Spook and Doctor Kitsch. As it happened, all of these names were unjust – he liked to walk alone, that's all, and he wore his hat pulled low across his eyes.

For twenty-two years he had lived by himself in a large house on Westmill Boulevard, almost a mansion, surrounded by high barbed wire. Late at night, returning from his travels, he would pace up and down in his study. A light shone from behind his back, his silhouette was framed in the window, his yellow eyes gleamed.

And that's how Johnny Angelo knew him. Sometimes, when he'd been out stealing turnips, Johnny would pause beyond the barbed-wire fence and watch while the Doctor

paced. The yellowed flesh, the black slouched hat – these things amused him and, later, he became aware of the Doctor beneath the gaslamps, or lurking up an alley, or moving silently behind his back, or simply crouching in the dark.

Johnny wasn't made uneasy. Rather he was intrigued, attracted: he thought the Doctor was cute. Therefore, passing him by on Mafeking Street, Johnny went slow and hoped to be accosted. His golden hair fell forward across his eyes, his teeth showed very white. When he looked up into the Doctor's face, the Doctor smiled. Then Johnny smiled in return and they shook hands on the corner.

The wind blew in spasms, the Doctor's coat was lifted high around his knees. Then he held Johnny's hand in his own, gently squeezing the fingers. 'Little boy,' he said. 'What are you called?'

'My name is Johnny Angelo: I live in the attic.'

'You have beautiful flesh.'

'I have a watch with five hands.'

It was almost teatime: Johnny Angelo wore his wine-coloured blazer with the yellow dragon emblazoned on the breast, his wine-coloured cap with the yellow stripe. He was almost ten years old. 'Of course, we could always go to my house,' the Doctor said. 'Once inside, we could eat toasted scones.'

'I think I'd like that,' said Johnny, simpering, and they walked together to the house on Westmill Boulevard, while leaves swirled around the ankles.

Beyond the barbed-wire fence, the Doctor's mansion stood black and gaunt and lonesome. Their footsteps echoed through the hallways and many empty rooms surrounded them, because the Doctor confined himself to a single room on the second floor and the rest of his house was deserted.

Hand in hand, the Doctor led Johnny Angelo out on to a balcony and they looked across the neighbourhood. Then Johnny shaded his eyes and he saw his own street, his own house, even the skylight of his attic. 'From this balcony I can watch everything that occurs,' said the Doctor. 'Even the Sunday morning markets, where turnip watches are stolen in their dozens.'

Johnny Angelo was not embarrassed. Standing close to the Doctor, he didn't feel threatened and he didn't feel tense. In fact, he felt more at ease than during any other phase of his lifetime, so he laughed out loud and the Doctor also laughed and then, still holding hands, they went inside the Doctor's study.

This room was the centre of the Doctor's whole existence. For twenty-two years without a holiday, he had paced from one end to another and all of his life had accumulated within its doors.

It didn't add up to much: on the hatstand, there were four slouch hats, all identical; pinned to a wall, there was the Doctor's medical diploma; in the darkest corner, there was a heaped confusion of books and journals and pamphlets, gris-gris calculations and secret cures; and hanging from the ceiling, there was a single candelabra.

Apart from these items, there were also a handful of applecores in an ashtray, three guttered candles and a phial of verdigris. When Johnny sat down in a velvet armchair, dust rose up in clouds and made him sneeze. Nonetheless, this room was not squalid. Just gently decaying.

Meanwhile, the Doctor had disappeared inside the kitchen and was preparing an afternoon tea, namely toasted muffins, buttered scones and cranberry jam. When he emerged once more, there were crumbs all around his mouth and his

yellow eyes were sheepish. First he took off his overcoat, his black slouch hat. Then he balanced his plate upon his knees, looking dainty: 'I am fond of elegance,' he said. 'Grace and style in all things, the avoidance of tedium.'

'I used to own a bright red suit,' said Johnny. 'I buried it in a bombsite.'

'Precisely.'

'I sit cross-legged on the floor and take many pictures. At four o'clock in the morning, I threw a brick through the window and my sisters were playing dominoes, the lightbulb was swinging in the draught. My eyes kept opening and shutting.'

Inside this room, everything was peaceful and Johnny sank down deeper in his velvet armchair. Soon he began to be drowsy and nothing mattered any more. Then the Doctor helped himself to a second buttered scone and spread it thick with jam. 'Doesn't truth get tiresome?' he said. 'When lies are so much fun.'

Johnny picked up a slouch hat from off the hatstand and placed it on his head. Straightaway, it slipped down over his eyes, skidded right to the tip of his nose and he looked ridiculous.

The Doctor laughed softly: 'Do you take my meaning?' he said.

'I think so.'

'Then have another muffin and come back again tomorrow.'

BEYOND THE BARBED-WIRE FENCE

In his own back room, Johnny Angelo played Snakes and Ladders with his sisters. 'Today I met with the Doctor,' he said. 'He fed me scones and jam.'

No one responded: his father was sitting in an armchair and his mother sat by the fire but neither made any reply. Meanwhile, the dice jumped and rattled on the table and motorbikes roared in the street outside. 'He lives inside a mansion,' said Johnny. 'He held my hand and led me on to a balcony. Our footsteps echoed through the hallways.'

'It's your turn,' said his sisters. 'Throw the dice.'

'He wore a black slouch hat.'

Johnny threw 9, landed on a snake and plunged all the way to 11. His mother was wearing a white nylon housecoat, scarred by many cigarette burns and his father was sunk in a secret dream. 'Then he told me his philosophies,' said Johnny. 'There was a candelabra hanging from the ceiling. There was a phial of verdigris.'

Even the verdigris drew no reaction: his mother sucked a jujube and Johnny was offended. 'Listen to me, I'm talking,'

he said. 'I'm explaining the way it was.'

'What was?'

'The Doctor: the way he entertained me, fed me scones and held my hand.'

His father was sleeping now, his mother was putting on lipstick. The dice span on the board and his sisters kept climbing ladders. Then Johnny Angelo was desperate and he felt his watch all snug and smooth inside his pocket, purring like a great fat cat. 'And he whispered in my ear,' he said. 'And he gave me wine, and he removed his black slouch hat, and his flesh was yellow like wax. When everything grew dark, he touched me with his hand.'

'It's your turn,' said his sisters. 'We're waiting.' Then Johnny got mad and he rose up without warning, he flung the board on the floor. Dice rattled against the windows, his father stirred in his dream. Johnny Angelo turned the table on its side and he kicked it and his mother sucked a jujube.

His sisters wept and Johnny went away. In the street outside, there were motorbikes everywhere and riders who wore black leather, with a silver crucifix that dangled from their throats. And Johnny Angelo walked through their midst, he wasn't scared.

On the dark side of the street, he sensed the Doctor beneath a gaslamp but couldn't trap him. Just behind his shoulder, just beyond his fingertips, the Doctor was elusive and Johnny chased him for hours, didn't come home till midnight.

At this time, Johnny Angelo was still a child but he did not think and he didn't speak like one. He had perfect white teeth, he had golden flesh and he walked by himself. He was repelled by squalor, drawn close by style. Already, he was conscious that he was set apart.

In school, he wouldn't say his prayers and his teacher was

insulted. 'Johnny Angelo,' said the teacher. 'Why don't you do right?'

'Because.'

'Because of what?'

'Because I'm Johnny Angelo.'

And the next afternoon, he returned beyond the barbed-wire fence, and walked through the echoing hallways. He stood on the balcony and overlooked the neighbourhood. 'I don't feel so good,' he said. 'Time keeps passing and my life goes nowhere.'

It was the most beautiful day. The sunlight was caught by the crystals of the chandelier and the study was filled with refractions, darting and flashing like dragonflies. 'Maybe I might help you,' the Doctor said.

'How?'

'Maybe I could show you another alley to run down. Maybe I could teach you the ways of style and then your life would proceed.'

He was eating a chocolate-chip cookie, the Doctor, and he smiled a yellow smile that was sneaky at the edges. Even in this warm autumn sunlight, he wore his overcoat. 'I might even create you afresh,' he said.

'Create me afresh,' said Johnny Angelo. 'I'd like that.'

'Johnny,' said the Doctor. 'I think you might.'

Inside the Doctor's study, the light was split into fragments and all the colours of the spectrum played upon the walls. Johnny Angelo moved in circles and his flesh was dappled like water. Then the Doctor munched a Turkish Delight and began to speak. 'This is a story of my youth.' he said. 'I hope you like it.

'When I was 25 years old, I travelled with Kid Clancey, the hired assassin. For four years we toured from country

to country, town to town, while the Kid shot to kill and I dressed his wounds.

'On the day that I first met with him, I was sitting in my bedroom, reading my medical textbooks, when I heard a gunshot in the distance and then footsteps pounding on the stairs outside. There was a ferocious hammering on my door, I opened up and in staggered Kid Clancey. Without a word, he went to the window, produced a pearl-handled Colt and broke the glass. Then he sheltered behind the curtain and watched the street.

'At first, I was too much surprised to speak but soon I recovered myself and I came up behind him. "Now hold on, stranger," I said. "What's going on here?"

'"I have just shot down Mario DeMario and now I'm being chased," replied the Kid.

'I didn't object. As it happened, I had never heard of any such DeMario and wasn't concerned, so I retreated from the window and went back to my studies.

'Kid Clancey hid behind the curtain, staring at the street below, and a confusion spread throughout the neighbourhood. Crowds swept up and down the boulevard, women screamed, dogs barked. Loudspeakers appealed for calm and lawmen assembled in squads. But time passed and nothing much happened – no shots rang out, no footsteps sounded on the stairs. Gradually the commotion began to fade. At the end of an hour, it had died out altogether and the Kid turned away from the window, he put away his gun.

'He stood behind me and placed his hand upon my shoulder. He was dressed as a gangster, complete with double-breasted suit, co-respondent shoes, and diamond tiepin, and his fingers were ornamented with many rings, his nails were freshly manicured.

'His hands were exquisite. Slim and strong and supple, they pulsed with a secret energy that was never exhausted. He had blue blank eyes, his face was expressionless. All of his life was carried in his hands.

'Inside my room, he touched my arm but didn't smile. "I wish to thank you," he said. "You saved my life."

'I reached inside the drawer and brought out a bottle. The Kid drank deeply, his eyes wide open, and then I drank as well. So we drew the curtains and smoked cigars and we didn't stop drinking until the bottle was empty.

'After midnight, the Kid went to the window again and the street was deserted, so we went down the stairs together and out into the night. At the bus station, we bought two tickets to Decatur, we rode the Greyhound and that's how I came to be Kid Clancey's partner.

'Why did I go with him? Because I thought he was nice, that's all, and because I thought I would have fun.

'When we arrived in Decatur, we sat for two days in a hotel room, drinking bonded bourbon. On the third day, the Kid made another hit and then we caught a train and journeyed through the Santo Grando, past Corinth and Holt and Pharisee, and so my life settled into its new pattern, I became accustomed.

'What shall I tell you next? For four years, I travelled with the Kid and never knew a single moment of happiness or unhappiness.

'Each time that we arrived in a different town, we locked ourselves inside a hotel room and waited. Kid Clancey sat on the bed and he filed his fingernails and polished them. There was a radio playing on his bedside table and I stood by the window, watching the street below. Three times a day, someone knocked on our door and we fed ourselves.

At night, I grew restless and wished I was drunk but the Kid remained motionless. He kept on cleaning his Colt and his hands were perfection.

'In due course, he went out and made his hit. Then he came back and collected me and we moved along. This process continued without a pause and had no end and no beginning.

'What was it like? It was like a dream. These hotel rooms, the streets below, the blue blank eyes of the Kid – all of this was a ritual that recurred and recurred again and recurred once more. City followed city, nation followed nation, death succeeded death in one endless motion picture. But don't believe that we were bored. We fulfilled our assignments, that was all that existed and, whenever the Kid was hurt, I healed him.

'There was never anyone like Kid Clancey. He was 28 years old and he had been an assassin for 9 years, he had already completed more than 80 hits in 7 nations and he stood at the summit of his profession. During all the years of his supremacy, he was unafraid of anything.

'But when we were halfway through the fifth year of our partnership, he changed. Without warning, his hands began to shake and he no longer sat upon his bed, he paced the floor instead. The secret energy departed from his fingertips, the pulse was extinguished. Then he began to miss. Three times in eight assignments, he failed and this was enough to ruin him, no more work came his way.

'What had gone wrong? "I do not know," said the Kid. "I only know that I used to feel fine and I don't feel fine any more. The truth is obvious: I'm finished."

'So he went into retirement and, together, we rode a Greyhound out of the circuit and settled in a two-bit town named Sanchez, where Kid Clancey bought a saloon and

ran a smalltime call-girl operation on the side. Meanwhile, I resumed my studies.

'I was not dissatisfied. Even in the days of his decline, I liked the Kid very much and was pleased to remain his partner, to give him aspirin when he sneezed. Therefore, we took it easy and time passed and our lives progressed without frustration.

'But the rules are not so simple – the Kid's former employers distrusted him, held him in contempt for losing his nerve and they sent three young assassins to end his life.

'When the Kid was just two days short of his 33rd birthday, he heard that the killers were locked in the Hotel Amsterdam and his hands began to shake again. Placing his drink on the bar, he went through into his office, took out his pearl-handled Colt and polished it. Then he opened the door and stepped out into the alley.

'Right then, a Buick '34 came round the corner and blocked his path. The headlights were turned full on, the alley was flooded with a blinding whiteness and the Kid put up his hand to shade his eyes. In that position, he was shot through his stomach and his leg and his chest.

'Then he fell down and lay without moving. His gun slipped through his fingers but his hand didn't shake any more, his eyes remained open, as blue and blank as ever. Footsteps approached him down the alley.

'I had been watching from the office but now I averted my eyes. Without delay, I went back through the bar, out on to the street and I caught the Greyhound back to Decatur, I travelled one last time.

'Such was the end of Kid Clancey.'

HEAT

Therefore, on his 10th birthday, Johnny Angelo became a gunslinger.

The Doctor took him by the hand, led him downtown and bought him the full uniform of a dude. High-heeled black boots with silvered spurs and glass studding up the front; tight black pants, narrow at the knee, slung low upon the hips; white frilled shirt with lace at the cuffs and on the breast; thigh-length black topcoat, as worn by Doc Holliday; black leather gloves, drawn tight, and a black stetson, and a pair of six-shooters that rested snug in the holsters of his jewelled black belt. With all of this, there came a pack of cards and five hundred caps for his guns.

It was an El Paso afternoon, the hottest day of that year. No one moved. Black men sat out on their doorsteps, drinking cold beer out of cans and young girls lay naked on their beds, oozing sweat in pure white rooms. Dogs went mad and schoolgirls meandered through town and dust climbed up their legs. Then the schoolboys came by on bicycles and bought them ice-cream at the corner stand, sat with them in

the corner booth of the soda fountain and maybe stole a kiss. One Coca Cola, two straws and the jukebox kept on playing The Little White Cloud That Cried.

Inside the toy shop, Johnny watched himself in a full length mirror, turning sideways and backways and spinning on his heel. Meanwhile, the Doctor stood at a distance and smiled his yellow smile. Then he went away, leaving Johnny Angelo to survive by himself.

Standing on the kerb, Johnny looked around him and his thumbs were hooked through his gunbelt and his feet were planted well apart. He peered out from under his stetson, squinting up into the sun, and then he moved off down the sidewalk, pigeon-toed, a slow strut, and all the time his hands hovered just above his holster, his trigger-finger ached.

He was 10 years old. He was 4 foot 5 inches tall and the heat was crucifixion. Sweat ran into his eyes and his white frilled shirt was already stuck to his back, his scalp crawled beneath his stetson.

Danger surrounded him: he moved slow and held his body tense, his senses all pared to their sharpest edges. Behind his back or around the corner or beyond an upstairs window, he was being watched, his destruction had already been planned. But then he was prepared, he refused to run. Gunslinging Johnny Angelo, he feared no man alive.

Black topcoat, black boots, black hat. Each time he turned a corner, the people turned to stare. Everyone watched but nobody laughed. Even at the age of 10, Johnny Angelo cast certain spells.

Slow-motion replay, he moved in a dream and no one moved as he passed on through. Men stopped and straightened as they dug roads, or froze as they entered their cars, one foot still on the kerb. Women held up melons like hand-grenades,

children stood with their sherbet sticks all dangling and slack between their lips. And Johnny Angelo slid through them all, not looking to left or to right, and dogs lay expiring in the heat.

Beneath his long black coat, Johnny was melting and his head was full of buzzing. Still, he passed through street after street, neighbourhood after neighbourhood, until he was almost back at the barbed-wire fence and he didn't falter. His hands hung just above his holster, his three-inch heels echoed on the paving. On his left wrist, his watch had five hands.

But then there came a show-down.

In the shadows behind his back, something moved without warning, a dog scratched itself and Johnny whirled in one movement, his gun came up out of its holster and bang, bang, bang, three shots rang out in the afternoon.

The dog ran away. Left by himself, Johnny was stranded on the sidewalk, his gun still smoking in his hand, his black glove tight as a sausage skin. And he bowed his head, bit his lip and straightaway, the spell was snapped.

Gunning down dogs in the open street: it has to be said, Johnny looked foolish. And it was a small girl aged 6, wearing blue jeans and a sexy sweater, who was the first to laugh. She sat on the kerb with her feet on the gutter, she pointed at Johnny Angelo with her forefinger and her laugh was clear like water.

Then everyone else laughed, too.

CRYSTALS

'At least I didn't miss,' said Johnny Angelo. 'Three shots in one second, three bullets through the heart: I killed him clean.'

'He was only a dog,' said the Doctor. 'You shot him with caps.'

'Doesn't truth get tiresome?' Johnny said, and he moved out on to the balcony. Inside the study, the Doctor was reading the evening paper and chewing on chocolate-coated caramels. After a few moments, he rose up in his black overcoat and took Johnny's hand. 'Come inside,' he said. 'There's something I want to show you.'

'What?'

'I want to show you some crystals.'

In one cobwebbed corner of the Doctor's study, there stood a cardboard box and, inside this cardboard box, there was a large white honeypot. 'This is my inheritance,' the Doctor said. 'It carries all my life.' And he held it up to the light and opened it and sniffed at it deeply. Sure enough, it was full to overflowing with fine white crystals.

Johnny Angelo stood out on the balcony and surveyed the neighbourhood. It was winter now, everything was smothered by fog and the Doctor's face was shrouded by his black slouch hat, except for where a few white crystals lay scattered about his nostrils like a line frost. 'This is a story of Monseigneur Pike,' the Doctor said. 'His mansion, his silver spoon, his magic honeypot.

'Monseigneur was a star of motion pictures, now retired, and he lived by himself in a house of 53 rooms. Every morning and every afternoon, he meandered through its corridors, stairways and chambers, and he used more crystals than any man alive.

'Everywhere that he went, he carried a silver spoon in his left hand, a honeypot in his right and, as he journeyed through his mansion, he kept dipping the spoon inside the honeypot. Immediately, a deep and satisfied sniffing would echo through the hallways and Monseigneur would sigh, would smile, would resume his wanderings.

'Over the years, the honeypot grew famous all over the county and Monseigneur's home was almost a shrine. Pilgrims converged from miles around and queued outside his door, hoping for a sampler. And sometimes Monseigneur would oblige them but more often he would only smile politely and turn away. Always, he quickly shut his door, hiding away with his honeypot, which was his whole existence.

'But then the time arrived when Monseigneur was old and his death came close. As to himself, he wasn't much upset by this, having fulfilled his life, but he was worried about the honeypot and he organised a special competition, in which the winner received a bottomless bowl of crystals.

'The rules of this competition were as follows: the contestants formed a queue at Monseigneur's door. They

filed past in ordered procession. They each received a free sniff at the honeypot. They then had to invent an original slogan, no more than 25 words in length, beginning with the words: "I like this honeypot because…"

Straightaway, a large crowd assembled to try its luck and the queue took several weeks to reach an end. As each slogan was delivered, however, Monseigneur only smiled politely and moved along and, when all the contestants had finally shuffled past, the honeypot had not been won.

'It was only at this late stage that news of the contest finally reached me and, of course, I decided to enter. So I travelled cross-country for two days and a night, until I came to Monseigneur's mansion and I knocked on his door.

'How come he was known as Monseigneur? He was old beyond age, wise beyond knowledge. His flesh was parchment, his eyes were shrivelled jellyfish. His skull was a deathmask and, yes, his age was only 74 but, in reality, he had moved beyond time. All the things that existed, he had seen them and touched them and passed them by. Every secret that was hidden, he had guessed it long ago.

'Monseigneur Pike, he wasn't reachable but I passed inside his house, I travelled his 53 rooms. Then he gave me the silver spoon, the honeypot and I sniffed.

'When the first crystals entered my nostrils, I sighed deeply and flowers bloomed in my brain. Flowers of black and flowers of white, petals so big and so soft that I climbed up on top of them, lay down with my eyes shut and, together, we floated.

'Flowers of beautiful evil: at once, everything that was squalid in me was cleansed away and all that remained was elegance. Journeying through the mansion, I sank deep in crystals and I smiled, feeling the fragrance spread. "I like this honeypot," I said. "I like it very much."

'"That's cheating" said Monseigneur. "You didn't give any reason."

'"I don't have a reason," I replied, sniffing once more. "But I like it very much."

'Then Monseigneur spread his hands out wide, a gesture of defeat. "That is not the correct answer," he said. "It's the best I'm going to get, however, and you can take the honeypot."

'One last time, Monseigneur sniffed deeply and crystals filled his brain. A very old man, he shook my hand and then he departed for some distant chamber, where he waited to die.

'I held the silver spoon in my left hand, the honeypot in my right and I went away from the mansion. The next day, I came to this town and I moved inside this house and I have stayed here ever since.'

Johnny Angelo was thinking of Kid Clancey. He was standing on the balcony and the Doctor was close beside him and the honeypot was standing on the balustrade. 'One day it will be yours,' the Doctor said. 'Just as I inherited it from Monseigneur, so you will receive it from me: one nose succeeds another and the line doesn't die.'

Johnny was thinking of Wyatt Earp and Sugar Ray Robinson and the Mad Monk Rasputin. Down below in the neighbourhood, there was his attic, his full-length mirror, his many turnip watches, all the things of his childhood, and now he placed his hand on the honeypot, wishing to test the crystals for himself, but the Doctor stopped him. 'Let's go inside,' said the Doctor. 'I have marzipan cakes for tea, and Chestnut Whirls, and Jasmine Dreams.'

FAT BLACK CAT

Johnny Angelo was 10 years old. Then he was 11. Then he was almost 12. Each day for two years, he went inside the Doctor's house, beyond the barbed-wire fence, and he learned everything that the Doctor was able to teach him.

Sitting in his study, standing on the balcony, the Doctor ate Love Hearts and told stories of Willie the Pleaser, the bigshot gambler who wore diamonds in his underwear; of Clarence Troy, the Pocatello Python; of Doctor Sax and Doctor Kitsch; of Avril Orchid, who plunged from the 53rd floor of her block; and Ryder Harte, the watcher, and Primo Carnera and Jay Gatsby, the richest man in the world; of Cuchulainn and the Baron Lambert, Babe Ruth and Akim Tamiroff; and the Silver Surfer and the Pinball Phantom; and Jill Irene Waddell who was the real thing; and Roscoe Fatty Arbuckle and Ferdinand de la Menthe; of Jet Powers; of Arfur, the teenage pinball queen; and Lim Fan, the clairvoyant, and Charlie Chase; and of Johnny Angelo himself, who was a legend in his lifetime.

So many styles, such various crystals: Johnny kept his

eyes fixed on the honeypot and, when he walked home in the dark, he rode with los Santos, the four tongueless brothers of the mountain El Gris.

Inside the back room, his sisters were playing Cotch, a three-card poker, ideal for the purpose of cheating, and Johnny was lying on his bed. Out in the alley, motorbikes were revving up and Johnny's eyes were opening and shutting. 'I'm leaving here,' he said. 'I'm moving on.'

His father was asleep in the armchair. His mother was reading Mary Grant's problem page. His sisters knew that he was watching. 'Listen to me,' he said. 'I'm going away.'

'You aren't,' said his mother.

'No, you're not,' his sisters said.

'Yes,' he said. 'I am.'

Up inside his attic, he sat cross-legged on the floor and he arranged his watches in rows and he took pictures of his reflection. Pictures of Johnny Angelo, at the age of 10, at the age of 11, in spring or winter or fall, smiling or pouting, moving or motionless, a small child.

He wore high-heeled boots with silver spurs, a stetson hat and a gunbelt. He wore a wine-coloured blazer with a yellow dragon emblazoned on the breast, a wine-coloured cap with yellow stripes. In class, he had inky pellets flicked at him. Dead mice were left in his desk. His locker had an obscenity carved deep in the wood: *Kick Me Says Johnny Angelo.*

Johnny, We Can See You.

Johnny Says Kick Me.

And on graduation day, he climbed the school flagpole, 53 feet in the sunlight.

He shinned up by his hands and feet alone, no ropes were employed and a large crowd gathered below, waiting to see him fall and kill himself. The headmaster, the board of

governors, the speechmakers: they stood in a ragged circle, gazing upwards, and many voices shouted for Johnny to come down. But he wouldn't.

Red suit on a red brick wall: when he got to the top, he looked out across the city, all of the parks and markets and boulevards, cathedrals and canals, stretched out like a map, and Johnny sat on a flagpole, high above everything. The sun shone, everyone was watching him and Johnny saw the barbed-wire fence, and the motorcycle alley, and he looked down in the faces of the crowd, he smiled and he waved.

Later, he sat with the Doctor and ate more sweets. 'I was satisfied,' he said. 'I wanted nothing else.'

'You looked good,' said the Doctor.

'I saw everything.' said Johnny Angelo. 'Everything.' It grew dark. The Doctor paced the floor, his yellow eyes glinted. 'Many years ago, Count Condu conducted experiments in a castle,' he said. 'He kidnapped young children from a neighbouring village and he strapped them down on a table, where he slit their throats and drank their blood as it spurted, still hot.

'He hoped to find a key to everlasting life, a magic elixir, so he slaughtered more than twenty children but then his luck ran out. He was found out and arrested. In punishment, he was walled up inside his own castle, where he remained forever. Perhaps he's sitting there still.'

And Johnny killed flies in the attic.

He held a rolled white napkin and, any time that he heard a fly buzz on the ceiling, he cut it down without blinking. He didn't ever miss. Passionless, he laid out his victims in rows and he didn't stop killing till he had collected 50 dead flies. Then he put them all in an old tin box and he bought a canary.

In due course, the canary ate the flies and sang delicious melodies. Together, they posed in front of the mirror, Johnny Angelo and the bird, and Johnny drifted in dreams of Laredo and the canary perched on his shoulder, crooning the gentlest lullabies.

So Johnny Angelo was soothed and, down in the Sunday morning market, he bought a fat black cat. Very sleek, very sly, with a purr of purest velvet evil, and Johnny brought it home in a luncheon box.

Up in the attic, the canary was singing and the cat was purring and Johnny was taking pictures. Then the canary was eaten by the cat and the floor was covered with soft yellow fluff.

The cat was not messy and the canary did not thrash its wings, did not make any sound. Stately in all its motions, this death was elegant and Johnny took many photographs of its reflection, he smiled.

Sunshine came through the skylight. The bird disappeared without trace and the cat licked its chops, lay down in Johnny's lap, and sunned itself. Its belly was full of good fresh meat and rumbled in contentment. Then Johnny lay down on the floor, his cheek was cushioned by feathers, so soft. He was wearing his gunbelt and his hair fell golden in his eyes. His fat black cat was purring.

Johnny Angelo and the cat. Each morning, they went to school together. Johnny leading, the black cat following, and the cat sat on the grey school wall, waiting through the day until Johnny came out again. Then they went home to tea.

They were happy.

This cat was Johnny's true servant and gave him its life. Then it began to steal for him. Sneaking through the market, it picked up liquorice sticks with lemon sherbet stripes,

or musical ties with scarlet flats and sharps on a sky-blue background, or big fat turnip watches. Smooth operator, it used a look of perfect innocence and policemen stopped to stroke it, stall-holders threw it sprats.

Big smug pussycat, it had great black eyes that glowed in the dark and it purred its velvet purr. Sitting on the school wall, it floated in heroic dreams of Johnny Angelo and it smiled. But then Johnny came out one afternoon and the cat was lying dead in the gutter. Some children had killed it with stones. Fat black cat that ate the bird that ate the flies and Johnny placed it in his luncheon box, buried it on the same bombsite where once he had buried his bright red suit.

He didn't cry. Sitting in the Doctor's study, he downed a glass of blackcurrant cordial and he spread his hands out wide, a gesture of defeat. 'They broke its legs,' he said. 'They cut out its tongue. They gouged out its eyes.'

The Doctor was calm. Just like always, he was logical. 'They killed one cat,' he said. 'You killed 50 flies.'

'Bullshit,' said Johnny Angelo, and he went away. This was the first obscenity that Johnny had ever uttered. It was not the first obscenity that he had ever thought, however, not by any means, and this was the truth; he planned revenge.

He was 11 years old. Then he was almost 12. Sitting in the back room, he thought of his dead black cat and he polished his guns. Up in the attic, he dreamed of explosions.

He went less often beyond the barbed-wire fence. The Doctor still had class, of course, and he still contained many mysteries but then, in the end, he only told stories. Swallowing gongons by the pound, he epitomised repose. Meanwhile, Johnny was hot for apocalypse.

And nights, the alley was full of motorbikes, of black

leather riders and the howling of the engines made the windows shake. A skull emblazoned on their backs, a silver crucifix dangling at their throats, the riders rode out in formation and Johnny approached their leader. 'I am Johnny Angelo,' he said. 'Let me ride.'

'No,' said the rider.

'Let me ride,' said Johnny again, but the rider laughed and left him behind. When the motorbikes were gone, the silence hurt his ears. And one more time, he lay down in the back room and shut his eyes. 'I'm leaving here,' he said. 'I'm going away.'

One more time, no one replied.

And Johnny stood out on the Doctor's balcony, he looked down on the neighbourhood. 'I'm sick of this,' he said.

'Of what?'

'Of going in circles.'

'Of me?'

'Yes,' said Johnny Angelo. 'Of you.'

The Doctor turned away. Inside his study, he opened up the honeypot and stuck his nose inside. Then the crystals flew up his nose and he sighed. 'Sniff,' said Johnny. 'That's all you ever do.'

But the Doctor only smiled. It was no part of his philosophy to get himself involved in insults and retribution. Therefore, he floated in the honeypot and nothing else existed.

Johnny wanted to hit him. White-faced, he came up close and hissed in the Doctor's face. 'Why are you hiding?' he said.

'I'm not hiding. I'm floating,' said the Doctor.

'Get mad,' Johnny said.

'No.'

'Why not?'

'Because,' said the Doctor. 'Because that would not be elegant.'

Then Johnny went down in the docklands and he walked all night long. He was wearing high-heeled boots with silver spurs, a watch with five hands, a stetson hat. He stalked the shadows. He shot from the hip. And he was the phantom that lurks in the graveyard, the vampire that flies like a bat. The white face at the window, the black shape beyond the balustrade and, everywhere that he passed, he dealt out death.

High above the waterfront, for instance, there was a disused church and this was the place where the tramps and the derelicts of the city stayed, surrounded by a graveyard wilderness.

When Johnny Angelo walked between the tombstones, it was almost midnight and the derelicts were sleeping on the steps of the altar, wrapped in rags. There was a smell of methylated spirits, there was a smell of death. There were cripples and retards and perverts, winos and mongols. There were men with no legs and men with sightless eyes and men covered with sores, all scabrous and running with pus.

Everywhere there was a terrible suffering.

On all of this, Johnny Angelo looked without flinching. Soon he came closer and the vagrants had lit candles at the altar, candles that flickered in the wind.

There was a man with no nose. He held a bottle of Sneaky Pete and, when Johnny Angelo stood over him, he opened his eyes. Then he saw the high-heeled boots, the studded gunbelt, the soft golden flesh. A phantom and a gunslinger, a vision of Death, almost 12 years old, and the man with no nose screamed out loud.

Delirium tremens: the man with no nose threw his bottle

at Johnny's head. Then he saw serpents, he saw black snakes that crawled on his flesh, and cobras that sucked his blood, and pythons that crushed his bones, and he clawed at his own eyes, the candles flickered and all this time he screamed an endless scream like an air-raid siren.

Then he rose up and he caught Johnny Angelo by the throat, meaning to throttle him. Then Johnny shot him with his pearl-handled Colt.

The cap went bang and the man with no nose staggered backwards, clutching at his guts. On the altar steps, he fell down on his knees, his mouth fell open and his heart gave out. His eyes changed, his face filled up with blood. Then he died.

Johnny Angelo had killed him.

The candles still flickered on the altar steps, shadows raced throughout the church. One man was weeping. Another dreamed of death. And Johnny turned aside, his gun still smoking in his hand, and no one stopped him, he went away.

Out in the graveyard, he sat on a tombstone and the wind tore at his flesh, he was cold. Child assassin, he was five foot exactly and he cleaned his gun, returned it to its holster.

Then he thought of the honeypot.

At dawn, he returned to the Doctor's house and knocked on the door. No one replied. So he went inside and his footsteps echoed in the hallways. And when he entered the Doctor's study, everything was arranged the same as before, except that the honeypot was gone and so were the four slouch hats. It was then that he knew the truth, that the Doctor had departed and would not return.

He stood out on the balcony but he didn't weep. One last time, he looked down on the neighbourhood and he saw his

own street, his own house. Just once, he recalled the man with no nose, the way he had screamed, the way his eyes had changed. Just once, he thought of the Doctor.

Then he went out past the barbed-wire fence and he walked down Westmill Boulevard, all by himself.

Part Two

CATSMEAT

At the age of 14, Johnny Angelo was a heart-throb. He had three-inch sideboards and he wore his hair swept high in a golden quiff, from which one lock detached itself and fell forward into his eyes. His smile was lopsided. And his mouth was full of the whitest teeth.

This is what he wore: scarlet silken shirts, open at the neck, and tight torero pants: white kid shoes with golden buckles; a photograph of Elvis Presley right next to his heart; a silver crucifix. All over his neighbourhood, he was known as Speedoo.

He was loved. Every morning, when he walked into class, all the little schoolgirls hung out of their windows and strained to catch a glimpse of him. Their skirts were rucked way up beyond their knees, their ponytails swung low. Waiting for Johnny Angelo, they scrawled his name in lipstick, one hundred times.

He was also greatly hated. On the far side of the schoolyard, right opposite the girls, there were classrooms full of young boys. And the things that the girls so adored, the white kid

shoes and the lopsided smile, these were the exact same things that the boys most abhorred.

Each day, Johnny was late.

Five minutes, then 10, then 15: he sauntered down slow and everyone waited. And he used a special walk, known as Shooting the Agate, where he hooked his thumbs inside his belt and he hunched his shoulders, he flicked his ankles out sideways at every step and, of course, there was a cigarette slouching from his bottom lip.

When he came into the schoolyard, he carried his books in a luncheon box, tied up in red braces, and he moved very slow, not looking to left or to right.

On one side of the schoolyard, the young girls stretched out their arms and pelted him with Jelly Babies; on the other, the boys took aim with their pea-shooters and shot him right between his eyes. Either way, Johnny kept on walking still.

But when he reached the portals, right before he disappeared, he half-turned. For the girls and the boys alike, he let one small smile flicker in the corner of his mouth, he let one hand trail behind him, fingers outstretched, and he Shot the Agate.

Somebody screamed.

Then he was gone.

During break, he sat on the schoolyard wall and young girls surrounded him. They did not speak to him or touch him but they stood a few yards distant, giggling, pinching each other or simply staring. Then he went back to the classroom and there were poems hidden in his desk:

Johnny Angel,
How I love him –
I'd do anything
To let him know.

And Johnny was formal, polite. But in the end, he only smiled and turned away, returning to the centrespreads of *Playboy Magazine*, women who filled his dreams.

He bought a pair of blue suede shoes and they filled his life. Sitting at the back of the classroom, he put his feet up on the radiator and he couldn't stop staring, his eyes were dazzled by blue and these shoes had pointed toes, sharp steel tips, pure white stitching. In every detail, they were perfection and the way that Johnny felt for them, it was like nothing since his fat black cat.

Each night, he spent 30 minutes cleaning them with a soft felt brush, one hundred strokes with his left hand, one hundred strokes with his right. Then he wrapped them in chamois leather and took many pictures of their reflections. And the time came soon when he didn't even wear them but carried them around in his luncheon box, tied up in red braces.

When nobody was looking, he took them out and held their softness against his cheek. He was happy then. But one morning he came into class and dirty words were scrawled on the blackboard: *Goodbye Blue Suede Shoes*.

Sure enough, the afternoon arrived when Johnny was working out in the swimming baths, diving off the high-board, swooping like a swallow, and then he came back into the changing rooms and the blue suede shoes were destroyed. They had been scuffed and splayed and spat upon, abused in every way imaginable and, scarred across the toes with a rusty penknife, there was an epitaph, as follows:

Adios Amigo.

Then a certain ritual was established, by which Johnny's enemies hid up an alley and each afternoon, when he walked home from school, they jumped out and hit him.

Each morning, he was screamed at; in the afternoon, he was beaten up. But Catsmeat truly loved him.

Who was Catsmeat?

Catsmeat was a mental deficient, who wore orange fluorescent socks, and he was an albino, with flesh as shapeless and soggy as sourdough. And one morning, when he leaned out of his window, he saw Johnny Angelo come into the schoolyard and he saw the blue suede shoes, the scarlet shirt, the crucifix, and Johnny half-turned, half-smiled, one lock of his hair fell over his eyes and his mouth was full of the whitest teeth. And Catsmeat said nothing but turned aside and he wept.

Inside the gymnasium, Johnny turned circles on the horizontal bar, beautiful slow parabolas, and Catsmeat watched him through the window, his nose splayed flat against the glass. He had a crewcut, he had pink piggy eyes. Every time that Johnny passed through a door, it was Catsmeat who held it open.

But Johnny didn't notice, he was busy thinking of his bright red suit, his blue suede shoes, his fat black cat. He combed his hair in the mirror. He practised his lopsided smile. He sat on the schoolyard wall, reading *Elvis Monthly*, and young girls surrounded him but he felt no lust, he went to the movies instead.

High in the second balcony, he sat in the dark and he watched Brigitte Bardot, her breasts and her thighs, her golden flesh. All through the afternoon, he sat without moving and her image flickered on the screen and this was the real thing, he travelled in her dream.

On his way home, he was ambushed and his blood flowed, while Catsmeat hid round the corner, and watched and wept.

Then it was a winter afternoon and Johnny walked home from school, waiting to get hit. It had been snowing and the streets were covered in slush, everything was slippery. Nonetheless, he Shot the Agate and his ankles flicked out sideways.

Catsmeat followed him.

The albino suffered from fallen arches and his legs were very short. Therefore, while Johnny floated up front, Catsmeat was struggling along in his wake, floundering in the wet, and three times he fell down on his back, where he trundled like an overturned turtle. But he persevered. Gasping, he broke into a trot and he waved his arms and, finally, he reached Johnny's side. 'Please,' he said. 'Can I walk with you?'

'No,' said Johnny Angelo.

Two blocks up front, all of Johnny's enemies were waiting in an alley, packing snowballs. Meanwhile Catsmeat was desperate, he kept slipping and scrambling, he fell down and got up again, and he clutched at Johnny's sleeve. 'Please,' he said. 'Please.'

'No.'

Right then, the schoolboys jumped out of the alley and the first of the snowballs flew past Catsmeat's ear. His pink eyes opened wide and he stood still just one second. Then he charged.

All soggy and shapeless, he ploughed along the pavement and straight into the alley, where snowballs smashed him at point-blank range. Still he kept going and he hit the schoolboys like a giant exploding doughnut, he bowled them over like skittles and they all fell down in the slush.

Then Catsmeat turned back towards Johnny, still running

as he fell, his fat face ecstatic, and everyone rose up and covered him, everyone started to hit.

As for Johnny Angelo, he walked on by.

AWOPBOPALOOBOP

When Johnny Angelo was 15, he went away from home. Up
in the attic, he left behind the full-length mirror, the camera
and the many turnip watches, all the things of his childhood,
and he found a room in Bogside.

On the night that Johnny left, his father was working on
his allotment, planting Sweet Williams, and it was February,
foggy and dank. Johnny zigzagged through the cabbage
patch, suitcase in his hand, and his father was sitting on
an orange box, reading the paper, and there was a dying
bonfire at his feet. Everything was damp and Johnny was
embarrassed. 'I'm leaving now,' he said. 'Goodbye.'

They shook hands across the fire. For just one moment,
they looked at each other and some current passed between
them, some spasm of recognition. Then Johnny turned aside,
and went on back through the cabbage patch.

His father sat by the fire and read the paper.

And the place that Johnny Angelo moved to was a cold-
water room on Cable Street, 11 foot by 8. There was a bed,
a table, a chair and, on the wall, a picture of Elvis Presley.

There was a wino next door and someone dying across the hall. There were many cats on the stairs.

Twice a week, Catsmeat came in and scrubbed the floor. He made the bed, dusted the mantelpiece, washed out Johnny's underwear. He continued to polish for a full hour and then, when everything was spotless, he started all over.

Meanwhile, in the caff across the street, Johnny sat close to the jukebox and the waitress had a crush on him. Every time that she passed him, she rubbed her breasts against his arm and Johnny smiled politely. In return, she let him play the jukebox for free and these were the records that he preferred: *Sweet Little Sixteen* and *Maybelline, Long Tall Sally* and *Yakety Yak* and *Chantilly Lace, Great Balls of Fire* and *Johnny B. Goode*.

Rock and roll music.

On December 21st, 1956 Johnny had walked down Waterloo Place and, inside an amusement arcade, he'd seen Little Richard singing *Tutti Frutti* on the scopitone.

He'd placed a nickel in the slot, he'd put his eye up close against the hole and Little Richard was there, a man in a baggy suit with trousers like a tent, 26 inches at the bottoms, and his hair back-combed in a pompadour, and he stood knock-kneed at a piano, pounding away with both fists, and he howled like a wolf, roared like a bull.

Squealing and shuddering, he put one foot up on the keyboard, his sweat dripped down between the cracks and he screamed, and he screamed, and he screamed:

Tutti frutti,
All rootie;
Tutti frutti,
All rootie;

Tutti frutti,
All rootie –
Awopbopaloobop
Alopbamboom.

December 21st, 1956: in that moment, Johnny's mind had upped and walked away. Trembling, he put another nickel in, watched once more and his eyes opened wide.

Awopbopaloobop, he turned around fast and put his fist straight through a hardboard partition. Alopbamboom, the noise was like gunshot and Johnny started running.

Then everything was different.

Sweet little rock and roller, Johnny wore a three-quarter length jacket with velvet lapels, drainpipe denim jeans, winkle-picker shoes, a Mississippi string tie and, of course, his scimitar sideboards, his golden quiff. This was his uniform and, on his table, there was a bottle of Coke, a jar of Brylcreem, a copy of *Elvis Monthly*, a bicycle chain.

Sitting in the caff, he blew the froth off his coffee and the jukebox kept playing *Heartbreak Hotel*. When it rained, the windows steamed over and the waitress touched him with her nipples. Motorbikes roared in the street.

At the end of two hours Catsmeat came in and they pulled wrists together. Then Johnny combed his hair, Shot the Agate and, everywhere that he travelled, Catsmeat shambled two steps behind him, carrying his schoolbooks, carrying his knuckle-duster.

These were fierce times.

On Friday and Saturday nights, the caff was filled with leather boys and the jukebox was played as loud as it would go. Young girls appeared in tight skirts and tight sweaters, bright red lipstick and candyfloss hair, piled up high in a

beehive. And Coca Cola was drunk direct from the bottle, and the windows were all steamed over, and the jukebox kept on blasting.

Good Golly Miss Molly and *Dizzy Miss Lizzy* and *Lawdy Miss Clawdy*: there was heavy necking in the corner booth, Willie did the hand-jive and then someone said that Bill Haley was King but someone else said No, it was Elvis. And there were voices raised in argument, there was a sudden scrimmage and a knife was produced. And then there was a circling and feinting and parrying, a flash of blades and someone screamed, someone fell down on the floor and began to bleed.

Johnny Angelo watched.

Upstairs, in his cold-water room, he mimed to *All Shook Up* and his hips went up and over like a roller coaster, up and over and down, up and up and over.

Catsmeat slept on the floor.

On Johnny's 15th birthday, he went down in the schoolyard and Catsmeat followed two steps behind.

On one side, there were young girls swooning; on the other, there were young boys throwing stones; and Johnny passed right down the middle, Shooting the Agate slow and lazy from his hip.

Inside the classroom, he approached the teacher and he laid down his schoolbooks on the desk, his luncheon box, his wine-coloured blazer with the yellow dragon on the breast, his ruined blue suede shoes. 'I'm 15 years old,' he said. 'I'm leaving here.'

'You can't,' said the teacher.

'Yes, I can,' said Johnny, and he did.

Down in the market, he payed his rent with his fingertips and his table was piled high with silver cigarette cases, cufflinks, diamond tiepins. Soon he grew wealthy and he

ordered double portions of froth on his coffee, he bought a cut-throat razor with an ivory handle.

The jukebox was silver and gold, it had coloured spangles that twinkled as it played. Johnny Angelo sat in the corner booth, and Catsmeat told him jokes, performed tricks, darned his socks, while good hard rock swept over them.

Then it was Friday night and *Jailhouse Rock* was playing at the Roxy.

The Roxy was a motion-picture coliseum of 1931, B. De Mille baroque, complete with sweeping stairways and marbled pillars and mighty Wurlitzers, cupids and gargoyles. These last years, however, it had begun to decline. The stucco was crumbling, the Wurlitzer was no longer used, rats ran in the aisles. Most nights, it was three-quarters empty, it was cold as a morgue and rain fell through the roof.

But on this Friday night, the queues stretched three times round the block and many hundreds were turned away. Only the leather boys were admitted, their pockets all bulging with rocks and knives and bicycle chains, brass knuckles and the final equaliser.

Tonight there was no popcorn sold, no drinks on a stick and there were no lovers holding hands. Instead there were policemen patrolling the runways, torches in their hands, and policemen on the balconies and policemen at all the doors. And then there were the leather boys, who divided up into blocs, some saying that Bill Haley was King and others saying No, it was Elvis.

Johnny Angelo was up on the second balcony, crouching in the dark, and he was combing his hair, he was smiling all lopsided. Then the lights went down and the screen was filled by pictures of Elvis.

Jailhouse Rock: Elvis played a truck driver who kills a man

in a fist fight and gets himself sent to the penitentiary. Inside the prison barbershop, his hair is shorn and his sideboards razored off entirely.

And the first lock of his hair to fall, this was the precise moment that the riot began in the Roxy.

High up among the gargoyles, the leather boys stamped their feet and the policemen flashed their torches. Elvis' sideboards were sheared down to the bone and girls began to weep and there was the noise of flick-knives snapping open. Then Elvis emerged with a crewcut and somebody jeered, saying Bill Haley is Best, and the very next thing his flesh was slashed with razors.

Johnny Angelo rose up, and Catsmeat beside him, and everyone began to stampede. The policemen formed into lines and swung their truncheons. Girls screamed and klaxons sounded and great hunks of stucco crashed down into the stalls, a gun went Bang and all this time the leather boys were chanting: El Vis. El Vis. El Vis.

Then Elvis was singing *Jailhouse Rock* itself, and his hair was long again, his sideboards black and shiny, and he switched his hips, he leered across his shoulder. Dancing on a rampart, sliding down a drainpipe, he squirmed and shook and shuddered, he strutted all over and this is what he meant: Fuck You.

Everyone was moving in the dark, and Johnny Angelo put his knee through the seat in front of him, the wood exploded, and he slashed at the cushions with his razor, and the stuffing came spilling out in handfuls, all grey and musty, and then someone was running towards him, a Bill Haley fan, wishing to hurt him but Johnny reached out real slow and he stuck a thick wad of stuffing straight down his attacker's throat, choking him.

There was blood on the floor. Catsmeat reached down and touched it. It was slippery in his fingers and, meanwhile, Johnny reached the edge of the balcony and went clean over the edge, grabbing a gargoyle by its throat, shinning down the stucco, and then he leapt into the runway, his knife still in his hand, and Elvis was leering, and Elvis was squirming, huge motion pictures, and a policeman was dying, his skull smashed in with a hammer.

Johnny Angelo stood still.

And Elvis was saying Fuck You.

So Johnny ran hard up the aisle and there was a great confused mass of flesh across his path but he smashed straight through, out the other side and on, until he came into a doorway and then there was a policeman, his face loomed up white and he swung his truncheon, he yelled for Johnny to stop. But Johnny didn't, he held his knife out in front of him and he kept right on, he ran directly through the lawman's guts. His knife went in deep and twisted. Then Johnny pulled it out again and the policeman fell down. Then Johnny went out in the street.

Outside in the street, it was empty and silent and still. Johnny's heels clattered down the pavement, he ran up an alley and he hid behind some trashcans. He sat down in the slops and wiped the blood off his knife. His knife had an ivory handle.

Johnny combed his hair.

HEARTBREAK HOTEL

'Fuck you,' said Johnny Angelo, and he lived in a cold-water room on Bogside, the hallway was full of cats and he smiled his lopsided smile. He flicked his ankles out sideways. He hid his eyes behind big black shades. He turned the jukebox way up high.

Most nights he went inside a club called Heartbreak Hotel, down in the docklands. High above his head, there was a disused church, where vagrants and derelicts stayed, and motorbikes were stacked in rows along the quays. The wind cut sharply off the river, blowing back Johnny's quiff like a plume. Everything was silent. Everything was still.

Heartbreak Hotel was a cellar, filled with a livid purplish light, and all the girls sat stiff-backed along one wall. Tight dresses and lipstick, they sported high-heeled shoes but the boys ignored them, preferring to huddle in their own tight circles, where they told dirty jokes and snickered, where they smoked cigarettes.

In particular, there was a rider named Ace, the leader of the pack. He wore a black leather jacket with silver studding

down the back, tight black leather pants, high black boots and he had a face like a weasel, all skinny and shifty and starved.

Why was he the leader? Just because he smoked a cigarette with perfect style and, down in Heartbreak Hotel, this was the only thing that counted.

The elegance with which the smoker inhaled; the length of time that the smoke remained in the lungs; the smoothness with which it was then expunged through the nostrils; the condition of the smoker, e.g. the absence of gasping or watery eyes; and, finally, the wrist-action with which the smoker dispatched the ash – all of these things were crucial and Ace was an artist, he couldn't be topped.

Johnny Angelo challenged him.

A beer-crate was placed in the middle of the floor and Johnny crouched on one side, Ace on the other. 20 cigarettes were laid out between them, a lighter and an ashtray, and all of the leather boys ranged in ranks behind Ace, and Catsmeat stood behind Johnny.

These were the rules: the contestants took turns to inhale and they continued to smoke without a pause until one of them cracked.

And Johnny was flash.

His style was full of flourishes, allusions, baroque embellishments. Just the way that he flared his nostrils and the smoke poured forth so smooth, this alone was enough to draw murmurs of admiration from the leather boys and Ace seemed crude by comparison. Nonetheless, he had lungs like india-rubber, he had stamina that was infinite and 8 cigarettes were smoked in succession but neither Johnny nor Ace gave ground.

Nobody spoke, no one moved: Johnny Angelo blew smoke

rings, then poked his finger through the hole, very idle, and a purple haze hung over everything. Ace sucked deep and Johnny watched him, stared him down until he sweated and his face was pinched like a ferret.

The 10th cigarette was completed, then the 11th and Johnny kept watching, and Ace kept sweating. Flicking ash, Johnny yawned and stretched and, halfway through the 12th cigarette, Ace just suddenly upped and quit. He ground out the butt beneath his heel, he walked away into the docklands. Then everyone sighed and the jukebox started playing, while Catsmeat wept.

At the age of 15, Johnny led the pack.

The leather boys drifted round the beer-crate and formed a ragged circle around him. Then Johnny let a very small smile flicker in the corner of his mouth, he let one hand trail behind him, fingers outstretched, and he led a parade of motorbikes.

At three o'clock in the morning, he emerged from Heartbreak Hotel and nothing stirred. All the ships were tied up, all their crews were down in the cabins and the quays were quite deserted. Very far away, the derelicts whimpered in their sleep.

Right then, out of silence there came an explosion like an earthquake, a sudden howl of engines, and the whole of the docklands shook. Windows rattled in their frames, loose bricks fell crashing into the street and then, out of the debris, Johnny Angelo came riding on a motorbike, a black monster on a black machine.

So many years, he'd listened to the bikes revving up in the alley and now he rode out front, black leather and black helmet, a yellow dragon emblazoned on his back and one word ELVIS, spelled out in silver studding.

Very slowly, soberly, the riders moved out of the docks and into Bogside and on through all the city. Everything was empty, all the streets were stilled and this was a solemn procession, Johnny Angelo first, then Catsmeat, then all of Johnny's followers, fanned out in formation, and they passed through like ghosts, not looking to left or to right.

Outside the city, they came to a long straight stretch, a hill that rose gently for almost two miles and then broke off in a sharp crest. And when the riders hit this stretch they put their feet hard down, the purr of their engines turned into a scream and their machines vibrated wildly between their legs, hurtling and howling and rearing back. And everyone was burning but Johnny most of all, he left them behind and, when he hit the crest, he flew straight off into space. 20 or 30 or 40 feet, he soared up high and everything was stretched out beneath him, everything, and his machine was exploding beneath him, and he hung there without moving, hovering like a great black bird.

Night-rider: he roamed the countryside, a phantom, a marauder, and his followers fanned out behind him, causing destruction wherever they passed. All night long, they rode without resting and, when dawn approached, they wheeled around, returning to the city.

While everyone was sleeping, Johnny passed by and sank down into the docklands. Along the quays, right to the water's edge and he came again to Heartbreak Hotel.

In the first light of dawn, a door opened and Johnny disappeared, went back into the earth from which he'd come.

ACE AND THE MIGHTY AVENGERS

Johnny Angelo was 15 years old. Then he was 16. Then he was almost 17. Each night, he emerged from Heartbreak Hotel and he travelled the countryside, his followers ranged out behind him.

He sat in the caff. He listened to the jukebox. He smoked cigarettes. He wore tight black leather. He kept combing his hair. Up his sleeve, he carried a flick-knife and, right next to his heart, a picture of Elvis Presley.

In Heartbreak Hotel, there was a purple haze over everything and the leather boys formed a circle, surrounding Johnny Angelo, who was their leader.

And Catsmeat wept.

Each time that Johnny passed him by, tears welled up in the cretin's eyes and Catsmeat hid his face. Such grace and such elegance, it made him tremble all over and he busied himself with his chores, ironing Johnny's shirts, darning Johnny's socks.

Late one night, however, Catsmeat went down in the High Street and he threw a brick through the window of

Musicland. And just as Johnny Angelo had once acquired a camera, so now the deficient reached through the neat round hole and picked out an electric guitar. This guitar was shaped like a spaceship and covered with golden spangles, tinsel highlights that glittered in his hands. Slung low on the hip, all shiny and unused. Catsmeat thought it was beautiful and he couldn't stop staring.

Pink piggy eyes and flesh like sourdough, he held this guitar like a baby, cushioned tight against his belly, and he walked on tiptoe. Under every street lamp, he stopped and stared some more.

In due course, he arrived at Heartbreak Hotel, where Johnny was sitting on a beer-crate, casting craps against a wall. Right then, Catsmeat came close and held out the guitar, 'Johnny Angelo,' he said. 'This is yours.'

'It is?'

'Yes, it is,' said Catsmeat. 'Yes, it is.'

A bit dubious, Johnny then took the guitar in his hands, looked it over, ran his fingers on the strings. Everyone was watching and he plucked a string at random.

A single note sounded.

Then Johnny smiled his smile.

And Catsmeat hid.

That same night Johnny Angelo went back to Bogside and shut his door. Inside his room, he stood in front of the mirror and he strummed, not learning how to play but learning how to move. How to drop his hips, how to grind, how to bury his guitar in his groin. Above all, how to twitch.

His legs were long and skinny, very fast, and he wrapped them tight in gold lamé. And as soon as he started to sing, they took on a whole private life of their own, they started to vibrate and they stretched like elastic, they flew.

Down in Heartbreak Hotel, Johnny Angelo stood on a small raised stage and his followers sat in the dark, not moving, just the tips of their cigarettes glowing red among the purple.

Then a spotlight came on and Johnny started singing, started strumming and moving his hips, but nobody heard him sing, no one heard him play: only his legs existed.

Legs that slithered like serpents, that bent back double, that tied themselves in knots. And ran, cowered, kicked and flaunted. And leaped up high and hovered and fell, and dissolved and reformed and dissolved once more, and they sprawled all over the stage, until they filled up everything.

Spider legs, puppet legs, clasped tight by gold lamé, and his spangled guitar kept glinting in the spotlight.

Somebody screamed.

And Johnny rode his motorbike all through the city, in the boulevards and alleys and freeways, in the mansions and the tenements, and Kid Clancey rode behind him, Little Richard and Monseigneur Pike.

At the top of the hill, he soared off into space, and his engine screamed, and he hung there, suspended like a black bird of prey, and everything was stretched out beneath him, everything.

He was 15 years old.

Then he was 16 and he led his followers against all the rival gangs of the city, the Black Marias from Jitney, the Shieks from St Jude, the Ricos from Shanty Canrush and, most especially, the Tombstones from Crescent Heights, who were led by Ace.

Riding out front, Johnny headed down an alley and Ace would be coming right at him, they'd meet in the middle. This was known as the Chicken Run, common practice

among the gangs, a shutdown in which one or other of the riders would always lose his nerve, would swerve away at the very last moment. But with Ace and Johnny Angelo, it didn't work like that: they kept right on going, they'd clash head on and their bodies were flung in the air, turning over and over, limp like rag-dolls.

Right behind them, their followers would also clash and then everyone fell off their bikes, and the riderless machines careened around the alley, tyres screaming, mowing down riders at random. In these ways, half of each gang was laid waste but those that remained rose up with chains and brickbats, rocks and knives and bottles, while Johnny himself wore a sharkskin belt, a crucifix and he beat Ace unconscious.

Week by week, victory by victory, he widened out his territory and no gang stood long against him. Finally, in desperation, the beaten riders all formed an alliance, the Shieks and the Ricos and the Tombstones, plus the Skulls from Lincoln County and the Compadres from Savoy, and they invaded the docklands, they laid siege to Heartbreak Hotel.

Johnny Angelo twitched.

Strumming his spangled guitar, he had long beanpole legs and he quivered like a jelly, while a single spotlight shone on him and his followers sat in the dark.

These followers were known as the Mighty Avengers. And Ace hammered on the door, calling them out, but Johnny went on singing and paid no mind.

Then all the gangs joined together and closed in fast, catcalling through the keyhole, throwing firecrackers and, finally, they started to break down the door.

Even so, Johnny wasn't disturbed. In his own good time,

he completed his song, his legs were still and he put down his guitar. He combed his hair, he took off his shades. And he walked to the door and opened it wide, he greeted Ace with a smile.

Very quietly, before Ace had time to react, Johnny gathered him up in both arms and carried him back across the threshold, bearing him as tenderly as a day-old bride. Everything stopped still. Everyone waited for Ace to fight back. But Johnny held him tight and looked deep inside his eyes. And Johnny smiled. And Johnny was gentle. And Ace just lay in his arms not moving.

All the way across the quay, Johnny carried him carefully and then, bending low above the gutter, he let him fall. Then Ace went Plop and Johnny turned away, went back inside Heartbreak Hotel.

Everyone was quiet.

The gangs stood around on the quays, uncertain, and then they got back on their motorbikes, roared off towards their own neighbourhoods, while in Heartbreak Hotel, Johnny Angelo picked up his guitar and his legs began to vibrate.

The Mighty Avengers reigned supreme.

And Johnny went riding by himself, just him and his machine, which he loved. The way that it howled between his thighs, the way that it shuddered, the way that it soared – all these things made him happy and he rode throughout the night, while the Doctor crouched behind his shoulder.

Up in Westmill Boulevard, he passed the barbed-wire fence and he remembered the honeypot, the black slouch hat. And it was true that Catsmeat loved him, that his followers obeyed him and young girls wished to touch him but then, after all, these people were mundanities and the Doctor belonged in a different class, the Doctor was a stylist.

Outside the fence, Johnny stopped and looked up at the Doctor's window, but no shadow paced the floor, no sound of sniffing reached his ears. Everything was empty.

So Johnny rode by himself.

He was 16 years old. Then he was almost 17 and Ace hid up an alley, the Tombstones ambushed him as he passed.

Nothing changed: at the age of 14, Johnny Angelo was pelted with snowballs and now he was caught in a crossfire of refuse, he was dragged off his bike and held against a wall. Then Ace and all the Tombstones took turns to beat upon him and they didn't stop hitting until he went limp.

When he opened up his eyes again, he had bruises all over his face, great lumps and abrasions, and his features were all misshapen.

He was ugly.

So he went back to Bogside and he locked himself in his room, where he stayed for a week without moving, hiding until he was flawless like before, and no one could get him to open up, not even Catsmeat.

Even when his wounds were healed and he'd returned to Heartbreak Hotel, he didn't ride by himself and he didn't smile. Everywhere that he went, he was protected by an entourage, black leather bodyguards, and he hid behind his shades, he sat in a purple cloud, where he dreamed of the Doctor. And, down in the cellar, deep inside the earth, he planned his revenge.

He didn't feel safe.

So he led the Mighty Avengers into Crescent Heights and he wiped the Tombstones out.

Ace was sitting in a caff and his gang was all around him. Johnny Angelo threw a smoke bomb through the open doorway. The bomb went Bang and the windows were

shattered, glass was everywhere. Dense smoke filled the caff, causing the Tombstones to choke and weep and stumble out in the street, where they were met by the Mighty Avengers.

The Avengers rode motorbikes, carried brickbats, hid flick-knives up their sleeves; the Tombstones were on foot, unarmed and unprepared. Accordingly, the Avengers formed a circle and began to drive the Tombstones backwards, herding them like cattle, pushing them out of Crescent Heights and into Jitney and on through Lincoln County, home of the freaks, to sumptuous St Jude and skidrow Jethro, exotic Savoy and further still, through Bogside and Cajun and Chinatown, until they reached the edge of the river.

Then Ace understood.

Trapped against the water, he began to run backwards and sideways and on, he zigzagged frantically and he crawled, he fluttered like an injured bird. Meanwhile, Johnny sat on his machine and kept on pushing, very calm and methodical, driving him right to the brink. Then he nudged him over the edge.

Again, Ace went Plop.

One by one, like the Gadarene swine, the Tombstones were driven into the waters, where they floundered, and the river was thick and black and putrid, it dragged them down.

Some swam to the other bank. Others were picked up by passing boats. Still others disappeared.

By this means, the city was purged of evil.

FLAMES

In the place where Johnny lived, the house was full of cats. In the hallways, on the windowsills, up on the roof. Hiding in the closets and sleeping in drawers. Sliding down the banisters, Siamese cats and Persians, marmalades and tabbies. Most of all, black cats. Fat black cats who were blind or scabrous or starving. Black cats who were psychotic and spent all their lives in fighting, gouging and killing.

Each morning, when Johnny woke up, there was a cat curled up at his feet, a cat in each of his shoes. Surrounded, he put on his clothes and went across the street to the caff, picking his way through all the ranks of sleeping or dying cats.

These cats disgusted him.

Inside the caff, he drank Coca Cola and listened to the Coasters. Outside, there were cats sprawled in the gutters and cats in the dustbins and dead cats splayed across the tramlines, lying on their backs with their legs in the air, blood still oozing from their mouths. It was seven o'clock, a very cold morning, and no humans were visible, only cats.

When Johnny went back in the street, the cats began to follow him. Wherever he went, there were cats beneath his feet and mangy cats ahead of him. If he ran, they ran as well; if he sat down and rested, they formed a circle around him, they waited.

Fat black cats: they sat all night outside his door. The smell of their excretions and the smell of their many diseases made Johnny Angelo squirm. Emerging, he threw stones at them and trod on them but they weren't upset, they merely regrouped and followed him once more.

This was because they loved him.

And it took an old lady across the hall to understand the reason, a woman who believed in the Devil, a woman who bolted her door against Evil each night and slept with a crucifix in her hand. She was 83 years old. Prayer was her existence and her only fear was Hell.

Then one morning she looked out of her window and there was Johnny Angelo in the street below, dressed up in black leather, with his golden quiff piled high and his smile all lopsided, and 50 cats walked behind him, animals that were twisted and scarred in every way imaginable. Creatures that were damned, souls that were lost, they trod on Johnny's heels.

Disciple of the Devil, Johnny Angelo switched his hips, flicked his ankles out sideways and the pussycats pursued him, mesmerised.

Then the old woman prayed.

At nightfall, Johnny sat on his motorbike and disappeared into the docklands. The cats sat down on his doorstep and licked themselves clean, waiting patiently until he'd return.

He felt trapped by them and abused them, he flattened them with his machine. Still, they loved him.

Cats with no fur and cats with broken limbs: beyond Johnny's door, they purred so loud that he couldn't sleep and then he was afraid, he didn't feel safe.

Cats were everywhere. They slept on his face. They pissed on his three-quarter jacket with the velvet lapels. Even inside the caff, when he stared out the window, they stared right back.

This was persecution and, when the waitress touched him with her breasts, he didn't look up. Even when he rode away on his motorbike, cats crouched on his shoulder.

Johnny Angelo suffered.

So he bought ten tins of cat meat, one can of paraffin and he mixed them both together. He went downstairs and he scattered the meat all over the street. Seven o'clock in the morning, it was raining and Johnny walked away.

Just like always, the cats pursued him and they ate up all the meat, even fighting among themselves for the choicest paraffin tidbits, and they lay down in the gutters, they licked their chops and composed themselves to sleep.

Then Johnny struck a match.

And when the old woman looked through her window, the street was full of burning cats. Bright red cats that hissed and writhed and crackled, screaming as they perished. 53 cats with flaming mouths.

And black leather Johnny Angelo, smiling benignly on death.

I AM THE COBRA

Everything was dangerous.

At the age of 17, Johnny Angelo left his back room in Bogside and moved into Heartbreak Hotel, hiding in a small back room with no windows, a room that was dark, dank and airless but very well protected.

Deep inside the earth, he lived like a mole and his bodyguards surrounded him. He slept all day and then he emerged at night, when he strutted and slithered and squirmed, or he plundered through the countryside, soaring off into space, having fun until the dawn.

He was safe. On stage, he wore a velvet suit and purple shoes. Each time that he smiled, someone screamed. Each time that he stuck his guitar in his groin, small girls wept and rushed the stage, stretching out with their hands, but the Avengers barred the way and Johnny wasn't touched.

Then he stood by himself on a bombsite, the same bombsite in which his bright red suit was buried, and also his fat black cat, and it was a windswept afternoon, and his hair was blown in his eyes, when someone sneaked up behind

him, a black girl who smelled of Voodoo.

As soon as she touched him, he turned around: 'My name is Yolande,' said the black girl. 'They call me the Cobra.'

She was very black indeed. She had slow black hands, and lazy black eyes, and smooth black flesh that rippled when she moved. She had a wig on her head, pink bouffant style, and hi-heeled scarlet sneakers. She wore a silver sequined dress, very tight, and she was sleek in all her movements, except in her smile, which was sudden like a serpent.

Touching Johnny Angelo, she came in close and breathed on him, a breath that made him restless. 'What is it?' he said. 'I'm busy.'

'I like you,' the Cobra replied.

'Everyone likes me,' said Johnny.

'I like you more.'

Stranded on the bombsite, Johnny turned his face against the wind, hunched up his shoulders and he walked down towards the docklands. Then the Cobra walked beside him, schlurping her hips, and there was desolation all around them, shelled-out houses, refuse dumps, corporation dugouts.

The Cobra had eyes like strange sins. 'I was born in Lincoln County,' she said. 'I've been travelling all my life.'

Down in the docks, the Mighty Avengers were patrolling the quays, revving up their engines, and Johnny was watching them, very far away. 'I was 8 years old,' the Cobra said. 'I started touring with a medicine show, travelling all over the nation, selling shoeshines and turning somersaults and, later on, I performed an exotic dance with snakes, hence my name of the Cobra.

'In downtown Decatur, I got married to a man called the Fearless Otto, a sword-swallower. It was my 16th birthday and I wore gardenias in my hair. All through that summer,

we worked the riverboat towns, such as Corinth and Sage and San Saul, until I was bored and left him and returned to Lincoln County, where I danced in Claessen's Follies.

'When I was 17, I was restless and I went back on the road with a Big Roll band, playing in dives and honky tonks, where I kicked up my legs by gaslight, and then I was married once more, this time to Mister Earl, a gambler, in Paducah.

'Mister Earl was a card-sharp. Very soon he got shot in a bar-room. Still, I went on travelling by myself, through Carter and Moose Jaw and Santos, El Paso and Sasparillo, until I was picked up in Tracy, arrested for vagrancy and sent to the reformatory, where I stayed for 3 months but then got bored and escaped.

'And so on, and so forth: I went on the road yet again, criss-crossing the nation, but when I was 19, I was tired and I came back home, where I worked in the market, selling yams, and I was satisfied. I danced each night away. I wasn't afraid.

'A week ago, however, I was walking at random and I saw you ride past on your motorbike, a black monster on a black machine, with all your followers fanned out in formation behind you, and you were smiling all lopsided, your hair was blown back in a plume.

'Right then, I went back to the market and dismantled my stall, scattering yams all over the street, and I packed up my belongings and put on my soulful dress, my pink bouffant wig, and started walking. For 6 days, I've tracked you down. Now I've found you.'

The Cobra was black, she smelled of Voodoo. Each time that she smiled, her teeth flashed very white and her black eyes were scary. Johnny was made uneasy. 'What is it you want?' he said. 'I'm pressed for time.'

'I am 20 years old, I'm restless,' she said. 'Let me take you on a journey.'

Johnny didn't answer. He kept on walking still and, when they came in sight of Heartbreak Hotel, he stopped and stretched his hand out across the docklands, as if to draw it up in his palm. 'I own this,' he said. 'All of this is mine.'

High on the hillside, they stood close together, Johnny and the Cobra, and the Cobra kept smiling, and Johnny turned away. 'I'm safe here,' he said.

'No, you're not,' said the Cobra, and she squeezed him softly, she was spooked. 'Not here. Not any place.'

She was ruining everything. Down inside the cellar, Johnny Angelo combed his hair and he was surrounded by Mighty Avengers, young men who smelled of axle grease. 'These are my disciples. They follow me everywhere,' Johnny said, but the Cobra didn't stop smiling, her teeth flashed white in the purple gloom. Then Johnny bit his lip, said nothing and he hid in his room without windows.

Still the Cobra pursued him. Deep down in the dungeon, she turned out the light and her eyes glowed red in the dark. Sleek black cat, she purred and she smelled of incense, sickly sweet, and Johnny felt drowsy, as though he'd been drugged. He couldn't move, he could not speak. He had no wish to struggle and he slid down in a dream, where he murmured, while the Cobra swallowed him whole.

CANDYFLOSS PINK

Johnny Angelo was sleeping. Then he was awake. Then he was halfway between the two, he was drifting and he travelled with the Cobra.

Every time that he opened his eyes, she was bending over him and smiling. She carried gris-gris in her breast, she touched him with her fingertips. She had smooth black flesh that rippled, so that Johnny was powerless against her, and she smiled a smile like sudden death.

For 4 days and nights, they remained inside this cell, lying in the dark, while the Cobra sucked his flesh, while she sighed and squirmed and murmured. But on the 5th day, they emerged into the light and they wandered all over the city, wherever the Cobra led them, and everything was changed.

Everything was made like a dream, exotic and strange and, on Chase Street, which was nothing in particular, the Cobra took him through bars and burlesques and bordellos, clip joints and casinos, opium dens, cockroach hotels and freak shows and funfairs. A thousand neon lights lit up the pavements. Millionaires smoked fat cigars. Derelicts lay

dying in the gutters. Champagne corks beat a tattoo on the ceilings but the shadows smelled of sewerage. Inside every man's pocket, a turnip watch lay snug and warm.

Standing on the corner, Johnny was jostled by big-time gamblers, by dudes and politicians, bankers and movie stars, dope fiends, acrobats and assassins and, everywhere that he looked, money was changing hands.

Love for sale: inside each mansion, there were gilded mirrors and chandeliers, white bearskin rugs, and music played very loudly, and rockets flew high above the houses and burst in multi-coloured stars, and all the colours were bright, orange and silver and pink, scarlet and midnight blue.

In his lifetime, Johnny Angelo had seen nothing like this, such glitter and extravagance, and he tried to hang back. But the Cobra drew him on, she licked inside his ear. 'Do you like it?' she said. 'Is it fun?'

'It's not real,' said Johnny.

'That's correct,' said the Cobra. 'It isn't.'

Yen-pox woman, her wig was like candyfloss, pink and sticky to the touch, and she smelled very strong of voodoo, which made Johnny sigh, and she sucked him in like toothpaste.

Strutting up front in her red sequined dress, she took his hand and led him through all the districts of the city, Savoy and Jitney and Crescent Heights, St Jude and the Shanty Canrush.

In Lincoln County, she brought him into a festering slum. Instead of open streets, there were only alleys, which wound in and out like a labyrinth, and the people lived in wooden shacks. Garbage was piled high against the walls, rotting slowly, and rats grew fat. Epidemics raged like plagues, the drains overflowed and, on each corner, there was sickness, madness and death.

This was the Cobra's birthplace and she liked it. Somewhere in the heart of the labyrinth she owned a single room and that's where she lured Johnny Angelo, that's where they remained.

In this room there was cowein and yen pox and gris-gris, the secret cures of voodoo, and reptiles in cages, poisonous spiders and serpents, and a metal bath-tub in which the Cobra wallowed, all black and sleek and shiny, while beneath her arms and between her legs, there was a tangle of hair like a jungle, a wild exotic undergrowth, coloured candyfloss pink.

Soaping herself slowly, she smoked yen and the room was filled with evil fumes. Very soon, she sighed and the pipe fell from her hand, it clattered on the floor.

While the Cobra was dreaming, Johnny sat by himself and crawling black snakes surrounded him, and dogs lay starving outside his window and, across the alley, crouching in the shade, there were cripples and spastics and mongols. It was then that he felt trapped and he ran out of the room, he plunged headlong into the labyrinth.

Straightaway, he was lost. In Lincoln County, everything looked alike and he blundered round in circles. Children clutched at his arm, rats nipped at his ankles. The smell was very bad and, after half an hour, exhausted, he sat down in the filth. There was slime on his white kid shoes.

In her own good time, the Cobra came and rescued him and took him back inside her room, where she licked him clean. Once more, she wallowed in the tub and she smoked bad yen, and Johnny lay with his eyes shut, and tarantulas crawled on the walls, scorpions made hissing sounds and he didn't move for a very long time.

How long did this continue?' Time meant nothing in

Lincoln County, each day was the same. But three times Johnny ran out into the alleys and three times he sat down exhausted. Three times he was covered in filth. Three times the Cobra brought him home and slowly licked him clean.

When all the yen was finished, only then, she led him back to Heartbreak Hotel.

By this time, he was very much changed. He no longer rode out with the Mighty Avengers, he didn't wear black leather and he didn't smile lopsided. Skulking in the back room, he bit his nails and picked his nose. Even with the light out, he kept his eyes shut.

And the Cobra ate him up. 'This is the truth,' she said. 'I am very fond of fun.'

She loved her candyfloss wig. Of all her possessions, this was the one that she cherished most and she never took it off. Every morning, as soon as she awoke, she would settle herself in front of a mirror and smile at its reflection. An hour would pass, maybe more: the Cobra sat without blinking, all alone with her pink bouffant, and she couldn't help but purr.

Johnny Angelo, meanwhile, was abject. He was aware of nothing but the Cobra. He didn't speak or eat or sleep without her approval. He didn't see, he did not think. At all times, he was drugged.

He dreamed many dreams of escape.

Way up in Crescent Heights, poised on the edge of a cliff, he sneaked up behind her and started to shove; in the Shanty Canrush, he purchased poison; and in his windowless room, suffocating, he laced his fingers round her throat. On each occasion, however, at the very last moment, the Cobra turned round and she smiled at him, she tickled him under his chin.

Then she took him on another journey, penetrating into neighbourhoods that Johnny had never seen, places that he

didn't even know existed and, in each of them, they passed through a different movie.

In Spanish Town, the week of the bullfights, the streets were full of roses and the young girls leaned down from their balconies, blowing kisses.

In St Sulpice, artists starved in garrets.

In gutrot Chicane, the Rube sat in his hotel room, polishing his guns, and Diamond Slim was killed on the corner, shot down as he stepped from his car.

Everything was total. On this journey, there was no middle course, there were only wild extremes. 'My best friend was Maria,' the Cobra said. 'She was known as the Suicide Queen. Every morning, without fail, she swallowed strychnine with her coffee but she still had fun, she never stopped laughing.'

In Pleasant Bay, riverboats passed by in the sunlight and the orchestra played waltzes, the women wore gowns down to their ankles. Beside the sparkling water, the Cobra and Johnny were strolling, eating ice-cream cones, when a sudden gust of wind whipped up and almost removed the candyfloss wig.

Fortunately, she reached up fast and saved it. In that moment, however, her eyes had shown fear, the first time that Johnny had ever seen her vulnerable and, for 10 minutes afterwards, she couldn't stop trembling.

Right then, Johnny Angelo saw his chance. But before he could take any action, they had left Pleasant Bay and travelled on through Tully Cross, through Fabian and Rouge and Tabasco.

The Cobra changed with every day.

In Little Italy, she took off her shoes and walked on a bed of burning coals, smiling as she did so.

In Musk, she healed the sick.

In Sancerre, she did a striptease on a table and she swilled champagne from the bottle, she used obscenities, she made love with any man that would take her.

After 3 months like this, Johnny was a shambles and he didn't wash, he grew fat, he stuttered. One by one, his teeth got loose.

Finally, in Bastion, he tried to sneak away and, slipping down the alley, he scrambled over a red brick wall and he fell down the other side. When he stood up, however, the Cobra was standing beside him: 'You're not safe,' she said. 'Not here. Not any place.'

The very next night, his revenge came.

In a waterfront hotel, they were playing cards and the Cobra kept on winning. Hour after hour, they sat without speaking and then, when it was already almost dawn, the Cobra's eyes rolled up without warning and she keeled over on the floor, fast asleep.

The rest was easy: Johnny reached out and he tugged at her wig, all pink and sweet and sticky, and he threw it on the fire, where it burned very slow and the flames licked up like the many tongues of a Chinese dragon.

Underneath, the Cobra was not bald, as he had hoped, but she had a coarse black stubble, which was not at all mysterious, and Johnny blew in her ear.

Everything was changed.

When the Cobra saw what had taken place, she wept most bitterly. 'John Angelo,' she said. 'Why have you burned my pink bouffant?'

'Why not?' said Johnny and he dressed himself like a riverboat dude, complete with satin waistcoat, string tie and St Louis Flats, fancy squat-heeled shoes with lightbulbs that winked in the toes.

That same morning, they returned to Heartbreak Hotel and this time they stayed there, they didn't travel any further.

In the small back room, the Cobra crouched in a corner, covering her skull with her hands, and she didn't smell of voodoo, she carried no cures in her breast. Her eyes did not glow in the dark, her smile was not like sudden death. She did not travel anywhere. She wasn't even a cobra.

She was only Yolande, an easy lay.

Teen Angel

When Johnny Angelo was 18, Yolande was his servant. Every day, she darned his socks and made his bed and laid out his various uniforms. Stubble-headed, she followed him everywhere.

She loved him very much. Outside his windowless room, she waited patiently and, as soon as he emerged, she caught him by the arm. 'Please,' she said. 'Can I have my wig back?'

'No,' said Johnny Angelo, and rode away on his motorbike, with his followers ranged out behind him and, everywhere that he went, he caused destruction.

Nothing was changed: he returned to Bogside, he sat in the corner caff, he listened to the jukebox. The waitress brushed him with her breasts. Elvis Presley sang *One Night*. Black cats covered the pavements.

He began to make money. Venturing beyond the docklands, he started playing in clubs and dancehalls all over the city. He hired a backing group and he wore a golden suit and he got his picture in the local paper. Squirming and slithering, he made his hair fall over his eyes, he let one hand trail behind him, fingers outstretched and, very soon, he had his own fan club. He acquired a girlfriend named Astrid, who had long blonde hair, tied back in a ponytail, and wore highschool sweaters, short shorts and bobbysox. Sitting in

the soda fountain, Johnny held her hand and she had eyes of baby blue; she kept on blowing bubblegum. One Coca Cola, two straws: in no time, she wore his ring.

They went to the beach and they went to drive-ins, where they watched Frankie Avalon and Fabian and Annette Funicello, and they shared a hot dog at the corner stand, and they danced the Madison and, after every date, Johnny Angelo kissed Astrid at her front door and then he turned away, fired his machine and he rode away into the night.

This was his Teendream and he gazed at the moon, he wished upon a star. At Heartbreak Hotel, meanwhile, Yolande crouched in the purple gloom, recalling the Cobra and, when Johnny returned, she crept up tight behind him, she licked inside his ear. Purring, she sucked at his flesh: 'You can't do that,' said Johnny.

'Why not?'

'Because you can't,' he said, and it was true that he was fastidious. Roaming the city as he did, looting and plundering, he had no place for lust and he changed his underwear three times a day, he washed behind his ears, and he slept in silken sheets, he sprinkled himself with cologne and he breakfasted on apricot juice, escargots, chilled white wine.

Anyone that called him names, they were beaten and thrown out in the gutter, while Johnny feasted on Kentucky fried chicken and flung the bones over his shoulder, a warlord, a waterfront caliph.

Beneath a starlit sky, Astrid wept in his arms and he kissed away her tears, one by one: 'Oh, Johnny,' she said. 'I love you.'

'Oh, Astrid,' he replied. 'I love you, too.'

On her birthday, he gave her a heart-shaped locket, in which there was his photograph and a lock of his golden

hair. Then, beside a fountain, their lips met in a burning kiss and Catsmeat waited on the corner, guarding Johnny's motorbike.

And this was only one of the ways in which Catsmeat made himself useful. Every door that Johnny approached, the retard passed through first, in case of ambush and, when Yolande sneaked out and bought another bouffant, it was Catsmeat that found it and burned it.

Factotum and jester and sometimes even confidante, he had his own special outfit, a cinema commissionaire's uniform, complete with braiding and shiny buttons, and he also had a sharp peaked hat, which he wore at a rakish angle.

Of course, he still had piggy eyes and puff-pastry flesh, he still wore fluorescent orange socks. No matter, he was satisfied and several months passed most peacefully, while Johnny rode his motorbike and twitched his legs like jelly beans.

He ruled the docklands. He commanded 100 Avengers. He was screamed at by small girls. He smiled lopsided for money each night. He was safe. He had the love of a wonderful girl.

Once again, however, a time arrived when Johnny grew restless. For more than 18 years, he had always remained inside this city and now he became bored, he wanted to move on.

One last time, he stood outside the barbed-wire fence, he walked the wall and he wandered on the bombsite, he sat in the corner caff and he watched Little Richard on the scopitone, and he swung from the balcony in the Roxy, and he passed among the derelicts, he hit the straight and he put his foot hard down and he reached the top of the hill, he soared up high and then he saw everything.

In Heartbreak Hotel, he packed his possessions and he

strapped his guitar on the back of his machine. The Mighty Avengers lined up behind him, and Catsmeat, and Yolande, who rode on Catsmeat's pillion, and Johnny Angelo waved them on, he moved out slowly from the docklands.

On the corner, Astrid was waiting in a white belted raincoat, and, when Johnny cruised by, she ran towards him, she kneeled down beside his motorbike. Her teeth were very white, her lips were very red: 'Take me with you,' she said.

Then Johnny looked grave. 'Someday I will return,' he said. 'When I am very famous, I will come back and we'll live inside a mansion, with a swimming pool, an orange grove and TV in every room.'

'Do you promise?'

'Oh, yes,' he said. 'I promise.'

In the shadow of Heartbreak Hotel, he kissed her lips. Then, with all his disciples behind him, he moved along and he passed out of the docklands, out of this Teendream for ever, and rode to Movie City, where he soon became a star.

Part Three

AM I CLEAN?

'I am the greatest,' said Johnny Angelo and, when he was 24, he rode on a golden cadillac.

Entering a city, he wore a suit of golden velvet, shoes of golden suede and his hair fell to his shoulders. Standing on top of his cadillac, he waved and smiled and blew kisses and, all around him, there were black-leather riders on black motorbikes, known as the Mighty Avengers.

Behind the golden cadillac, there came a long black limousine, in which sat Johnny's intimates, Catsmeat and Yolande, and his hair-stylist, his masseur and his valet, his astrologer and his tennis coach, plus a selection of pretty young starlets.

And behind the black limousine, there came an open wagon, which was filled with varied performers, Johnny Angelo's private circus, complete with clowns and jugglers and tumblers, belly dancers and dwarves, contortionists and bearded ladies and, also, his mother, his father and his two older sisters.

Finally, behind the open wagon, there came a series of

trailers, in which were caged wild animals, who roared and shrieked and howled, who screamed abuse through the bars.

Very slowly, this cavalcade nosed through the crowds and, when it reached the heart of the city, the wagon opened its doors. Music played loudly, the voice of Johnny Angelo boomed from a dozen hidden loudspeakers and out rushed freaks of every description, hunchbacks and midgets and spastics, stringbeans and albinos, who ran among the crowd and showered them with confetti, and pulled faces, turned somersaults and gave out countless autographed pictures of Johnny Angelo.

Raised high upon his Cadillac, meanwhile Johnny held a single white rose. Smiling rather sadly, he cast it high into the air where it hung for a moment, hovered, and then it dropped down in the street, where it was torn apart by a thousand clutching hands, while Johnny passed by.

Once inside his dressing room, he took 2 full hours to prepare himself. Everywhere that he performed, it was his habit to send a team of interior decorators ahead of him, who equipped his rooms with gilded mirrors and chandeliers, Persian rugs, Egyptian tapestries and a satin chaise longue for Johnny himself, on which he now reclined, sucking on a liquorice stick.

And first, his stylist combed his hair, one hundred strokes with the left hand, one hundred strokes with the right, and then drew it back in an 18th-century ponytail, tied up with a black velvet bow.

Second, his beautician painted his eyes, using liner and shadow and thick mascara, and coated his teeth with sparkling white oil, and powdered over his golden flesh, and lastly touched his mouth lightly with lipstick.

Third, his manicurist shaped his fingernails, and his

masseur toned up his muscles, and Catsmeat read him poetry, and Yolande licked inside his ear.

Finally, his valet dressed him in a suit of baby blue velvet, with pants so tight that it took him 5 minutes to get them on, and buckled blue suede shoes, and white kneesocks, and his jeweller hung him heavy with monogrammed bracelets, diamond earrings and, of course, a silver crucifix.

In Johnny Angelo's life, everything was a ritual and, just before he went on stage, he faced his astrologer, who consulted charts and Tarot cards. If these turned out badly, the whole performance was cancelled. But if the omens were auspicious, nothing on earth could stop him and he smiled his golden smile, Sun God Johnny Angelo.

On stage, his followers were already raging and the auditorium was filled with entertainments of every kind. Simultaneously, there were trapezists and trick cyclists and high-wire artists, trampolinists who bounced into the balconies, belly dancers who strutted their stuff by candlelight, and wild animals who prowled the aisles, chimpanzees and llamas and baby leopards, and there were liveried servants who scurried everywhere, distributing capons among the audience, sweetmeats and guavas, pomegranates and fat black grapes, and that wasn't all, there were also swordswallowers, human torches, boxing kangaroos and, most important of all, there were goatskins full of rough Algerian wine, which were passed from hand to hand, until everyone was flushed and roaring, howling for Johnny Angelo and then, without warning, the lights went out.

In a single mauve spotlight, Catsmeat emerged from the shadows and climbed up into a podium, a pulpit. He wore a white silk suit, a pink carnation in his buttonhole, and he was round like a human doughnut, he had pink piggy eyes.

Inside this auditorium, there were ten or twenty or fifty thousand small girls, all of whom lived for Johnny Angelo, and now they began to scream, they began to weep and wring their hands. Lost in the dark, they called his name, they fainted, they bayed. Down on their knees, they prayed.

For several minutes, Catsmeat said nothing. Basking in his pool of purple light, he felt no urgency, he was happy here. Smirking, he picked his nose and, even when he finally made his announcement, it carried no hysteria, it was almost conversational: 'Johnny Angelo,' he said.

Somewhere in the wings, trumpets played a Purcell fanfare, very stately, and Johnny was revealed, standing motionless on top of his golden cadillac, one arm raised, just like the Statue of Liberty.

Solemn and slow, he travelled across the darkened stage and nobody screamed, every sound was stilled. Very stern, he froze the audience and he held them like that, he permitted no kind of levity. But then, without warning, he suddenly jack-knifed and he jumped up high in the air, he flew and, in that instant, even as he was airborne, everything exploded.

Lights flashed and flames leaped up and mirrors glinted all over the auditorium, blinding and distorting, and a hundred musicians thumped, strummed and blew, and bass drums rolled like thunder, and electric guitars wailed like sirens, and then Johnny hit the ground, his legs began to tremble.

The noise was frightening: out of the dark, there came wave after wave of a sound that was screaming, yet resembled no scream that you'd ever heard. It had no rise and fall, no variation, almost no emotion, and it shattered all the windows, so that the audience was showered with splintered glass, and it went on for ever, it was quite relentless.

And this was the truth of Johnny Angelo, that he was all

things at once, masculine and feminine and neuter, active and passive, animal and vegetable, and he was satanic, messianic, kitsch and camp, and psychotic, and martyred, and just plain dirty.

He twitched and squirmed and shuddered. He ran his hand down inside his thigh and tickled. His head was tucked in against his shoulder, very coy, and he pouted, he fluttered his eyelashes. He blew fat kisses from wet red lips. He staggered with emotion. He fell down on his knees, grovelling in the dust, and then his hips rose up and over, he raised himself, and his baby blue pants split open from knee to crotch, the girls glimpsed golden flesh. Or he sang songs of heartbreak and he buried his face in his hands, moving very slow, like a man in an underwater dream. Or he leered and he scowled, he ground his groin and every defenceless virgin in the world was raped, he beat them and he whipped them, he kicked them in the guts and stomped them underfoot and fucked them till they fainted. Or he minced. Or he slithered his legs like serpents, he stretched them out like tentacles, and he bent them back double, he tied them up in knots, and he sprawled them all over the stage, nothing else existed. He blasphemed. He wept. He cowered, begging for mercy: 'Am I clean?' he said.

And the screams got louder and louder and louder. Down in the darkness, the small girls were rending their hair, were tearing their own flesh and they writhed in religious ecstasy, and their bodies were racked by spasms, their eyes rolled up, and there were some who pissed themselves, there were others who were covered in vomit. A sordid detail, but true, there were many who ripped the legs from their seats and thrust them under their skirts, mauling themselves most horribly.

Johnny Angelo's hair was undone, it tumbled down around

his shoulders, and he was dripping sweat. His mascara ran, his lipstick was smeared all over his face. His clothes were torn in many places and his golden flesh was soggy and his face became a swamp. His eyes went blind. His mouth hung open. When he was 24, he was ugly.

He was pelted with jelly babies and hairclips and cigarette butts, teddy bears and coins. A gilt bracelet hit him full on the mouth, splitting his lip, and blood flowed over his face. Blood stained his blue velvet suit, blood fell on the stage, blood got in his eyes and he stumbled, he collapsed in a heap.

On his knees, he clutched at his heart and, taking out a white silk handkerchief, he soaked it in his blood, he let it fall into the audience.

With a last convulsive effort, he tried to rise, just for a moment, he almost made it, he staggered 3 steps forward but then he suddenly crumpled and fell down on his back, spreadeagled, his arms and his legs stretched out in the shape of crucifixion.

Catsmeat ran on in his white silk suit, and others behind him, and they carried Johnny Angelo, limp and shattered, from the stage; just as they reached the wings, however, he revived and he threw them all off, he came storming back on his stage and he grabbed the microphone and he reached out with his bloodstained hands: 'Am I clean?' he said. 'Can you touch me?'

It was then that the small girls rose up and stormed the stage. Policemen with linked arms formed a barrier and tried to force them back but were soon overwhelmed by handbags and broken bottles, nails and teeth and stiletto heels. Within 5 minutes, the cordon was smashed and the girls surged forward in their hundreds, in their thousands and tens of thousands.

Flames sprang up everywhere, and the music kept getting louder, and trapezists swung low, dropping stink bombs, and wild animals rampaged through the aisles, jackals and muskrats and skunks, mongeese and kangaroos, while Johnny bled in the background.

And the first girl to reach him, she clutched at his feet and he turned around, he kicked her full in the face. 'Am I clean?' he said, and then his followers surrounded him. At the very last moment, they rescued him.

They carried him to his dressing room, where he slumped in an armchair and didn't move. His hair hung down in sodden rat-tails, his face was slabbed with paint and sweat. His mouth was full of blood.

Outside, the girls were baying like wolves and then they hammered on the door, they began to break it down. Very soon, it buckled under the weight of blows, the boards split open and hands reached through, grasping, clutching and, one last time, Johnny Angelo arose. He wiped the blood from his face. He spat on the floor. He climbed out through the window and dropped down in the alley, where his cadillac was waiting, and he scrambled inside, he was safe.

Up front, there was the golden cadillac and, all around it, there were black motorbikes and, behind the motorbikes, there was a long black limousine and, behind the limousine, there was an open wagon and, behind the wagon, there was a zoo.

Slowly and with dignity, the procession moved off and it passed through the heart of the city, it headed out towards the open countryside. Inside his cadillac, Johnny Angelo fell asleep and girls climbed on the roof, clung to the handles, pressed their faces tight against the windows. They scrabbled with their fingernails. They clambered everywhere. They fell

down in the dirt. They were trampled underfoot, they were hit by flying stones, they were thrown beneath the wheels. Always and always, they screamed.

And inside the auditorium, when everyone else had gone, there remained one last girl, who was crying. She sat in the aisle, surrounded by refuse, by stale sweat and vomit and urine, and she whimpered softly. She wept for a very long time.

PRANKS

Although his fans adored him, Johnny Angelo also had many enemies, who described him variously as a menace, a maniac and a moral degenerate and, every time that he caused a riot, they rose up fiercely against him.

They wrote letters to the papers, they organised petitions, they set up pickets. When Johnny did the splits and his trousers were ripped from knee to crotch, questions were asked in parliament and his concerts were banned in many cities.

Was he disconcerted? On stage at the Gladstone Armoury, he unzipped his flies real slow and the aisles were littered with swooning puberts.

And this was the truth, that he travelled by himself, locked inside a private movie, which contained his cadillac and his velvet suit, his fans, his circus and his mansion, and nothing else had any meaning for him.

Within his movie, Johnny was a sultan, all-seeing and omnipotent, and he passed through a hundred cities in a hundred days and, everywhere that he went, he left chaos

behind him, and that was his only purpose, to cause explosions.

Each morning, before he hit the road, he sent out a posse. A random assortment of Mighty Avengers, acrobats and freaks, they headed for the next city on his route and prepared for his arrival.

Lifesize effigies of Johnny Angelo were carried through the streets, loudspeaker vans toured the suburbs and free souvenirs were given away by the hundred. More important than all this, however, a series of pranks was played, throwing the whole city into turmoil.

Hearses careened wildly down the High Street, for instance, while masked gunmen riddled the crowds with dummy machine guns and plastic bombs were thrown through windows and the pavements were splattered with ketchup. Sirens howled non-stop. Itching powder was dropped from skyscrapers. Bank-notes were scattered by helicopters. In stores and bars and stations, the multitudes were sprayed with Dayglo paint and, meanwhile, 50 miles away, Johnny Angelo lay in bed, munching a crab-paste sandwich.

The rest was simple: when he rode into town, Johnny was met by utter confusion and, given the circus and the motorcade, the blaring music and untamed animals, not to mention the final apocalypse of his own performance, hysteria was swiftly turned to flat-out anarchy.

Seated in the penthouse suite at the Hotel Splendide, he ate oysters with champagne and he looked down 43 floors to the streets below, where rioters ran wild with knives and clubs and razors, lit torches and sawn-off shotguns. Burning and looting at random, they threw bricks through windows and overturned cars and beat up on racial minorities, they raped defenceless virgins, they wallowed and grovelled in

filth, and Johnny Angelo sighed, very far away.

Violence and glamour and speed, splendour and vulgarity, gesture and combustion – these were the things that he valued, none else, and his tours turned into full-scale odysseys, and Johnny himself was seen almost as a messiah, whose message was a single word: excess.

In Plankton, his followers sneaked out at dead of night and scattered tintacks on the boulevards, deflated car tyres by the thousand, planted white mice in the subways; in Sabine East, the TV studios were stormed and captured by the Mighty Avengers, who then staged an orgy on camera; and finally, at sacred Magdalena, Johnny spat in church.

Of all his outrages, it was this last, minor in itself, that most incensed his enemies. Goaded beyond endurance, they determined not to rest until he'd been banned outright, his circus dismantled, his records deleted and he himself left friendless and derelict, exiled for ever.

To this end, they cursed him up and down the nation, they heckled his concerts and defiled his photographs and scratched his records with hairpins, and they spread foul rumours about his private life, they bribed his musicians to play out of tune, they hissed the very mention of his name.

Politicians and priests, journalists, retired colonels and strict-tempo bandleaders, they gathered close together in their common cause, regardless of race or religion, and the ruin of Johnny Angelo became their only dream.

'This man is a monster,' said Sir Aubrey Challenor. 'More than a man, he's a symptom,' said Dr James Purdie.

'It's people like Angelo that have brought this country to its knees,' said Lord Morly, the motor magnate.

'Man or myth?' asked the Sunday Echo.

'He is the anti-christ,' said the Reverend Groat. 'In the very

strictest confidence,' said Bobby Surf, who wore a toupee, 'he is a fairy.'

Johnny Angelo was not alarmed: riding in his cadillac, he ate chocolate bonbons and scratched himself, he stuck out his tongue at meter maids and then, at Sloat, he pissed in the soup.

Criss-crossing the nation from coast to coast, he covered half a million miles each year but never tired of causing chaos and he rampaged like a reborn Ghengis Khan, a souped-up Saladin or Attila the Hun.

Furthermore, for every insult that he suffered, he gained revenge in full. Sir Aubrey Challenor, for instance, speaking in public, was attacked by unknown marauders, who sneaked up tight and razor-slashed his braces, thus causing his trousers to fall around his ankles.

Lord Morly, who was a cripple, was stripped naked and deprived of his wheelchair; the Reverend Groat found his altar defiled; Bobby Surf lost his toupee; and many others besides were found out, cornered and purged.

Stern and unforgiving, Johnny lived like a warlord and his opponents were crushed without mercy. In private, however, he was not always so harsh. To his fans, whom he trusted, he appeared as almost a saint.

Any young girl who knocked at his stage door, she was sure of his kindest attention; any gifts that he received, be they sweets or flowers or furry toys, he was often moved to the edge of tears. Busy as he was, he was known to drive 500 miles to see a sick supporter on his deathbed and, whoever was killed at his concerts, stifled or trampled underfoot, it was always Johnny Angelo who sent the biggest wreath.

And day by day, week by week, his enemies pursued him but he didn't slow down, he never looked back. When the

crowds milled around his golden car, surrounding him, he didn't even blink.

'Fuck you,' he said.

JOHNNY ANGELO SPEAKS

There follows a transcript of a press conference given by
Johnny Angelo, sitting in his suite at the Hotel Excelsior, on
April 14th, 1964:

'What is your favourite colour?'
'My favourite colour is baby blue.'
'Are you pleased to be here?'
'It's wonderful to be back.'
'How do you feel about your latest record?'
'I'm so very happy to see it in the charts, it's a thrill, and
I wish to thank all my loyal fans, who put it there and make
my life worthwhile.'
'How is your tour going?'
'Great business, just great business.'
'Any amusing incidents?'
'Just one so far: in Decatur, a little girl came to the stage
door and asked to see me. Of course, I try to meet my fans
whenever possible, I make it my duty, but imagine my surprise
when in came a very small child, no more than 8 years old,

who was clutching a battered teddy bear, and she curtsied, she stepped right up to me, bold as brass, and she said to me, Johnny Angelo, she said, please will you give teddy a kiss, because teddy wants to marry you.'

'Are you happy?'

'I am very happy.'

'Why aren't you married?'

'I believe that the right girl has not yet come along. Someday I hope to meet my dream and fall in love but, until that happy time, I will endure by myself.'

'Are you very rich?'

'My wealth is beyond all reckoning.'

'What is your temperament?'

'I am very sensitive. Sometimes almost too sensitive. I am a leaf blown by the wind, a naked nerve, and the merest breeze may bring me pain.'

'What is the nature of your appeal?'

'I am the world of dreams, the Thousand Nights of Arabia, and I am all things at once, all heroes and all villains. I am the Wonderful Wizard of Oz, the sneaky Doctor Strange, the secret Count Mordo, who flies by night, and the glamorous Mr Universe. I provide, and you may quote me on this, a teenage fulfilment of fantasy.'

'In other words?'

'I fuck.'

'What are your ambitions?'

'My personal ambition is happiness; my professional ambition is likewise.'

'Who do you admire?'

'Among my favourites are Lord Byron and Elvis Presley, the Mad Monk Rasputin, Howard Hughes and Our Lord Jesus Christ.'

'What are your hobbies?'

'I am partial to pinball.'

'Where is your family?'

'My mother is dead, my twin brother is also dead and my father is an oil tycoon, who lives by himself on a very large estate. When I was only 5 years old, he ran away with a waitress and I was left to keep us alive. For years, we scrabbled and starved in a rat-infested basement, until my mother died of TB and my brother ran off to sea and my two sisters turned to alcohol, sousing themselves in gin, the first sad step on the road to prostitution. By God's good grace, I was spared and I persevered until things began to break my way. When I was 21, I rode on a golden cadillac, I was worshipped by millions and I travelled to my father's distant estates. For 3 days and nights, I drove without stopping, until I arrived at a long winding driveway and, at the end of this driveway, I drew up in front of a house like a palace. I knocked on the door. For some minutes, I waited in the cold but then the lock turned and a face appeared, the face of my father. I looked deep into his eyes. I smiled, just as I was going to embrace him, however, he suddenly shrank back and his eyes were blank. "Who are you?" my father said.'

'What happened then?'

'I went away.'

'Did you weep?'

'I returned to my fans, who love me, and I learned to live again.'

'Do you believe in God?'

'I do.'

'What is your preferred foodstuff?'

'My most favourite is knickerbocker glory deluxe, which consists of vanilla ice-cream, chocolate and coffee

and strawberry, poured over with hot chocolate sauce, and crushed pineapple sauce, and butterscotch and melba sauce, plus a turret of fresh whipped cream, sprinkled with pistachio and topped with a morello cherry, the whole thing combining into a fantasia.'

'What do you value?'

'It is sacred to be clean.'

'How many cars do you run?'

'I own 7 cars.'

'Are you paranoid?'

'I am fastidious. I am a creative artist, which means that I am condemned to solitude, for inspiration is loneliness, and I am repelled by squalor, I cannot live with ugliness or tedium.'

'Do you sleep in the nude?'

'I refuse this question.'

'Are you lonely?'

'All men are lonesome.'

'Do you like women?'

'I do not.'

'Why not?'

'In my view, a woman is a vulture and she is full of shit, she's a wheedler and whiner and twister. The man who trusts her, consigns himself to hellfire and she will gobble him up like popcorn. Plus, her body disgusts me and the way that she fucks is distasteful, all the ways that she screams and scratches and smells, with no sense of dignity – these things repel me and it is also true that a woman will destroy you, casting you aside as soon as you're squeezed dry, and she is dirty in her habits, her flesh is soft and sloppy.'

'Have you ever been in love?'

'Once, I was worshipped by a girl named Astrid, who sat with me in the soda fountain, and we drew Love Hearts on

the steamed-up window sipping Coca Cola, one bottle, two straws. Very soon, she wore my highschool ring and I kissed her lips by moonlight, I wished upon a star.'

'What went wrong?'

'Her folks did not agree. A child of the ghettoes, I came from the wrong side of town and I rode a motorbike, I wore black leathers. When her father saw me, he locked Astrid up in her bedroom and threw away the key.'

'Are you embittered?'

'I am saddened.'

'Do you hate?'

'I am weary of bullshit, for not a day goes by without some fresh plots being laid against me, some flagrant fabrication, which tries to sabotage my records, my concerts, my private life and will not quit until I am dead.'

'Why don't you fight back?'

'I am a pacifist.'

'Who are your friends?'

'My oldest companion is Catsmeat, who acts as my MC, my jester and general factotum. Even though he's a retard, his loyalty is boundless and I cherish him, I do indeed.'

'What is your sign?'

'I am an Aquarius.'

'Do you prefer blondes or brunettes?'

'Just so long as they're female, I'm satisfied.'

'Are you frightened of death?'

'I am frightened of nothing: death tracks everyone, after all, it is insatiable but I believe I am prepared. When it shows its face at my window, I will not hide beneath the bedclothes.'

'Do you believe in magic?'

'Ask me another.'

'Do you have any heroes?'

'I recall with affection my twin brother, Jason, who became a missionary and disappeared in the African jungles. Roaming through the swamps, he was caught by headhunters and his brains were sucked out through his ears.'

'Are you serious?'

'I am.'

'What will you do next?'

'I may become a leader of men. Riding on my golden cadillac, I would bless the crowds and bring them wealth, good luck and happiness, just like my fans, they would love me very much and, in return, I would treat them as my children.'

'Do you like oysters?'

'I enjoy the sensation when they slip down my throat, soft and slimy as the sperm of a worm, but they also make me sick to my stomach.'

'What is your most especial quality?'

'I am a magnet. Every time I walk in a room, the people turn and stare, they can't help themselves, and I draw them on behind me, a Pied Piper of Hamelin.'

'Do you have many servants?'

'My circus numbers 53.'

'Will you live for ever?'

'I don't believe so.'

'What do you think of fun?'

'This is my philosophy: live for today, tomorrow may not come and, therefore, I party every single day, feasting and carousing, travelling the highways, causing riots everywhere I go.'

'Tell us a story.'

'It was in Waterloo Place that I entered an amusement arcade, put a nickel in the slot and placed my eye up close against the Scopitone, where Little Richard was pounding

the piano, performing Tutti Frutti, and his trouser-cuffs billowed out like sails. Right then, I discovered the truth.'

'What was the truth?'

'Awopbopaloobop Alopbamboom.'

'Awopbopaloobop?'

'Alopbamboom.'

'What are your beliefs?'

'I believe in God, I believe in my fans, I believe in Johnny Angelo. I also believe that a time will come when we will overwhelm all obstacles and no more squalor will survive, only style.'

'What are you like?'

'I am terrible, I am tender.'

'Do you run from adversity?'

'I spit on it.'

'What is your favourite sport?'

'I am fond of chess and karate, archery and wrestling but, most of all, I am thrilled by motorbike jumps.'

'What is a motorbike jump?'

'The method is as follows: riding on my black machine, I roar up a long ramp and fly straight off the end, hurtling over a line of 10 cars, placed end to end, and landing safely on the other side, a jump of more than 40 yards.'

'Isn't this dangerous?'

'I have broken my leg in 3 places, fractured my wrist, dislocated my shoulder and, next time, it may well be my neck.'

'Why do you do it?'

'Coming in to land, just for one moment, it's true that I touch infinity.'

'Are you frightened of the dark?'

'I am.'

'Why do you cause riots?'

'I'm fond of fun.'

'Are you evil?'

'Among the cripples of Waterside, horrified by their suffering, I touched my silver crucifix and I caused the lame to walk, I caused the blind to see.'

'Do you eat sweets?'

'I love chocolate bonbons.'

'What is your stance on drugs?'

'I abhor them and hold them in contempt, since they befuddle the brain, rot the bones and poison the bodily fluids, until the user becomes a travesty of life.'

'Are you left-handed?'

'I am.'

'Will your enemies be triumphant?'

'Any person who attacks me, he only does me a favour, for persecution stings me and, when I am angry, my energies are infinite. Once the greatest, always the greatest, that is proven fact.'

'Why are you hated?'

'Because I'm Johnny Angelo!'

'Do you believe in an afterlife?'

'This is my afterlife.'

'What are your politics?'

'I hate human garbage.'

'Are you fond of animals?'

'In downtown Pharisee, I was seated in an all-night Laundromat, when a young girl saw me and came to sit down beside me, cradling a puppy in her arms. A very sweet 16, she had eyes of baby blue but I could tell that she was sad and her tears fell down like silver stars. Then I held her hand, I asked her why she was troubled and she told me the

truth, that her dog was sick and close to death.'

'What did you do?'

'At 3 o'clock in the morning, weeping, I held the animal tight in my arms, where its eyes turned up and it died.'

'What do you want?'

'I seek the magic honeypot.'

GUNS AT LA COLLINA

Riding on his golden cadillac, Johnny Angelo travelled all over the nation and, everywhere that he went, he was received as a hero. 'I am the greatest,' he said.

He lived in a mansion with 50 rooms, which was named La Collina, and it was surrounded by electric fences and electric gates. It was covered by neon lights, glowing red and blue and gold in the dark, lighting up the countryside for miles around, and its grounds were patrolled by guard dogs, Irish wolfhounds and Alsatians that would tear out a man's throat, and its doorways were barred, by uniformed guards.

Apart from Johnny's own entourage, no one entered this mansion for any reason. Agents and producers and accountants, journalists and songwriters alike, they were kept waiting outside the gates and Johnny Angelo sent them their instructions by messenger. However, if they were in favour, they were also given a bowl of nourishing broth, a chocolate chip cookie and an autographed picture of the artist.

Inside a darkened room, meanwhile, Johnny sat all day without moving. Reclining on his chaise longue, he sipped

beer through a straw and he played with a Siamese cat, holding
it up by its tail and swinging it in circles. The curtains were
drawn tight and he hid behind dark glasses. He watched TV
and he read comic books. He chewed on fat black grapes.

When he'd first bought this mansion, he had spent one
million dollars on embellishments and he was surrounded
by jade and silk and tortoiseshell, jewelled caskets and sable,
spurious old masters, heart-shaped candelabras and grand
pianos.

Scattered throughout the house, continuous movies of
Johnny Angelo were projected on the walls and, on the ceiling
of his bedroom, there was an outsize portrait in oils, which
showed him in his blue velvet suit and buckled blue suede
shoes, walking on clouds.

In every room, there were hidden microphones and close-
circuit televisions and two-way mirrors, so that Johnny could
keep in touch at all times and nothing remained a secret, no
plots could be laid against him.

There were bars across the windows.

At the same time, he was slovenly in his habits and the
floors were littered with old socks and discarded beer cans,
torn newspapers, cigarette butts, and stains, of brown and
green and yellow and, everywhere, there were smells of
staleness, smells of decay.

Sitting in the dark, Johnny dangled his Siamese cat, swung
it slowly like a pendulum, while the cat turned and twisted in
the air, trying to scratch his eyes out.

At night, he dined in his banqueting hall, where the
walls were hung with trophies, with shields and spears and
scimitars, and the windows were covered in cobwebs, and
the ceiling was too high and too dark to be seen, so that the
hall was like a huge black pit.

Down the middle of this chasm, there ran a long oak table, big enough for 40 people and, at the farthest end of this table, all alone, Johnny Angelo sat and feasted, dining by candlelight, a single patch of light in a great swamp of black.

He drank wine from a flagon and he ate a chicken carcass with his fingers, chewing through flesh and bone and gristle, giblets and all and, when he was done, he cast the remnants over his shoulder, where they were devoured by three Great Danes.

A falcon sat on his shoulder and Johnny wore a foxfur jerkin, a crucifix, a pair of rancid jockey-shorts. Grease dripped from his fingertips, wine dribbled down his chin. Candlelight flickered on his face and, medieval warlord, he belched, he farted, he clapped his hands just once.

Straightaway, the hall was filled with light, the falcon flew up into the rafters, and Johnny's followers ran amok, tumblers and jugglers and clowns, female impressionists, ventriloquists, the whole resident circus, and liveried servants brought in sumptuous bowls of fruit, overflowing with lychees and pomegranates and Chinese figs, and the musak machine played madrigals.

What else? Yolande danced naked on the table, Catsmeat played with a yo-yo and 4 giant Negroes stood guard in the doorway, juggling with lighted flares, while trick cyclists rode backwards into the fireplace, hunchbacks bared their humps and, finally, a pyramid of dwarves climbed on to Johnny's shoulders, whispering prayers in his ears, and their tongues quivered like aspen leaves.

The wind squawled in the rafters, causing the lanterns to squirm and sway, and Johnny Angelo was carried to his couch, where he stretched out like the Emperor Nero, and many beautiful starlets soothed his brow, and licked the

grease from his fingers, and stuffed his mouth with delicious tidbits.

All his life was a Hollywood movie, nothing else was relevant and, in his banqueting hall, the entertainments lasted halfway through the night, in every corner, bodies were coupled at random, midgets with behemoths, starlets with spastics, and glasses were smashed against the walls, wine spread in a lake across the floor, the mansion rang with obscenities.

Johnny Angelo took no part.

At the bottom of the pit, everything was frenzy but he didn't speak, didn't smile. Surrounded by profanity, it's true that he was bored.

He sat all day without moving. He watched old movies on TV. He blew smoke rings. He lay face-down on a mattress in his swimming pool, gazing at his own reflection.

He was afraid of being killed.

Every morning, among his fan mail, there were also demands for blackmail, claims for breach-of-promise and promises of instant assassination. Obscenities were scrawled in his driveway. Beards and moustaches were added to his posters. On stage, when the small girls rushed forward, he was caught unawares and his blue velvet suit was splattered with rotten eggs.

One time, he was ambushed in his dressing room and kidnapped by students, who held him up for ransom. Or again, in the middle of the motorcade, a conspirator burst from the crowd and threw a home-made bomb, which landed at Johnny's feet and fizzled but failed to explode.

Then Johnny Angelo hired gunslingers, silent men in dark glasses, who followed him everywhere, and he ordered bullet-proof windows for his golden cadillac, and he set up a

searchlight, which swept the grounds throughout the night. Even so, he didn't feel safe: 'My death stalks me,' he said. 'One day, it won't be long, Catsmeat will come to wake me and my throat will be slit, my heart will be riddled with bullets.'

He trusted no one. He had no friends. He used no lovers. When he slept, he stayed by himself and there were guards outside his door, bars across his windows, wolfhounds howling in his estates. For a very long time, he lay awake and he gazed at the ceiling, where Johnny Angelo walked on the clouds.

He passed through the 50 rooms of his mansion. He wallowed in a sunken bath. He consulted his astrologer.

'I'm sick of this,' he said. 'It's time to change.'

Then he went back on the road and he visited 30 cities, in 30 days and, in each of them, he rode on his golden cadillac, he wore his suit of blue velvet, he pouted and squirmed and grovelled on his knees.

Inside the auditorium, flames leaped up, freaks rampaged in the aisles, wild animals ran amok. Later on, escaping through his dressing-room window, it was then that Johnny Angelo felt alive.

THE GREAT CHESTER FIRE

Even so, he wasn't satisfied.

It was true that he lived to cause havoc but it was also true that he couldn't repeat the same riots over and over again, for that would be tiresome and self-defeating. Night after night, he was forced to come up with bigger and wilder sensations, a process that was most exhausting, and it wasn't long before he was bored again, just the same. He did not quit.

At the Corinth Coliseum, he staged his entrance inside a monstrous egg, which was fired from a cannon and, when it hit the stage, it shattered in a hundred pieces and out stepped Johnny Angelo, newly hatched.

Or again, at the Philo Empire, he performed in a gilded cage, locked up with man-eating tigers; and at San Badino, he landed by parachute.

Still he was restless. And he knew that, in the end, such diversions were irrelevant, that his true quest was for final explosion. At the same time, he knew that nothing is final but death, except that he didn't wish to die, not yet, and so

he was caught in a stalemate, and all his pranks were wasted, which made him sad.

What remained? Trapped like this, he had no choice but to persevere and, at Polack, he swung down on stage by a silken rope, leaping over the balcony and, at Samson, he loosed wolfhounds on the audience and once, at the New Holt Regal, he wept.

Finally, in windswept Chester, he staged a striptease. His suit of baby blue velvet, his blue suede shoes, his white kneesocks, his monogrammed bracelets and golden rings, his silver crucifix and the scarlet ribbon that tied up his hair: all of these items were peeled away in turn, until only satin underwear was left, at which point the curtain was lowered without warning and policemen rushed out to make an arrest.

Seeing their leader in danger, the Mighty Avengers hurried to his assistance and the lawmen pulled him one way, his own supporters pulled him the other, until he was likely to be torn in half.

Despairing, Johnny threw a left hook and it landed on someone's nose, breaking it. Without delay, the policemen then brought out truncheons and whistles, which the Avengers countered with brickbats, flick-knives and bicycle chains and, in seconds, the stage was turned into a pitched battlefield.

Out in the dark, meanwhile, small girls were screaming and surging forward, and bottles were flying, and rival gangs were fighting hand-to-hand, and then the cages were unlocked, the wild animals broke loose.

Within 5 minutes, the auditorium had turned into one great whirlpool, which sucked in everyone, and the carnage was terrible to behold. Lawmen were stabbed in the back, young girls were stampeded, and commissionaires dropped

dead of heart-attacks, and the lights were fused, and blood-crazed beasts roamed the aisles and, in conclusion, the whole of one balcony collapsed, spilling its occupants more than 40 foot in the stalls.

Who could describe the horrors that ensued?' The floor was piled high with the injured and the dying, whose groans and shrieks and prayers were drowned out by the enveloping uproar, and still the battle raged without let-up.

Barbarians rushed wildly through the darkness, destroying at random, setting fire to anything that would burn, curtains and seats and clothing, and very soon, fires raged unchecked all over the Chester Palladium.

As for Johnny Angelo, he was surrounded by a tight circle of bodyguards, so that he could watch the action undisturbed, and he put his clothes back on, he placed cologne behind his ears, he combed his golden hair.

This was a true explosion, after all, this was just what he'd sought and the flames began to lick at his feet, the smoke began to choke him.

At the Chester Palladium, those who didn't plunge to their deaths were trodden on, those who weren't stabbed were garotted and those who weren't savaged by leopards were burned up like kindling. Looking down, Johnny gazed upon a holocaust.

Then the Avengers lifted him up, bearing him high above the debris, and they carried him back to his dressing room, locking the door behind him. Once more, he slid through the window and slid down in the alley, where the limousine was waiting, and he rode home to his mansion, and flames lit the sky behind him, and faint screams reached him through the night.

He knew serenity then. Inside his banqueting hall, he sat

by himself, while candlelight flickered on his face, and he waited calmly until the lawmen arrived and took him away to jail.

Of course, he could have escaped. Doubtless, it would have been easy to climb back inside his limousine, round up his circus and head for somewhere very far away, some place where he could hide in safety. It would have been very easy, yes, and it would have been sensible but then, inside his movie, such stuff was meaningless. Inside his movie, it was apt that he should suffer.

He sat in the half-dark, therefore, and his falcon sat on his shoulder, and his servants brought him food, a side of venison, a saddle of beef, and a flagon of rough wine, and a bowl piled high with fruits, aesthetically arranged, and his Great Danes were asleep in front of the fire, the floorboards creaked and Johnny prepared to be martyred.

Midnight passed and still the policemen didn't arrive, still Johnny Angelo waited patiently and he thought: I will be captured, yes, and I will be put in bondage. I will be tormented and my name will be legend. Soon enough, I will die.

Because, in the end, it was only the movie that mattered and no such thing as reality, nor the prospect of pain, could break in on his cadillac dreams.

Fingering his crucifix, he ate fat black grapes and sure enough, at 2 o'clock, a small army of policemen surrounded his mansion, ready to bust in by force, but Johnny offered no resistance, he welcomed them gladly.

They charged him with indecent exposure, incitement to riot, resisting arrest and assaulting a police officer. When they put on the handcuffs, Johnny Angelo smiled his golden smile.

IN BONDAGE

Buried under the rubble of the Chester Palladium, there were more than 20 bodies and many thought that Johnny Angelo deserved to be lynched. In the end, however, he received no more than 90 days in jail.

How come he got off so lightly? Basically, he escaped because, although his moral guilt was plain, legal blame was hard to prove. After all, he had kept on his knickers, he had given no verbal provocation and he'd given himself up willingly. Even his left hook had been thrown in self-defence.

For all these reasons, it was not possible to destroy him for ever and everyone was most disappointed, not least Johnny Angelo himself, who had set his sights on martyrdom.

Just the same, when he saw what was actually involved, 90 days began to seem ample. For a start, he was parted from his followers, stripped of his rings and his bracelets, prised out of his blue velvet pants and then, something he hadn't reckoned with, his golden hair was cut.

Exactly like Elvis in Jailhouse Rock, he was clipped down

to the bone and, when he opened up his eyes, his hair stuck up as stubble, all rough and raggedy, like a cornfield after harvesting.

It was then that he almost wept. But he didn't. Instead, he pursed his lips and cast a giant spitball on the barber shop floor, an offence that cost him a day in solitary confinement.

He didn't speak to anyone. During morning exercise, however, he Shot the Agate real slow and everyone stared at him, warders and convicts alike, even the prison governor, when Johnny went back inside his cell-block and, just before he disappeared, he half-turned, half-smiled and let one hand trail behind him, fingers outstretched.

Uniformed in a suit of many arrows, he sewed mailbags all day long, coarsening his hands, and at night, he lay alone in his cell, drowning in the smells of the latrines.

By his own orders, he received no visitors and he did nothing that wasn't strictly necessary. He ate and he slept and he watched, that's all.

He made a calculation, as follows: if he counted numbers very slow, it would take him 60 days to reach a million and this is how he filled his time, moving his lips in a private rhythm, a pattern that no one could understand.

And outside his mansion, his followers auctioned a head of golden hair, falsely reputed to be Johnny's own. At 50 dollars a lock, they grossed more than a million dollars and, even then, there remained a queue more than two miles long, which reached far down the hillside, curling around like a serpent.

At the end of a week, Johnny Angelo had counted almost to 100,000 and, at the end of a month, he was well past a quarter million. Lying awake in his cell, night after night, it

was then that he felt stranded and, for the first time in many years, he began to recall the Doctor.

He returned beyond the barbed-wire fence. His footsteps echoed in the hall. His hand paused on the banister and he faltered, he was frightened but he persevered and nothing was changed, nothing at all. Not the emptiness nor the balcony, not the hatstand, not the black overcoat nor the black slouch hat. Not even the honeypot.

Things began to turn tough: every day, he sewed mailbags; every night, he lay awake; both day and night, he kept on counting slowly, until he reached half a million.

Very soon, his fingers were scabbed and misshapen, his flesh smelled stale. His clothes were covered with arrows and his hair stuck up like a wire-brush, all his companions were evil and, no matter how hard he scrubbed, he did not feel clean. After each meal, he vomited.

Latrines and bedbugs and pigswill for lunch, such things had no place in any motion picture and Johnny felt betrayed. Martyrdom was one thing, after all, but this slow erosion was something else entirely. Caged, he began to fall apart.

Everything was different: in the courtyard, he didn't Shoot the Agate but huddled in a corner, twitching, and he couldn't sleep, and he believed that he was laughed at, he lost count of his numbers and, worst of all, he could not stop shaking.

All the time, he kept remembering the Doctor, and his yellow flesh, his yellow eyes, and his study at tea time, so safe beyond the fence. And the cranberry jam, the buttered scones and muffins, the Jasmine Dreams, and the Doctor on the sofa, telling stories, his voice soft in the afternoon.

Standing on the balcony, Johnny looked out across his

neighbourhood, thinking of turnip watches, and motorbikes revving up in the alley, bright red suits in the sunshine and cards slapping on the table, hour after hour, when the Doctor crept up behind him and put his hands over Johnny's eyes, blinding him.

Johnny Angelo wept.

But on Thursday afternoon, when he visited the jail, the Doctor was unchanged. Seated behind the grill, he wore the same old overcoat, the same slouch hat, and his flesh was yellow like parchment, like old papers found in an attic. 'Johnny,' he said. 'I've missed you.'

'What do you want?'

'Many times I've read of your exploits, I've watched your exhibitions on TV and I've meant to get in touch with you, except that I've kept forgetting.'

'And now?'

'But now I've remembered.'

Underneath his arm, the Doctor carried a little black bag, which contained something heavy, and Johnny looked at it steadily. 'I may say that I've been proud of you,' the Doctor said. 'It was me, after all, who created you.'

'What's in your bag?'

'On Mafeking Street, the wind blew in spasms and my coat was lifted high about my knees. Your golden hair was blown into your eyes. Everywhere that we walked, newspaper kept clinging to our legs and I taught you, I made you afresh.'

'Tell me,' said Johnny Angelo, growing impatient. 'Why have you come here?'

'I have brought you a present.'

'Show me.'

Inside the small black bag, there lay something not quite

like a box, not exactly like a jug, nor yet a tub or jar: 'Of course,' Johnny said. 'A honeypot.'

'That is the correct answer,' said the Doctor, smiling shyly, and he brought it up close against the grating, where Johnny might touch it with his fingertips. 'In a house of 53 rooms, all alone, there lived Monseigneur Pike, a star of motion pictures, who carried a silver spoon in his left hand, a honeypot in his right and, everywhere that he wandered, a deep and satisfied sniffing was heard.'

Through the bars, Johnny reached out and clawed, feeling for the pot itself, which just eluded him. 'In one month, you will be freed,' the Doctor said. 'Straightaway, you will receive your gift and every happiness will then be yours.'

Very soon, the warder came and the Doctor put the honeypot back inside its bag, clicked the lock and he went away, smiling his yellow smile.

Left alone, Johnny Angelo counted past 600,000, on past three quarters of a million. And his flesh was still torn, his senses still befouled but, out in the courtyard, he stuck his thumbs back inside his waistband and he hunched his shoulders, he strutted very slow. Passing the latrines, he sniffed crystals.

So he survived, and the time came soon when he was given back his velvet suit, his blue suede shoes. When the gate swung open, Johnny put his hand up to shade his eyes, dazzled by the sudden brightness, and all his followers were waiting for him, arranged in formation, and there was also his golden cadillac, and many hundreds of schoolgirls, who waved white handkerchiefs and whimpered. A small army, they filled the street solid for several blocks, waiting for Johnny to wave his hand and smile, and the sun was shining brightly. It was the most beautiful day.

Standing outside the prison gate, however, Johnny gave
no sign. Instead, he pulled up his overcoat collar, he tugged
down the brim of his hat and he disappeared inside his car,
driving home to La Collina without a word.

His golden hair was gone and he could not smile. Inside
his mansion, he sat all day without moving and, while he was
motionless, he held a mirror up in front of his face. He didn't
run, didn't jump, did not burn. Instead, he only slouched and
schlurped and did the mooche half-hearted. Shorn, he was
pathetic.

He waited for the honeypot.

On the third day of his confinement, he received a visit
from the Doctor, who brought with him his little black bag.
Something that Johnny had not noticed in jail, the Doctor
was a very old man, a walking corpse: 'In his house of 53
rooms, Monseigneur Pike sniffed deeply and, one last time,
the crystals bloomed in his brain,' he said. 'Then he shook
my hand.'

'Never mind that,' said Johnny Angelo. 'Where's the
honeypot?' And he reached out greedily, as though he'd tear
open the bag, grasping the pot by force.

But the Doctor was too quick: backing away, he clutched
the bag to his bosom, he shook his head sternly. 'Not yet,' he
said. 'You can open it after I've left.'

'When will that be?'

'Straightaway.'

'Where will you go?'

'I am tired,' said the Doctor, sniffing, and crystals bloomed
in his brain. When he gave the pot to Johnny, he touched him
lightly, a touch as dry as dust, and then he shut the door, he
went away to die.

Johnny Angelo sat by himself, surrounded by pictures of

himself, and he thought of elegance. At the age of 25, he opened the honeypot slowly and he looked inside.

It was empty.

NEON ARMADILLO

At La Collina, Johnny waited for his hair to grow and, meanwhile, he was helpless. Stubble-headed, he was not robbed of his essence, like Samson or the Cobra, but he wasn't beautiful and, when he wasn't beautiful, he was filled with self-disgust.

Accordingly, three months passed by in total inertia, while he roamed through the many rooms of his mansion, a mirror always in his hand, and no one could get in to see him, not even his fans and closest followers.

Outside, his enemies had triumphed: his concerts had been banned throughout the nation, his records withdrawn, his memory abused and his picture removed from public places. 'The dragon has been slain,' Lord Morly said, and everyone cheered.

None of this seemed to bother Johnny Angelo, however, whose face remained expressionless, and he gazed at his own reflection, and he dined alone by candlelight, and he watched himself walking on clouds, he waited, he was patient.

At last, in the middle of a heatwave, he looked once more

in his mirror and his hair hung smooth and golden to his shoulders, it shimmered and it glowed.

Then Johnny smiled and he called his circus all around him. 'I am still the greatest,' he said, his hair tied back in a scarlet bow, and he led them away from La Collina, a mighty cavalcade.

For five days and nights, they travelled without stopping, until they came into the desert, a place named Armadillo.

Sixty miles from Gulch City, 80 miles from Magdalena, Armadillo was nothing but sand but here, with the remnants of his great fortune, Johnny built a neon sculpture, a monstrous effigy of himself.

A hundred and eight feet high, it glowed with sixteen colours and it wore a suit of baby blue neon, it was hung with a neon crucifix and, high above everything, visible at a range of 100 miles, it featured a flashing neon sign, and the slogan it spelled was as follows: JOHNNY ANGELO in silver, I AM THE GREATEST in gold.

Furthermore, this was not just a monument, it was a lived-in palace and, the moment that he entered its toe, the visitor was lost in a world of neon delight.

All the organs of Johnny's body were traced in appropriate colours, red for the bloodstream and blue for the lungs, gold for the flesh, puke green for the intestines and purple for the heart. And in the liver, there was a gambling salon and, in the pancreas, a cinema and, in the bladder, a discotheque. In the brain, there was a lecture hall. Inside the genitals, predictably, there were scented boudoirs.

Everywhere that the visitor turned, he was dazzled by bright lights, which formed pretty pictures or spieled strange messages, and music blared in every limb, kaleidoscopes unfurled at every corner and, 24 hours a day, the name

JOHNNY ANGELO kept flashing overhead.

As for Johnny himself, his bedroom was placed in his own left eye, and hour after hour, he gazed out across the desert, brooding, while his circus disported and roistered down below, having the time of their lives.

Sometimes he brooded about his imprisonment, sometimes he brooded about his enemies and sometimes he brooded about his bright red suit. Most of all, however, he brooded about the empty honeypot and what it might possibly mean.

Detail by detail, he delved back through all the sequences of his movie, looking for his mistakes, but he could find nothing crucial. Perhaps some errors in emphasis, yes, and a few missed chances. Even some moments of tedium. And then, of course, his journey with the Cobra. And the time when he shot from the hip and it was only a dog. And when KICK ME was scrawled on his back. But again, what did it all come to? Surely not an empty honeypot. Surely not.

So he looked across the desert, unsatisfied, and he walked the red brick wall, and the sun shone very brightly, he held a turnip watch all snug and safe inside his palm. And he threw a brick through a plate-glass window, the hole was perfectly round, and he hid in the attic, he lay with his eyes shut. Motorbikes roared outside and the Doctor stood beneath a gaslamp, on the far side of the street, and his face was shadowed by his hat. Johnny Angelo took photographs, his father sat by the bonfire. In his hotel room, Kid Clancey sat without moving, polishing his guns, and Johnny was a jackdaw, who owned a watch with five hands, and he wore a wine-coloured uniform with a yellow dragon emblazoned on the breast.

At tea, there were Chestnut Whirls and Monseigneur Pike had crumbs on his waistcoat. From the balcony, it was

possible to see everything. Perched on top of a flagpole, Johnny saw everything. In the graveyard, he buried his fat black cat and derelicts clawed at his feet. Dead mice were left inside his desk and he rode on a motorbike, he sat in the corner caff, where the windows were all steamed up, where the waitress licked inside his ear. In the darkness, small girls screamed and Johnny jumped over the balcony, soaring off into space. Catsmeat had pink piggy eyes. Elvis Presley smiled lopsided. Catsmeat was beaten to a pulp. Melting in the heat, Johnny was a gunslinger and his hair fell over his eyes, all golden, and he smoked the most cool cigarette in the whole of Heartbreak Hotel.

From Lincoln County, there came the Skulls and, from Spanish Savoy, the Compadres and, from Jitney, the Tombstones. Black monsters on black machines, they howled in the night, causing destruction wherever they passed, and Johnny Angelo trembled, slithering like a serpent. On the bombsite, he stood with bowed head and shot the Doctor dead. In the windowless back room, he was safe.

What else besides? His guitar shaped like a spaceship, and Ace, who was dropped in a puddle, and Astrid, with her eyes all full of silver stars. The Cobra and her candyfloss wig, her smell like voodoo, her smile like sudden death, and cats with flaming tongues, who hissed and writhed and crackled, and Johnny himself, Johnny Angelo, who rode away to Movie City.

All of this, and very much more: a journey, an odyssey, with every detail perfect. And yet. And yet Johnny brooded in his own left eye, he cast a spitball in the sand.

In his thighs and arms and belly, his disciples lived for fun alone. They swam up and down in his arteries, they prayed in his armpits and orgied in his scrotum and, everywhere

that they went, neon flashed and flickered constantly, so that nothing looked the same, not ever.

From time to time, overwhelmed by sensation, a strongman or bearded lady would go insane and leap screaming through the vents of Johnny's suit, tumbling sixty feet to their deaths. In general, though, morale was very good and the circus endured through all disasters, even when the fuses blew or sandstorms whipped in their faces or, once, when the whole of one kidney exploded, killing five outright and injuring fourteen others.

Nor did Johnny Angelo absent himself entirely. Once a week, he descended the sweeping stairway of his throat, a single white rose in his hand, and he strutted on his collarbone. Again, he snarled and squirmed and grovelled on his knees, twisted his legs like rubber bands, buried his guitar in his groin. Yet again, he smiled his golden smile and then, launching himself without looking, he swooped and soared and ricocheted, span and trampolined, all the way down to his diaphragm.

Climbing back inside his eyeball, he returned into solitude but he didn't brood any more, he got drunk on neon instead. Safe in the effigy, he spat out blood, he shouted out obscenities and he threw away the honeypot, hurling it far into the desert night, up and away and on, until it disappeared.

And this much was true once inside the movie, he was caught for ever. At the age of 26, excess was his life, to which he was committed, and it was too late now to change. 'I will die as I have lived,' he decided, very solemn, and swore to turn his back on doubt and analysis.

On the following morning, he called a meeting of all his followers and, seated on his lower lip, he swung his legs, he kicked his heels. He wore a white silk suit, white kid shoes,

a pink carnation in his buttonhole. With every word that he spoke, his neon mouth moved in time and, smiling, he made a speech, as follows: 'I am sick and tired of tedium.

'For much too long, I have sat and thought and tied myself in knots, until I don't believe in anything, but now I wish to plunge back into insanity. Even so it's not enough simply to repeat my past, to go back on the road and shake my hips and make small girls scream. If I'm going to come back at all, I have to come back more extreme. This time, therefore, I mean to make an ending, a final explosion and, when it's done, I shall cease.'

Leaning back on flashing white teeth, Johnny Angelo paused to survey his supporters, who stood knee-deep in sand. Truthfully, he could not deny that they were motley but this was no time to quibble, he thought, and he let fall a rose. 'I shall cause a revolution,' he said. 'As soon as possible, I shall recruit an army, a full-scale crusade, and then I shall march on Decatur, I shall overthrow tyranny and replace it with fun.'

At Armadillo, he stood up straight, drew back his shoulders and, V for Victory, he spread his fingers wide. 'If I win, I shall blow the world apart and, if I'm killed instead, I won't complain,' he concluded. 'Either way, I will not be bored.'

While his circus applauded politely, whistling and waving handkerchiefs, Johnny returned to his eyeball, where Catsmeat served him with tea and scones. 'Johnny Angelo,' said Catsmeat, loyally. 'We shall overcome.'

'I'm sick of this,' replied Johnny.

'Sick of what?'

'Of everything.'

Nevertheless, he sent out messengers into every corner

of the nations, envoys who spoke behind their hands, who whispered and passed out pamphlets in underground cellars. Lurking in doorways, they hissed and, very soon, the first recruits began to arrive at Armadillo, straggling up by bicycle, in worn-out wagons and even on foot.

Within a week, there were more than a thousand of them and, by the end of a month, there was truly a small army 10,000 strong, all eager to perish for Johnny Angelo.

On the other hand, they were hardly what he'd had in mind. Somehow he'd imagined that he would collect an elite, commandos and ghurkas and American marines, men who had fought in five continents and, therefore, he was disconcerted to find, peering out through his navel, that the desert was full of mutants, of mongols and morons, of the blind and deaf and dumb, the sexually perverted, the criminally insane, and thousands of midget schoolgirls, hardly past puberty.

By any standards, these were the scrapings, strictly the flotsam and jetsam of society: 'Human garbage,' said Johnny Angelo. 'I might have known.'

And his first impulse was to scrap the whole project, to disband the crusade and hide inside his mansion, where he might sit in the dark and sulk. On second thoughts, though, he saw that this was not possible. Having launched an apocalypse, he couldn't yawn and go home to tea. Once the greatest, always the greatest: he'd said that himself. Backsliding was unthinkable. Trapped, he sighed deeply but walked out in the sand and began to train his troops. Dressed in a uniform of black barathea, he carried a swagger stick and divided his men into small platoons, each according to his gifts.

First of all, there came the Mighty Avengers, and then

the specialised performers such as jugglers and trapezists, acrobats and snake-charmers and so forth, and then the mass of schoolgirls, who might serve as cannon fodder and then the walking wounded, all those in wheelchairs or on crutches, and then the wild animals, and then the very riff-raff, the humanoids and human vegetables and, last of all, his mother and his father, his sisters.

Every day for two months, he lined them up and drilled them and shouted obscenities in their faces, until at least they could march in formation, without tripping over their feet, bumping into each other or all falling down in a heap.

Even so, they were a rabble, they always would be and the very sight of them made Johnny squirm, so that he soaked the desert in spitballs as big as pennies.

From his bedroom, he watched the moon and thought dark thoughts. Gnawing at the end of his pencil, he wrote small sad poems, which took him nowhere, and he played his old hit records, relics of his golden age.

And then, when he was almost 27, he looked in the mirror and there, unmistakably, he saw the first fine wrinkles forming round his eyes, the first sag beneath his chin. When his stylist dressed his hair, he noticed clusters of golden hair in the comb and, swinging like Tarzan on the hairs of his neon chest, he had a blackout, he lost his fingerhold and dropped like a stone. If it hadn't been for a budding paunch, which broke his fall, he would certainly have plunged to his doom.

That settled it: of all catastrophes, old age was the worst and, right then, he quit wasting time. Blindfold, he stuck a pin in a calendar and chose a date for the coup d'état, just 17 days ahead.

After that, he felt more serene. Now that the die was finally cast, he relaxed, he combed his hair and made out his will.

Also, he wrote a letter to Astrid, his teenage dream, all full of passionate lovewords, and he composed his epitaph: To all who pass that they may see – Rock and roll was a part of me.

Down in the duodenal tract, meanwhile, casting craps against the wall, Catsmeat was humming tunelessly and Johnny tousled his hair, cuffing him like a lapdog. 'When I'm dead,' Johnny said, 'will you visit my grave?'

'I will,' replied Catsmeat.

'And will you shed tears?'

'Yes, I will.'

'And will you bring me flowers?'

'I will bring yellow roses and I will lie down beside your tombstone. I won't move until I'm dead myself.'

In all the years of their acquaintanceship, almost half of their lifetimes, this was the most conversation that they'd ever had, Catsmeat and Johnny together, and now, while Catsmeat wept, Johnny Angelo stroked his cheek, quite tender.

Then he was calm. He was almost content.

INTO THE VALLEY OF DEATH

On the 17th day, Johnny Angelo rose up early and entered his golden cadillac, which turned its nose towards Decatur, the capital of the eastern plains, and his army formed itself in ranks, following wherever he led.

Mutants and misfits, spastics, dwarves and dope fiends, and performing seals, and half-hand bigshots, and paranoids, schizoids and drooling athetoids, and singing dogs, and peglegged, softshoe shufflers, and all the beasts of the jungle, man-eating tigers and cheetahs, jackals and serpents and lynxes, and rats blown up like balloons, haemophiliacs and bigamists, and poisonous spiders, and hennaed drag queens, and astrologers, card-sharps, assassins: these were the disciples of Johnny Angelo and, to each of them who stretched out their hand, he gave some kind of weapon, be it a gun, a knife or a hand-grenade, a brickbat or a garotte.

Festered and pocked and gangrened, they gazed into his eyes, trusting him, and he gave them his blessing: 'With God on our side,' Johnny said, 'we shall not suffer.'

High above his head, his effigy burned and sparkled,

flashed and made explosions. On every side, as far as he could see, sand lay unbroken and nothing stirred. 'We shall overcome,' said Johnny Angelo and, from Armadillo, he rode out to conquer the world.

What was his plan? Quite simply, he meant to advance on Decatur, drive directly into the heart of the city, walk up the steps of the Town Hall and capture it. If nobody tried to stop him, he would then control almost half of the whole nation. On the other hand, if he met with opposition, he would not shrink from a holocaust.

From Armadillo to Decatur, it was 94 miles and the journey took almost a week, during which time Johnny Angelo remained in his cadillac, while his army stumbled behind him in the dust. Sadly, a very great number got lost along the way. Each time the crusade passed by a bar, a score or more would desert and there were also many deaths, caused by sunstroke, exhaustion and plain decrepitude; just the same, more than 7,000 fighters arrived at Decatur, a force sufficient for all of Johnny's schemes and, in a golden September sunset, they camped beside a river, just outside the city limits.

That same night, seated beside the campfire, Johnny warmed his hands in comfort, chewing on a chicken bone, and his astrologer laid out Tarot cards. The priestess for mystery, the eremite for loneliness, the moon for fear: 'Johnny Angelo,' said the sage, 'you are doomed.'

'Will I suffer?'

'You will perish.'

'Then will I be shamed?'

'You will die as you have lived,' the astrologer said, and Johnny was not dissatisfied, he felt something close to relief. In the end, it didn't bother him, whatever might befall him,

just so long as it wasn't undignified, and he threw the scient a sovereign.

Beside the river, he gazed at his own reflection. His army was asleep, the campfires were burning low. Across the water, Decatur was also slumbering, all unaware, and everything was still, Johnny held his breath.

Right then, without warning, he brought up his forefinger, shooting fast and hard from the hip, and he drilled his image six times through the heart.

Then he lay down in the long grass and slept, dreaming of the waitress in the corner caff, who steamed up the windows, put a dime in the jukebox and her breasts flopped down around his head, as soft and warm as earmuffs.

He woke at dawn and it was one of those mornings when everything is made anew, when the air is as clear as crystals in a honeypot. Watching the first rays of sunlight on the water, feeling the dew against his cheek, Johnny didn't understand, could not conceive that this was his ending, when everything else was newly reborn. Rubbing his eyes, he found a ladybird in his shoe and nothing made sense.

But when he scrambled to his feet, he found his disciples already prepared. Pale sunlight glinted on their helmets and their shields. A light breeze fluttered their banners, butterflies settled on their shoulders and the Mighty Avengers rode along the ranks, keeping order, while their engines purred like pussycats.

As soon as Johnny Angelo stood up, the throng produced three cheers, throwing their caps into the air, and then he was trapped, he could do nothing but climb inside his cadillac and cross the bridge into Decatur.

Shuffling and shambling, the crusade passed through the sleeping suburbs, on through the slums and the business

districts, Chinatown and the markets, and very soon, almost before the city had started to stir, they were already approaching Constitution Square, the very hub.

The federals were waiting.

Johnny was not surprised. Optimist as he was, he had hardly supposed that 10,000 men could march unnoticed for 100 miles, especially men as garbled as these. Nor had he wished it, truthfully, for the closer he came to the crunch, the less he wished to survive, the more avidly he dreamed of death.

On this most beautiful morning, he jumped out of his cadillac, and he climbed up on the roof, he raised his hand and led his disciples on, across the square, up the steps of the Town Hall, into the valley of death.

And the federals shot them with machine guns.

In memory of Johnny Angelo, it would be pleasant now to turn this into an epic, to write of thrusts and ripostes, swaying fortunes, valorous deeds and of Johnny himself, leaping like a dolphin, cutting great swathes through the enemy until, at last, pinned against a wall, he expires of a dozen gaping wounds but dies with a smile, famous last words on his lips.

The truth, unfortunately, was very different. At the first volley of gunfire, the freaks stopped dead in their tracks; at the second, they began to back away; and at the third, they turned around and ran like hell, out of the square and all the way back to the river, into which they dived without looking, and the confusion was truly horrific.

What could you expect? Stampeding, they lost all sense of discipline and fled in one monstrous mêlée, everyone jumbled together, all tangled and collapsing, and the weak were trampled by the strong, and the strong were run down by the Mighty Avengers, and the Avengers were eaten by

wild animals, who broke out of their cages. Very soon, the streets were jammed solid with new-mown corpses, a human barricade, and the stragglers couldn't get past, they could only scrabble with their fingernails, squealing like pigs with their throats slit, while the federals took aim and shot them one by one.

Even those who reached the river, still they did not escape. Cripples and cretins that they were, they could not swim and they drowned in their hundreds, a pitiful sight, while the water turned pink with their lifeblood.

Of all the proud 7,000 who set out in the morning, less than half survived to see the afternoon. As for the federals, they did not suffer a casualty and, when they had mopped up the remnants, they went off to the pub for a pint.

But what of Johnny Angelo?

When the federals first opened fire, his heart beat very fast and he rode his cadillac straight ahead, aiming right at the heart of the enemy ranks. He was afraid of nothing, he spat on death. He drew a pair of long six-shooters from out of his breast and, exulting, he let them blast at random.

Seeing the federals duck and take cover, he laughed out loud and looked back over his shoulder, shouting encouragement to his troops. But his troops weren't there. Already, they were halfway back across the square, begging for forgiveness, and Johnny was left on his own, just him and Catsmeat, who was driving.

What could he do?

He hid.

To die like this, after all, where was the point? Gunned down in a massacre, unnoticed, unremembered, it would have been downright wasteful and he took fast refuge in his car, taking potshots through the window, while Catsmeat

gunned the engine and they ran away, they escaped.

They were not killed, although the cadillac was riddled like a sieve. They weren't even wounded and the federals could only gnash their teeth, while Johnny Angelo burned back across the desert, free as a bird.

What remained? Once they had thrown off all pursuit, they returned to La Collina. In reality, there was nowhere else that they could hide.

An empty mansion, surrounded by electric gates and fences, guarded by wolfhounds, honeycombed with radars, close-circuit TVs and hidden microphones: Johnny sat all day without moving and Catsmeat baked him Jasmine Dreams.

Nothing moved, nothing made any noise. Somewhere in the 53 rooms of his home, Johnny was stretched out on a chaise longue, was looking at his fingernails, was waiting. On his bedroom ceiling, he was walking the clouds.

And after three days, a week or a month, the federals arrived, a whole platoon of them, forty men, and they surrounded La Collina. Beyond the electric gates, they carried sten guns and tear gas and pineapples, they hovered in helicopters and spied through periscopes, they shouted through loudspeakers: 'Johnny Angelo,' they cried. 'Come on out.'

Johnny didn't reply.

In his banqueting hall, a falcon sat on his shoulder, cobwebs covered the windows and he dined on artichoke, iced avocado soup, salmon en croute with ginger, roast piglet with spiced cherries and fresh wild strawberries, washed down with a bottle of Château Y' Quem '45. And when he was quite satisfied, only then, he rose up and dressed himself all in black leather, a reminder of Heartbreak Hotel, and high black boots, tight black gloves, a lowslung gunbelt with holsters on both sides.

In these holsters, there were pearl-handled Colts, and Johnny Angelo watched himself in a full-length mirror, tying his neck scarf, and he combed his hair, he sprinkled cologne behind his ears, just for himself, he smiled his smile.

At the front door, he shook hands with Catsmeat. At the very last moment, he almost kissed him instead but then he drew back, blushing. In the whole of his lifetime, he had shown no true affection, not once, and he turned aside, he stepped out of the mansion.

At the age of 27, he met with the federals.

THE END

Outside La Collina, there was a very long driveway, more than 500 yards in length, which led to the electric gates, and Johnny Angelo walked down it slowly, his hands above his head. Beyond the gates, the federals did not move.

On either side of the driveway, there were parklands that were tangled like a jungle, all full of swamps and creeper and monkey trees and, through the undergrowth, there roamed many animals, badgers and rodents and skunks, felines and doves. High above everything, the mansion hung like a shroud and, for fully five minutes, Johnny went on walking.

About 50 foot from the gate, he stopped. The federals stared at him, he stared back at the federals and neither side made any move. Time passed.

At last, growing bored, the federal captain stepped forward, a man in a scarlet uniform: 'Are you coming out?' he asked. 'Or do we come in?'

Then Johnny Angelo dropped his hands, whipped his Colts from out of their holsters and let fly without looking. In the space of a second, twelve shots were fired and twelve

federals fell down in the dirt, where they died.

There was a silence.

Then the federals fired back and Johnny was hit in the shoulder, in the thigh, in the hip and in the guts but he wasn't killed outright, he was only maimed and he crawled along the ground, crablike, until he reached the shelter of his golden cadillac, which was parked just inside the gates.

Behind the cadillac, he wiped the blood from his lips and, both slowly and painfully, he began to reload. Everything was still and he listened to the animals moving in the jungle, he was surrounded by secret stirrings. Just for one moment, he shut his eyes and was still. Then he stood up. 'I am still the greatest,' said Johnny Angelo, and he started to shoot from the hip.